To Conrad

Dreams of Glory

Thanks for believing in me

By

Lawrence Bear

PublishAmerica
Baltimore

First printing

ISBN: 978-1-61546-433-3 (softcover)
ISBN: 978-1-4489-9557-8 (hardcover)
PUBLISHED BY PUBLISHAMERICA, LLLP
www.publishamerica.com
Baltimore

Printed in the United States of America

Dreams of Glory

1

Dreams, I sometimes wondered, what they are and what they mean.

Dreams, are what every boy has growing up, a dream to play in the National Hockey League. If you owned a pair of skates, and went skating till who knows when. These were probably your dreams, your future. If you listen closely enough, our hearts speak to our dreams. If its what you desire, and if you had skated in the frigid weather, through supper and till your mom had to come and get you. Then maybe this is what your dreams were probably telling you.

Sometimes when we dream, we may not understand them. Or what they are telling us. What they really are, what I believe, a glimpse into our future, they are a peek to what we are supposed to do. We sometimes face obstacles, and we sometimes let them defeat us. Sometimes we watch as our dreams drift away. This is a story of my dream, to play in the National Hockey League.

This story takes place in Cranberry Portage, a small community in Northern Manitoba. Frontier Collegiate Institute. I played for the Mohawks hockey club in the Saskatchewan High School League. It is mid season and I am about to head back to school, after spending Christmas holidays with my mother. Listen closely, as you are about to embark on a journey. Through my eyes I would like to share, what it is like to be a player with that dream.

As I sat and waited for the driver to load the bus, I waved at the guy's who brought me to the depot. They waved at me and saluted, with a smile now on my face I couldn't wait for spring break to come; I was already lonesome. Soon the bus was departing Winnipeg, I was watching for Bill and the guy's if they were to wave once more but they were gone. Once we've reached the city limits, I heard a honk from a passing vehicle. To my surprise looking out the window, it was Billy and the gang holding a sign. This had read "Go get em', Rob." Honking as they passed by, that sure picked my spirits up. Once again they waved at me; I waved back with a tear now in my eye, watching as they turned off the next turn. The next few hours were long.

It was early that morning, while the bus stopped in Neepawa for a few moments. I began to think about Candice Peterson. The girl I had a crush on for quite sometime. During my visit home for the holidays, we hung around together. I saw her more often than my own mother. I would often cancel out on the guy's, who would go out of their way to hang out with me. Billy one of my friends, came over one night and asked me why I wouldn't spend sometime with them. After all they were my cheering squad, at all my games in the city before I joined the Mohawks in Cranberry Portage. I told Bill that I would meet up with the guy's the next day at the drop in centre. That night I went to visit Candice; we shared a special moment together for it was the last time I had seen her.

The bus's destination was Flin Flon; it was seven AM when it arrived in Cranberry Portage. The driver's voice had awakened me, announcing that he was stopping for twenty-minutes. Tired as I was from the twelve-hour bus ride, I slowly got my bags together. I don't know why I waited till the last minute to go back; I knew school started the day I arrived back in town. I stood outside the depot on Main Street and stretched out for a moment.

"How was your break?" Someone had said behind me.

I turned around startled.

"Oh it's just you. What are you doing here?" I asked with a smile.

"Came to get you." Waylon my fellow teammate had said.

"You didn't have to come and meet me you know. And how in the world did you know I would be here?"

"The wind told me, the great spirit of the Earth." He babbled.

"What!" I looked at him with a wry smile.

He laughs and shrugs his shoulders.

"Your mother told me, when I had called for you last night."

That made me laugh and I was glad to see him there, he grabbed a bag and we talked on the way back to the Collegiate. When we got to my dorm room, I threw my bags on the bed. Waylon asked if I wanted breakfast, so we headed to the cafeteria. We sat by the window along the stairway, which led to the study hall. We chatted about what we did over the holidays. I also told him about Candice, he sat quiet staring at me.

"So you had sex with this chick?" he asked.

"What? Had sex! Now what kind of question is that? Let's just say, umm it sure was the best gift I gotten this year."

"Are you stupid or something?" Waylon said smiling nodding his head.

"What?" I said to him. "Maybe she was in the spirit of giving."

"Man, you really are something aren't you?" He chuckled. "What about Lisa?"

I was speechless, I had totally forgotten about her. I didn't know what to think I tried to gather some thought.

"What she doesn't know wouldn't hurt her."

Just then Darryl walked into the cafeteria.

"Hey ladies! What's up?"

"Not much, Robert was just telling me what he got for Christmas." Waylon looked at me with a smile.

"So did Santa give you what you wanted?" Darryl asked.

"Humph, yah! You could say that." I smiled.

"Oh shit! Look at the time. We better get going, or we'll be late for class. Are you coming Rob?" Waylon asked.

"Nah, I think I'll just go back to my room and catch up on some shut eye. Besides I can always copy from you."

"We'll see you at break then." Waylon said to me, as they both walked off into the direction of the school.

When I entered the dorm, the morning buzzer sounded to start the first class. I sat on my bed thinking of Candice and Lisa. How in the world am I going to explain it to Lisa if she ever found out? To my surprise, Lisa knocked at my window. I opened the window for her.

"What are doing here? Don't you have a class?"

"Yes, I just wanted to see you. Waylon told me you were back and so…here I am," she said.

"Waylon…" I said under my breath.

I snuck her in through the side door, since girls were not allowed in the boy's dormitory. I looked outside to see if anyone spotted her sneaking in. She gave me a big hug and kiss.

"I missed you," she said.

I smiled and gave her a little hug; she then pushed back and looked at me.

"Is something wrong?" She asked.

"What do you mean?"

"You don't seem glad to see me!"

"Of course I'm glad to see you; I'm a bit tired from the bus ride. That's all." I said to her.

I held her hand and sat down on the bed. She stood in front of me. I gazed into her eyes. She wore a red-buttoned top. Feeling guilty I tried to hide it, but as I talked a little. My voiced sounded funny, but I quickly cleared my throat. Trying to think of something fast; then I asked if she thought maybe it was time for us to get serious, since we were only together for 4 months. But I was a hockey player, the one who gets what he wants and desires. So I thought it would be quick and easy, I mean to get rid of the guilt. She thought about it for a while but I urged her. Then she gave in, but told me she hasn't done this before.

I began to unbutton her top so far and kiss her neck softly. She pulled my top off and then pants; I sat there with only my boxers on. She then backed away, slowly undressing herself. First taking her top off, showing me her bra. Then she took her jeans off, showing her lace panties. "My God" I thought. She aroused me when she took off her bra. I then rolled her onto the bed, kissing her and caressing her breast gently. I slowly moved down her body, feeling her quiver made me more excited. I removed her panties and I took my boxers off as well. She moaned for me to put a condom on, when I did she laid me on my back. Slowly getting on top of me riding me. Making out, she took control of the moment. With all the excitement, I didn't realize I moaned Candice's name. Lisa stopped and looked at me; she got off and began to put her clothes on.

"What's wrong?" I asked her, not knowing what I said.

"You moan some other bitch's name and you have the fucking nerve to ask me what's wrong," She stood there waiting for an explanation, but when I didn't answer.

"You fucker…How could you?" She began to cry; I didn't know what to say. I just sat there with my head down. She looked at me with tears in her eyes. "Why?" She sobbed and walked out the door.

"Lisa wait." I tried to grab her.

"Don't touch me. Leave me alone." She ran out the dormitory.

I quickly dressed and chased after her. I finally caught up to her by the cafeteria, when I grabbed her she screamed for me to leave her alone. Causing a commotion I tried to reason with her to quiet down. Some students gathered to watch. Feeling a bit embarrassed, I reached for Lisa to explain. Then she kneed me in the groin. As I lay there in pain, I could hear some snickers and a few awes. Moaning and groaning I tried to get myself up. I slowly made my way back to my room, when I got there I lay on the bed trying to recover. I thought about what had happened, what an idiot I was. I didn't mean for this to happen, Candice was…well it just happened. It wasn't supposed to but it did.

"I hope she doesn't get pregnant," I thought. I didn't use a condom that night, everything happened so fast. The time passed, with the first break, Waylon popped by to see me. He sat on my desk wondering what to say.

"You're not going to believe what happened to me," I said to him.

"I heard." He looked at me, trying to hold back his smile.

"So I see. It hurt like hell."

"Oh man, are you okay?" he asked while he laughed at me.

"Yah sure, thanks for laughing you jerk off." I laughed with him.

"Here, Lisa wanted me to give this to you," he said handing me a letter.

I opened it and began to read it.

Dear Robert,

There's so much I could say right now, but I won't. If this other girl didn't mean anything, then why did you sleep with her? But since you're such a complete asshole, I hate your guts. I thought we had a thing going I guess I was wrong. You hurt me, I don't know, I guess this is it between us. If you cared at all which you don't. You should've thought about us before screwing this Candice chick.

I gotta go, see you around I guess,

Lisa

The buzzer sounded to end the break.

"Is there anything you want me to tell her?" Waylon asked before leaving.

"Tell her that I would like to talk to her so I can explain."

After he left, I sat at my desk hoping she would speak to me. As it would turn out, the day seemed to drag. I spent most of the time in my room, thinking of everything. Then I thought of calling my uncle Terry, who lived in Scanturbury, Manitoba. It's a small reservation, north of Winnipeg on highway 59. He was part of the reason I came up here to the Mohawks hockey club. He inspired me, he always told me, "*Never give up, follow your dreams*" He would push me to higher limits, just to see if I could achieve them. I looked up to him. I'd play every game for him. I phoned him after every game, he would be glad to here about it. Even though I was pointless in a few games. He'd just give me a little pep talk, to encourage me for next game. I was leading scorer for our hockey club. I had thirty-two goals and thirty-eight assists, a total of seventy points.

Being a father of two children, he always had time for me. My father died of Tuberculosis when I was six years old. I guess he felt he should fill the gap or something, but he was always my uncle. I headed towards the link way to use the payphone; I bought a soda from the drink machine along the way. I was dialing his number, when someone tapped on my shoulder. I turned to see who it was, with the receiver still in my hand.

"You wanted to talk to me, Asshole!"

"Lisa, would you just hear me out, could we go some where and talk." I asked as I hung-up the phone.

We went to the hanger, where the hockey club stores our equipment. Also it's where most of the boy's hang out, to play table tennis or pool. I knew no one would be there; we went inside and sat on the couch next to the drink dispenser. I tried to think of something sensible to say.

"So, this is what it looks like in here," she said looking around the place.

"Lisa, I know..." I pondered on what to say. "What I did was wrong, I'm sorry. I never meant for this to happen."

"Oh yah, now tell me how you managed to get in her pants huh? Or did you lay some sad story, like you're telling me right now?"

"I don't understand why you are so upset."

"You're a fucking two timing asshole, did you understand that?" She pointed her finger at me.

"Look, I said I was sorry. Do you not hear I'm sor—ry," Pretending to sign language.

"If you want to act like a bitch, then go ahead. But you know what else, I'm only young once. There's plenty fish in the sea. You go your way and I'll go mine." I said, before leaving her there.

How she felt, I don't know. She believed I was in love with Candice. I thought for moment, maybe I was. Anger and confusion came over me. I didn't know what to think. I sat in the link way for a while, and then I went back to my room. A week had passed by and I still haven't spoken to Lisa. It was in my room, I began to think about her. I noticed she wasn't at our two home games at the barn. That's what we called our arena across the highway, from the Collegiate. Passing by it, you would think it was a barn. Its shape and that tin covering it with half of it brown; it's just ugly.

Those two games, I didn't play too good scoring only one goal. The coach was upset with me. He told me to shape up and get my head in the game, or he'll bench me to let someone else play in my spot. I wanted to tell him what I was going through, but I certainly did not want to sit. I took his words seriously. Although he was a bit hard on us at times, other than that he was a cool guy.

2

I remember one time at the Canadian Professional Hockey School, which was held at the Hylander Sportsplex every summer. I attended the School there, a couple years before I went to Cranberry. That summer I got to know the entire staff. The following summer, I went back to the hockey school. The instructor's told me that I had improved a lot from the summer before. It was a couple of weeks later when Walter Hutchison. Manager of the hockey school had asked to see me in his office. I stood at the doorway before he asked me to sit down.

"Mr. McKay, how are you feeling today?" he asked, sitting back in his swivel chair.

"I'm fine sir, just fine." Not sure of why I was summoned to his office.

"I see you've improved a lot from last year. Impressive!" Twirling his pen between his fingers.

I sat there, wondering what he meant. But was eager to hear what else he had to say.

"You know Mr. McKay," He stood up and walked around to the front of his desk, leaning on it. "I regularly don't do this, but consider it a favour."

"Don't do what sir?" I asked.

"I have a friend, who is looking for players this fall. Player's like you. He needs hard worker's and from what I seen in you. You're exactly the player he need's."

"What…What do you mean? What are you saying?" I asked with excitement.

"What I'm saying Robert, is that he'll be here tomorrow, to have a look at you. He sounded quite thrilled, to hear about you."

I was so excited; I didn't know what to say at first. I jumped out of my chair to thank Mr. Hutchison. With a huge smile, I hugged him and thanked him again. That whole day I was lit with joy. When the other instructor's heard the news they wished me luck. I told my mom that evening about the good news that a scout was coming to Winnipeg to watch me play. I couldn't sleep a wink that night. The next day, I had asked my mom to stay with me at the hockey school. I was getting nervous. I told her how I was feeling.

"Pretend he's not there, just be you," she said.

"He's going to be watching me play this afternoon, I'm a bit scared. What if he doesn't like the way I play? What if he came to town for nothing?" I said feeling discouraged.

"I'm sure you'll do fine. I have to go to work this morning; I'll be there after lunch. Play like you would, if Terry were watching you."

"Yah, but this is different mom. This is my future, the most important moment in my life. I've always dreamed for a chance like this, an opportunity like this only happens once in a lifetime. I have that chance to grab a dream. I want it. I want it so bad," I said.

She looked at me and gave me a hug.

"I'm sorry son; I didn't realize this means so much to you."

"More than anything mom…More than anything." I said, as tears formed in my eyes.

She wiped my eyes and smiled.

"If only your father were here. He'd be so proud; to see how determined you are."

On the ride over to Hylander, I started to feel sick. I tried to relax and stay focus. The morning wasn't too bad; we skated for an hour and a half. The last ten minutes, Mr. Morris made us do the lines. We started from the goal line, to the blue line and back. Then to the red line and back to the goal line, then to the far blue line and back to the goal line, at last, to the far goal line and back.

After that, without any rest he said to give him ten push-ups and ten sit ups, and then go for a light skate. Dry land training was scheduled for the rest of the morning. After lunch was the big game, the butterflies were in my stomach. While some of the group went across the street to A&W, I stayed and ate up stairs in the cafeteria. One of the girl's, who we got to know, had told me that some guy was talking about me.

"What did he say?" I asked her.

"He was talking to Walter Hutchison this morning. I over heard him saying you would be a key factor with his club. What ever that meant," she said.

I started to think, "He's here." this is it; my future is in his hands. I quickly ate and went to the dressing room, to retape my sticks. When it was time for the game, I sat there looking around at the other guy's. Before we cleared out of the dressing room, I put a towel over my head. I took a deep breath, held it in for a few seconds and let it out. I closed my eyes, visualizing myself putting on a great performance.

"Okay, boys let's get out there and have some fun," an instructor yelled out.

"Its show time." I said to myself.

We skated around to warm up our legs. I skated by the windows where people could watch. When I saw my mother, I had this feeling go through my body. It gave me the inspiration I needed. I waved at her and she waved back smiling. The guy's on my team lined up along the hash marks, shooting at the goalie to warm him up. I stood on the side watching. Looking around the rink, I then caught a glimpse of Mr. Hutchison talking to someone. They were upstairs watching us warm up. The ref blew his whistle to start the game. Once the puck dropped, it was end-to-end rushes.

We changed on the fly, once my line got on the ice. I had skated my heart out. I made a few nice moves to get around the offence, skating down the left side. Leading a two on one, I dragged the defence into the corner, where I made a perfect saucer pass to the front of the net. Leaving my line mate all alone, but was robbed by the goaltender's quick glove, as he tried to go upstairs on him. Through half the game, I was pointless. Feeling frustrated, I broke one of my sticks as we came off for line change.

"Relax Rob! You got to relax. Focus, stay focused." I thought to myself.

I then thought of Terry, wishing he were here. I remembered one of his games, when he played against Grand beach Dune Buggies. He was on break away until the defence chasing him, hauled him down. Hurting his shoulder as he slid into the end boards, the ref ruled a penalty shot for Tomahawks, The team he played for from our hometown Scanturbury. Slowly getting up, he just smiled.

He skated towards Terry Jr. and me and stopped at where we were sitting. "Pick a corner squirt," he asked Jr. "Blocker side!" was his response. Skating to center ice, he waited for the ref's signal. Terry gave us one last smile and winked when the ref blew his whistle. Skating down hard, not giving the goaltender a chance to set up. He faked going to the right, which was the goalie's glove side. Then with one quick move, he snapped a wrist shot over the goalie's blocker to put his team up one goal. He circled back to the net and picked up the puck he scored with and tossed to me. "That one was for you," he smiled at me again. The Tomahawk's won that night, with Terry scoring the game winner on his penalty shot. Remembering his smile brought my nerves at ease.

Our line was back on the ice, I was now relaxed and feeling comfortable. It was half way through the third period, when I got my break. The play was in our zone; I stole the puck and streaked down the left side. I cut across the ice between the red and blue line, as I got to the hash marks on the right side. I let a zinger of a slap shot go, over the goalie's right shoulder. "Bingo, Top corner."

"He shoots He scores." The instructor, acting as coach had said to me when we got off the ice for a line change. "Nice shot McKay!" He patted me on the shoulder. I was relieved I finally got a goal, to get a point for that matter. Before the game ended, I also added an assist. I felt totally down, like my game wasn't good enough. Depressed as I was leaving the dressing room, I remember thinking. "There goes my future."

As I entered the lobby, I had seen Mr. Hutchison along with Mr. Boyle speaking with my mom.

Hey Mr. Boyle's here, I haven't seen him in two years, since he was my instructor the first time I had attended the Hockey School. Where's this guy Mr. Hutchison was telling me about, I thought. I felt very discouraged and doubtful.

"There's your man now." Mr. Hutchison said; when he caught a glimpse of me.

Mr. Boyle smiled at me; I looked over to my mom who also had a big smile when I approached them.

"Hi Mr. Boyle, how are you doing?" I said to him.

"Call me Jamie Robert! I see you've improved, you looked pretty impressive out there."

"Thanks, but I feel I didn't play well enough out there." I had said.

"Oh!" Mr. Boyle looked at me. "And why is that?" he asked.

"I just wanted to impress the scout, which was watching me. But I guess I blew it."

"Don't be so hard on yourself Robert," Mr. Hutchison said, patting me on the shoulder. "Mr. Boyle is the man I told you about."

I felt my jaw hit the floor; I didn't know what to say. I just stood there feeling stupid.

"So...Mr. McKay! Are you interested in our hockey club?" Mr. Boyle asked with a smile.

"Uh..." I looked at my mother. She seemed more excited than I was. "Yes, I would be honoured to play for you."

"I already explained everything to your mother. You would be well looked after. Your education, room and board is spoken for. All you have to pay for is the bus fare there." Mr. Boyle said with a wink.

"Thank you for making this possible Mr. Hutchison." I said.

"Ah, it was nothing." He smiled.

That evening, I told my friends the exciting news.

"So Rob, if you ever make it to the big league. You would give us tickets right?" Joey asked poking me in the ribs.

"Why of course he would," Bill added.

"Don't be so stupid, we're his cheering squad."

"Well Rob! Since you wouldn't forget us...I hope you don't," Jason had said. "We'll treat you tonight. Let's just say, it's a going away gift. Lori is having a party. What do you say fellow's?"

"Its Miller time let's party and get **DRUNK!**" They all shouted.

Being sixteen was the time of my life. These guys were two to three years older than I was. I was in grade ten at the time. They were Varsity boys. A couple was repeating grade twelve, but my age didn't matter. I had loads of fun that night. When we arrived at Lori's, everyone screamed; "Congratulations, Rob." I was in total shock. I felt like a celebrity or something. I was part of the in crowd, instant recognition. Bill piled five shooters of Tequila on each other. He called it. Count down to stardom just looking at them made me sick. I was trying to back out, but the guy's wouldn't let me.

"Come on." Joey taunted. "Come on, I'll do some with you! Bill pour me some, pretty boy here is to shy to do it by himself."

"First one to win, well...Will get me for the night!" Lori added to the stakes.

"You might as well come over here sweet cheeks, he'll not do it." Joey said.

One night with Lori Chartrand, "Wow!" that was my inspiration. She's one of the hottest chicks in school, Elmwood's finest honey around. I was raring to go it was a count down from five. Soon as I heard number one, I shot back a shooter, before I could taste it. I downed another, then another. After the shooters were gone, Jason made me chase it with a Budweiser. The taste finally caught up to me. I felt my face go into a knot as I began to gag.

The guy's laughed and then cheered, when Lori shoved her tits into my face. I wiped my watery eyes, brushed my hair back with my hand. I grabbed Lori, smothering her with a kiss. The whole party was screaming my name. Bill and the guy's were shouting "**Pretty Boy**" My own cheering section all right; they were party animals. After a few more drinks, the rest of the evening was blank.

As I recall, I was sick the next morning. I sat up wondering where I was. I was at home, "How did I get here? Bill must have brought me home." I thought. I stayed in bed the whole day. Billy popped by later that day, to sort of check on me.

"Man! You look like shit." Bill said with a laugh.

"Yah...You smell like it!"

"Bite me; the guy's are heading to the drop in later. Feel up to it?"

"Not really! But I'll probably go." I said.

"I'll see you there then?"

"I suppose, hey! By the way, how did I get home?"

"Get lost! You mean you don't remember?" He laughed.

"What's so funny?" I asked.

"Lori; Lori brought you home. You two were all over each other. It was probably the best night of your life. And you don't remember a damn thing! Rob, you're an idiot." I laughed to myself, as I lay on my bed, wondering about the guy's. I wished they were there with me in Cranberry. Also I just wish I could remember that night with Lori. It haunts me to this day.

Lying there, Candice suddenly popped in my thoughts. I began thinking about that night with her. I remember it like it was yesterday. I was talking to her on the phone that evening; we were talking for some time. Somewhere out of the blue, I asked if her parents were home. She responded "No" Then I asked if it were okay to come over.

"What's on your mind, you devil."

"Oh you don't want to know." I said in a savvy voice.

"Mm sounds interesting. You know where I live, see you in ten sailor," she said before hanging up. I phoned one of my friends. I explained what had just happened. What was supposed to be a joke, turned into reality? He asked if I was going to go. I told him I wasn't sure of what to do.

3

"You mean this is your first?" he asked.

"Are you for real? I've done it many times. It's just.... I can't believe she wants me over."

"What the hell you waiting for, get going. She's expecting you."

"Oh yah! Yah, I'm only visiting that's all," I said.

"Okay there, what ever you say. Send her my love and kisses, all over her pink parts." Jason had said.

"What is that suppose to mean?" I asked.

"You should know! Call me later."

Candice wasn't too far; she lived fifteen minutes away. When I arrived at her place, I stood at her door. I knocked a few times. "What am I doing, what about Lisa?" I thought. I was home for Christmas break and here I am knocking on another girl's door. I was about to leave, when the door opened.

"There you are; what took you so long?" She asked.

"I had some things on my mind."

"Oh, something dirty I hope," she said, biting her bottom lip.

She invited me in, escorting me to the living room. I sat on the couch and made myself comfortable. She asked if I wanted something to drink.

"Sure, what do you have?"

"Let me see, I have Coke and umm J.D." She had said.

"J.D! What is that?"

"Jack Daniel's!" She said with surprise.

I sat there looking at her dumb founded. She gave me a weird look.

"Alcohol!" She said.

"OH…I'm sorry, no thanks. Coke is fine."

She handed me a can drink and went to the stereo. I was so embarrassed, feeling stupid. I took a big shot, thinking of what to say to her next.

"What kind of music do you like?" She asked.

"Mm doesn't matter," I said.

Playing a tape, she turned to me. It was country; I looked at her shaking my head. She laughed; laughing with her, I tried to stop it. Wrestling her on the couch, I looked into her bright hazel eyes. My lips pressed on hers. My hand caressed her breast, her body shifted around as she was getting aroused, kissing her on the chin, then her neck. Then I began to slowly remove her top and kissing her, moving down her cleavage to her stomach. With a moan, she pulled me up kissing me on the mouth again. We were on the couch naked, her hot body pressing up against mine. She rolled me on my back, to get on top thrusting onto me. Hearing her moans made me get even more excited. We rolled over and it was my turn. This was my first time with a girl, or at least I think it is. I only wanted to remember this moment. I don't remember that night with Lori Chartrand, so that doesn't count. Everything with Candice seemed so perfect. I was too embarrassed to let her know she was my first. Thinking she might laugh or not even bother with me at all. I didn't know what to think. As long as I was with her, I didn't care. The sensation was great; I forgot I hadn't put a condom on. Not pulling it out, I came inside her. Kissing her on the lips one last time, I told her that she was incredible. She smiled at me, as we lay there naked for a while.

"I've always fantasized about this moment with you." I whispered in her ear.

She turned around to face me. Kissing me,

"Me too!" She had said with a smile.

Lying there on my bed, I thought to myself. "I hope she doesn't get pregnant." I decided to go to the Mess hall, sit around the lounge and listen to music. Debating with myself, whether I should phone her or not.

Grabbing the receiver, I was hesitant at first. It was nearly a month since I've spoken to her. "What do I say?" I thought. Curiosity had gotten the best of me. I decided to call her, I needed to know the truth if she was pregnant. I felt my heart beating, scared and breaking out into a cold sweat. I was hoping she would answer the phone.

"Hello!" She answered.

"Hey, how are you?" I asked.

"Fine, and who's this?"

"It's me...Robert."

"HI," she said with excitement. "Where are you?"

"I'm in Cranberry Portage."

"When are you coming back?" She asked. "There's something we need to talk about!"

"Not till spring break, listen before you start. It's probably the same thing I want to talk to you about. The reason I'm calling is to ask about the night we slept together."

"Oh..." She went quiet.

"Candice.... Candice. Are you there?" I asked, thinking she hung up.

"I'm here," she said.

"I just wanted to see how you were, and to see if...well you know?"

"What are you talking about?" She asked.

"Look this is not funny, this is serious. We didn't use protection that night, and it's possible you..." I was afraid to say it.

"Well it's too late for that now." She exclaimed.

"What do you mean? Too late!"

"I could be." She left it at that.

"Is it mine?"

"Of course it's yours, who else's would it be?" she shouted before hanging up on me.

I was in total shock, how do I know she's telling the truth. Then again she wouldn't flip out the way she did. This cannot be happening. "What in the world am I going to do?" I thought. I'm too young to be a father. I'm only sixteen; seventeen is just around the corner. Great, that's just great. I spoke with her for ten minutes and she cuts me off by hanging up. What a bitch, she cost me $ six-eighty five on the damn payphone.

How was I supposed to explain this to my mother, let alone Uncle Terry? Both of them would be really pissed. My hockey dream was suddenly put on hold. Then again, Candice might be lying. My head was a complete mess. I couldn't think straight. My schoolwork began too fall behind. I was starting to miss some classes on a regular basis. I was losing it; I needed to talk to someone, but whom? I was too scared to phone home. "Why me?" I thought. I had a future to chase after; my dreams of glory seemed so distant. Feeling tears roll down my face, suicide crossed my mind. I broke down and cried, I had no idea were I stood. I cried myself to sleep.

The next day, I built up some courage to phone Terry. He was the only father figure I had the one person I could really talk too. I strolled down to the link way to use the phone. It rang for sometime, but he wasn't home. "Maybe I shouldn't tell him, not yet anyway." I said to myself as I sat by the phones.

There was a dance that evening at the gym. I thought about going with Waylon and Darryl. I usually had gone with Lisa, so I was undecided. I headed back to my room, feeling depressed. My entire world was yanked from under me. It was after supper when Waylon came by. He sat quiet for a while, as if he was searching for words. He just sat there staring at me.

"What are you thinking about?" he asked. Taking a shot from the Mickey he pulled out from his jacket.

"A lot of things," I wanted to tell him, what was going on. "Girls bud! Just girl problems."

"Don't worry about Lisa man! Why don't we go to the dance, take a load off your mind. Then we'll go see Darryl down at the dock." Waylon said.

"Yah! I guess your right. I'm probably thinking too much," I said to him.

Waylon was already half-cut. I guess he didn't eat after all, I didn't mind. He was about to take another shot from his Mickey, before I swiped it from him.

"Let's go then," I said taking a shot.

We were taking the long way around to the gym. Waylon wanted to finish his Mickey first. It was chilly outside, but the whiskey we had kept us warm. Waylon stopped suddenly.

"Wait a sec!" Waylon said holding out his arm. "I forgot. Lisa wants to see you."

"I don't want to see her!" I had said, moving his arm out of the way.

"It'll only be a minute," He said. "She's waiting for us in the link way…Oh look, there she is now." Lisa was walking toward us. I turned to Waylon and gave him a look. I didn't know how to react. "What the hell does she want now?" I thought. When she approached us, I noticed she too was intoxicated.

"Fu—ck," I looked over at Waylon. "Doesn't anybody eat?"

I did not want see or talk to her. She tried to kiss me. But I pushed her away. She acted like nothing happened between us. She was practically trying to screw me on the spot. I pushed her away again before she finally quit.

"Here Rob! Have another swig."

"No thanks. I think I had enough for tonight. I'm just going to head back to my room."

"Is it because I'm here?" Lisa said, as she hung on to Waylon for balance.

"What do think sweet cheeks? I was perfectly fine until you showed up."

"You're such an asshole! I only wanted to have some fun." Lisa blurted.

"Are you blonde? We broke up," I looked at Waylon with a shrug. "Broads."

"Fuck you Robert! I'll leave, if that makes you happy."

"Oh don't trouble yourself, because I'm going. Thanks for a wonderful evening Waylon!" I said turning to walk away.

"Rob wait, I didn't mean…"

"Let him go Waylon, he can't help it if he's such a prick!" She yelled.

"You're a bitch!" I shouted back.

Waylon stood there, staring blankly at us. He probably felt shitty for what had happened. It wasn't his fault; I had no intention to get him involved in our argument. I was going through a tough time. I headed back to my room and retired for the evening.

Two more weeks had passed by. I missed two hockey games during that time. I finally broke down and told Mr. Boyle about my problems last week. I told him I couldn't play, not the way I was feeling. I needed some time to straighten myself out, also to catch up on some schoolwork. I already missed too much. Mr. Boyle understood my situation and granted me time away from hockey.

I was sitting in the T.V. room of our dorm, when Paul Beardy walked in with the mail. Paul was our Supervisor. We rarely talked to him; he spent most of his time reading books. He wore black clothes with his black cowboy boots. He was tall and skinny; His hair was short, black and spiked. He must have been in his early twenties, because he still had some acne.

"Okay guy's here's your mail." Paul had said, tossing the bag on his desk.

He called out everyone's name, tossing our mail to us.

"Mr. McKay," He said looking at me. "Looks like you have some fan mail." He chucked a stack of envelopes at me. I sorted through the mail. Some were from my grandparents and my mother, Terry and one letter from Andy. Then I seen Candice's letter. I stood up from the couch and went to my room. I quickly opened it, not knowing what to expect. But on the other hand, hoping it was good news. I skimmed through it. She told me, she was sorry for leading me on. Our night together was a one-night stand; also she was already seeing someone when she slept with me. The feeling I had, was confusion and hurting. I felt used; here I thought we had some sort of chemistry. It felt like someone had closed their hand on my heart. She also said she was nine weeks pregnant. That it was Todd's, her boyfriend.

She explained to me that she went to get an abortion, how she was too young to be a mother. She went on to say, how sorry she was for involving me. She still wanted to be friends. I crumpled up the letter; I was too hurt to finish reading it. I sat there thinking, I suddenly realized. I no longer need too worry about being a father. It seemed a lot of weight was lifted off my chest. I was relieved.

"Oh God! What a ride." I sighed. "Lisa…I have to talk to her. It's been a month since I've spoken to her." I thought to myself.

Right now, I couldn't think about her. I had my hockey career too worry about. I went to the hanger before the team left for practice in the Pas. I stood there and watched as the bus was being loaded with our hockey gear.

"Don't forget mine." I said.

Mr. Boyle turned and smiled at me.

"What are you doing here?" he asked.

"I just miss the game, I want to play again."

"What about your grades? I thought you needed time to study?" Mr. Boyle had said.

"I received a letter today; it made me think about my future. It turned my upside down world, right side up. I realized where my heart is. And it's set on hockey."

"Well that's good to hear McKay, but that doesn't change anything. Your schoolwork comes first. Once your grades improve, I'll let you play," he said.

I was stuck for words. The last three weeks was a roller coaster ride. I thought he would be glad to see me, further more to do what I love the most; too play hockey. I watched as the last guy boarded the bus. Mr. Boyle along with Mr. Patterson was making sure everything was packed. I started walking back to the dorms.

"McKay!" Mr. Boyle shouted to me.

I stopped and looked at him.

"Get your ass on the bus!" he said.

It sure felt good to hear him say that. Without any hesitation, I ran to the bus.

"McKay," Mr. Boyle stopped me, before I jumped on the bus. "If you don't mind me saying; Lay off the girls a little, would yah!" He said with a smile.

During practice, Mr. Boyle had made us skate hard. We were to get ready for the big game next week. The Melville Millionaires, they were the top team in their division. This would be the first time our teams would meet, we play there and they too play at our place on Sunday. Wade McCormick was the new scoring leader. Wade was a tall and hefty center, which was his advantage point. He stood six foot four, six five on skates.

He was the big hitter and power forward for the Millionaires. He was their Goliath. I was behind sixteen points, with twelve games left. It was a new game and it was called Catch up! I think I could catch him. Even if I played injured, which I hope never happens.

I missed two weeks, but it felt like a month. I was a little out of shape, we were only half way finished through practice and I wished it were the end. I don't think I ever sweated like that, well. Not since hockey school anyway. When practice was finally over, I leaned over the boards in exhaustion. In the dressing room, I slowly took my gear off. Taking only my skates and shoulder pads off. I sat back in the stall.

4

"Well boys. That was one hell of a practice," Mr. Boyle had said. "Get some rest, cause tomorrow. We've got some dry land training after school."

We all moaned. Yep! It sure was great to be back. I missed all the excitement in the dressing room. I forgot how hard some practices were.

"Man! I swear. One of these days, my fucking legs are going to fall off. The way Boyle is skating us." Blaine Warner had said.

"It's good to see you too Blaine."

"Yah! Fuck you McKay!"

"Ah quit your complaining: If you played in the WHL. You would have to work much harder than this! So Shut-up!" I said before jumping in the shower.

After I got out of the shower, I gathered my gear together and got dressed.

"Hey! Nice speech. But you forgot to ask for cheese with your wine." Waylon had said.

"What! Your old lady's cheese was right here." grabbing my crotch.

"You sick bastard…Talk about my mom like that!"

"What! Get out of here, that's not what I meant," I said as I laughed. "By the way, I found out the truth about Candice. She's not pregnant, well not anymore."

"What do you mean? Not anymore." Waylon had said.

"She had an abortion. She had lots to say, but I didn't finish reading it."

"Was it yours?" Waylon asked.

"She told me, it was her boyfriend Todd's."

"Whoa! Back up a little; she had a boyfriend? And you cast your line in her?" Waylon asked with excitement.

"Cast your line?" I shook my head. "I didn't know she was seeing anybody!"

"You are one crazy guy. Hey, you old smooth. Give me some pointers."

We all boarded the bus. Sitting by the window, I thought about Candice. I tried not to, but I couldn't help it. Here I was, acting like a jerk. All she wants is to be friends. We were beyond friendship and that's what she thinks of me. "Maybe I should call her, it's the lease I could probably do." I thought. Once I get rid of this guilty feeling, hopefully things would be back to normal.

When we arrived back to the collegiate; I put out my gear, to air them out and then I went back to my room. I needed to study for midterm exams. Candice began to float around in my head, was I falling for her. Or was it a guilty conscience about her letter. I had mixed emotions; I was beginning to feel lost. Suddenly, I found myself in the link way. I sort of drifted in here. Standing by the phones, I debated with myself, whether to call her or not. Then I seen Lisa, I wanted to talk to her. She was along with one of her girlfriends. I called out her name as I approached them. She took one look at me and continued on, like I wasn't there. Calling her once more, I pleaded for her to listen.

She said something to Kristen, and then she left. Lisa stood there waiting, I felt scared to approach her, and she was still hostile. It was hard to swallow, feeling a big lump in my throat. I explained everything to her, although she had a few words to say herself. But I told how much remorse I had toward her. I asked if we could start over again. "Lisa, I'm so sorry for what I put you through. I know it's hard to forgive me. At least try to find it somewhere to forgive me. Look, you don't have to say anything right now. I just want us to be friends again. If you want, I'll be in my room studying. So I hope to see you later!" Then she just left without a word.

That evening, I studied; sometimes glancing out the window, wondering if Lisa was coming over. Reviewing some recent chapters, I hoped where going to be on the exam. As time quickly went by, I found myself sleeping face down in my textbook. It was four in the morning; I dragged myself to bed. The following morning, I went over some notes before I had a shower. I skipped breakfast, so I could study a bit more for my history exam. I only needed sixty percent to pass; I hoped all the studying I've done pays off.The exam was held in the gym that morning. Feeling nervous and tense, "I could do it." I said to myself as I tried to shrug off the pressure. Thursday January 27th marked the date of the exam. Mr. Dumont's tests during the semester; were usually difficult. We had two hours to complete. Our English literature was held in Mr. Patterson's chemistry lab that afternoon. As the day passed, I finished my exams with great confidence. I couldn't wait till the morning, as our marks would be posted on the billboard in the link way.

I barely slept, I needed to know if I passed or not. I was hoping to pass, so I would remain on the team. It wouldn't look good if I failed. I would be a disgrace. Now the pressures were beginning to build. Having to study for Math and Biology, made everything seem more difficult. When morning finally came, I couldn't look at the billboard; I was too afraid. When I saw my name, I went across the page with my finger. History 80%: English 62%. I almost fell over; I was in shock. When it sunk in that I passed, I was practically jumping up and down.

Thinking to myself, "All I need is a passing mark on these last two courses. I hoped I studied enough, I just want to remain on the team." That Friday was a long one. The day seemed it wouldn't end: both exams were extremely hard. There were times where my mind went blank. Finally completing my most feared tests of them all, fearing the worst. I now had the weekend too sit and wait for the results. We had the weekend to think about, whether we passed or not. The teachers probably had a ball; Watching us walk around all worried. I eagerly waited for Monday to roll around. When the marks were posted, there was a line up. Everyone was anxious as I was. Hoping I passed when I seen some faces turn from excitement to almost nothing at all, I felt sorry for them.

I was crossing my fingers, looking for my name. I did same thing, running my finger across the page. Math 71%: Biology 75%. I was lit with joy, but before I could jump around. I thought about those who failed. I waited till I was in my room, yelling and screaming; my hands in the air like I just scored a goal. I was ecstatic. I'm staying on the team. As the day went on, some students had gotten a second chance for redemption. They received re-examination. "Teacher's pet." Monday was the last day for our exams. We had term break for the remainder of the week. Some students left for home. Our hockey team had to stay, because we had important game on Thursday February 3rd. facing the top team in the SHSL league: The Melville Millionaires. Mr. Boyle scheduled to leave Wednesday afternoon.

The night before leaving, one of the locals from the team decided to have a party at his house. Brian McLeod was his name. He invited everyone from the team along with who just wanted to party. It would be the first party I had attended since arriving here in September. I was to shy to go to other parties. This one was no different, I was still nervous, but Waylon and Darryl accompanied me. We arrived at Brian's around eight-thirty. Brian announced us in, acting as the butler.

"You're an idiot." Darryl had said to him.

"Thank-you sir. I do my best!" Brian replied. "You want something to drink, a Budweiser perhaps?"

"Sure!" Waylon and Darryl had said

"Then get it yourself, the fucking kitchen over there." Brian had said.

We turned and looked at one another laughing. Brian the goof that he was always made us laugh.

"Hey guy's," Dwayne called to us. "How's it going? Wait till you see the whoa." tripping over a chair. We couldn't help but laugh, as he stumbled to get back to his feet.

"Where in the hell did that come from?" He said before leaving, totally forgetting he was talking to us.

We went into the kitchen where Jason and Crystal were hanging. Waylon sat down by Crystal, chatting about some school stuff. I glanced around feeling a bit out of place. Jason was asking me how I did on our mid terms. Sitting there, hearing the music blasting. I drifted away, thinking about my old gang back home. No wonder I was feeling lost; I was missing my boys.

"Hey Rob!" Jason shook me. "You feel alright?"

"Yah! I was watching those girls dance."

I said hi to Crystal and moved away from the kitchen. I wondered around the house. The whole place was kicking, I thought about leaving.

"Hi Robert." Lana Campbell said as she tapped me on the shoulder.

"Hi Lana!" I smiled.

"Enjoying the party?" She asked.

"Yah, it's alright."

"Would you like a drink? Since I see you're without one." She asked.

"Uh, sure. A Coke will be fine."

"Come on!" She looked at me. "Have a real drink. Rye or something."

"Not right now, maybe later."

"I'll mix it light for you; A little Rye and Coke. How about it? Come on try it, you'll like it." She implored me.

"Okay, you've talked me into it; But only one." I looked at her and smiled, shaking my head.

"Great, have a seat. I'll be right back." Lana had said.

I sat down at the table, watching some drink their brains out. Then out of the blue, this one guy leans over me and was about to puke. I pushed him away from me as I dodged the mess he made. Brian wasn't too happy to see what had happened. Not that the guy dirtied the floor, but watered his tree plant as well. The poor guy was thrown out the door on his face. To add insult to injury, the tree plant was thrown on top of him. I laughed to myself. Then Darryl sat down beside me.

"Hey! Is this a great party or what?"

"I've been to better ones." I had said.

"Ouch! That hurt. So are you having any fun yet?"

"I was, up until some bozo almost threw up on me."

"What! Oh man…I wish I were here when that happened. That's just great; I'm missing all the fun."

"Here you go" Lana had said, handing me a drink.

"Hey Lana, what's new?" Darryl asked.

"Mm, not much: just trying to get your friend drunk!"

"You told me, you were not going to drink." Darryl looked at me. "I'm just mingling, he say's." He was making quotation marks with his hands.

"What? I'm only having this one!"

"Yah, okay there Rob," he said, winking at me.

"Excuse me boys." Lana had said, tending to her friends, who were calling her.

"Hey, what's up?" Darryl had said, looking at Lana.

"What are you talking about?"

"Don't play dumb, spill the beans. Give me details?" He implied.

"She's just a friend! Holy cow, I can't even talk to a girl without you or Waylon, thinking something."

"Not around here bud! What? Are you from the city or something? Oh yah I forgot," Darryl had said. "You're forgetting. This is a small town, people love to gossip."

"I was only talking to her. What's wrong with that? I was just being polite by talking to her." I said.

"Ah, I was only messing with yah!" He smiled. "I'll see you later." He got up and left.

"What an asshole!" I thought. I sat there for a moment feeling upset with Darryl. Then Lana came back with a couple of friends.

"Robert, come hang out with us." Lana had said grabbing my arm.

I took a quick sip of my drink, as she led me around the house. I was beginning to feel comfortable as Lana kept me entertained. I did not realize how late it was, a couple of hours passed by so quickly. I still had the same drink in my hand. I only finished half a glass. I put my glass down on the end table, as it was too warm to drink. Lana dragged me around the house, we played games and stuff, and some were drinking games. But she drank the whole time. I was having a great time, this was one party I didn't want too forget. It was a little past one in the morning, when I told her I was leaving.

"Do you have to leave?" She asked. "It's still early. Come on; stay a little bit longer. I was just getting started!" She pleaded.

"I'm sorry, I can't. We're leaving tomorrow. Besides, I'm getting tired."

"Well, since I can't talk you in to staying. Can you walk me home? It is kind of dangerous for a girl like me, too be out all alone." She requested.

"Where do you live?" I asked with a smile.

As we walked down the street, she babbled something about movies. I wasn't listening; my mind was elsewhere. Then she invited me to watch a movie with her sometime. I wasn't paying any attention to where I was going, when I suddenly realized. I was lost.

"Where are we?" I asked.

"Just a little ways more." Pointing to a house that over looked the lake.

The scenery amazed me; it was a full moon. You could almost see clear across the lake. Her house stood along a small cliff that peered over the frozen lake. It was beautiful.

"Thanks for walking me home. I had a wonderful evening. I hope you enjoyed yourself as well," she said.

"I should be thanking you. If you hadn't shown me around, I probably would have left a long time ago. You made me feel, how should I say this, special. I was comfortable around you." She smiled at me and kissed me on the cheek. I stood and watched her walk up the stairs, slowly closing the door behind her. I was about to leave when I realized. I had no clue to where I was. I knew I had to walk the opposite direction of the lake. It was a small town how could I get lost. It took me almost an hour to get back to the dorms. I snuck in through the back so I wouldn't get caught outside past curfew. I probably should have gone back for Waylon and Darryl, but they might have left after me. I quietly snuck into my room and went to bed.

5

The morning after, Waylon and Darryl somehow got in my room. I felt someone tapping my arm and whispering for me to get up. Slowly opening my eyes to see who was bothering me, my visual was blurry at first. Rubbing my eyes, about six inches from my face, was the hideous mask I ever seen. I Jumped out of bed nearly pissing on myself: Darryl fell over laughing. Waylon barely pulled his mask off, he was laughing so hard.

"You Asshole," I shouted. "Are you trying to give me a heart attack or something?"

"If you could only see yourself," Darryl said laughing. "Your eyes were like saucers."

"How did you guy's get in here?"

"Through the door, duh." Waylon said as he snorted with his laugh.

"Man! Don't you two ever sleep," I said while rubbing my eyes. "You guy's reek. Go shower or something."

"What are you talking about, we just left Brian's." Darryl said.

"Holy shit! We're leaving this afternoon. You guy's, Boyle is going to be pissed at you."

"Oh my God really? Ha would you relax, Boyle wouldn't leave with out the rest of us anyway," Darryl had said.

"The rest of us? You mean some of the others are still drunk?" I asked them.

"Yup! Now. Let's talk about you and Lana Mm." Darryl said with a stupid smile on his face.

"What's this?" Waylon had said.

"Rob here was with Lana last night." Darryl said.

"Whoa. Whoa, hold on just a minute. I was only talking."

"Sure, sure. Come on, huh." Darryl expressed.

"Leave him alone. I'm sure he has some explanation for his behaviour. Is that right Robby?" Waylon now adds to the discussion.

"Nothing happened!" I looked at them. "Believe me."

"Come on man! You could tell us, we're your friends!" Darryl implored.

"How about. Nah!" I said

"Jeez, you've been hanging around us too long, to be talking like that." Waylon had said with a chuckle.

"Yah! All I wanted to know was did you kiss her?" Darryl continued.

"Oh for the love of Pete, would you let it go already! Let's just go have some breakfast." I said to him.

"Okay, okay." Darryl had said. "Then you'll tell us?"

"Oh go to bed already." I said to him.

We were walking to the cafeteria, passing Darryl's dorm. He decided to go to his room. Waylon punched him in the arm and kicked him in the ass.

"Its about fucking time, I'm tired too. But you kept me up. Asshole! I just got my second wind. And you decided to go to bed. Jerk off!" Waylon stammered.

I was shocked at the way Waylon spoke to Darryl. I never heard him talk that way before. I stared at him blankly, searching for words.

"What?" Waylon had said, after seeing the expression on my face.

I shrugged my shoulders.

"Phfft." Was the only word that came from my mouth.

"He was sickening all night," Feeling he had to explain I guess. "You don't know him like I do. And believe me, he can be a real asshole at times. Like now for instance, I had to put up with that all night."

"Whoa, okay there. Ease up! You're starting to slobber all over me." I said.

"Fuck off Rob!" Wiping his mouth. "Don't start with me now." He chuckled.

"Good thing you didn't pass out!" I said to him.

"Why is that?" he asked.

"You would have probably drowned!" I said as I laughed.

"Fuck you." Grabbing me to wrestle.

After wrestling around, we continued toward the cafeteria. Suddenly Waylon began to stagger. I asked if he was okay; He just blamed the Whiskey. His second wind ran out, he began to run sideways to regain his balance. But fell flat on his face. I tried to hold my laugh in but couldn't. Trying to help him back to his feet, I asked if he was okay, the only thing I heard from him was a gargle.

"Waylon! Snap out of it. Come let's get you back to your room."

I struggled to keep him on his feet. As both of us now, staggered towards the dorm.

"Wait, wait a second. Stop; you're going all over the place," he said.

"You sure you can walk then?" I asked.

"Oh absolutely," he said with his eyes closed.

"Let's go then!" I laughed. "Before someone comes."

"Right behind you slick!" Giving me thumbs up, before falling over again.

Lying there, rolling on his back. Calling me over to him.

"You know what Rob? I think I better go to bed."

"Well don't fall asleep here! Man you were fine a few minutes ago. What happened?"

"The whiskey snuck up on me. Oh! I think I'm going to be sick."

"Come on get up before you choke. Lets go, you have three hours to try to sleep it off." I said as I helped him to his feet.

Walking back to the dorms, I wondered how the other guy's were. Mr. Boyle isn't going to be happy. Darryl along with Waylon reeked. When it was time to leave for Melville, half the guy's were late. Boyle was furious, he shouted at us. Telling us how disgusted he was, too see half the team still cut. He made us grab our hockey bags and run to where the bus waited for us. He gave us twenty minutes to reach the bus. If we didn't make it, the bus would go ahead another kilometre. I was one of the first one's to make it. Mr. Boyle patted us on the back as we boarded the bus. As for the other's, the one's that were hanging over, they ran 2km's more. When everyone was on the bus, and settled in: Mr. Boyle gave us shit again.

"You boy's make me sick!" He said scratching his head. "I'm not here to baby sit. I'm here to coach, not to run around looking for you. What you did, is an embarrassment to this hockey club. It stinks in here, I don't know about the rest of you. But I sure don't want smell that stench all the way Melville. So what I'm going to do is, make everyone run one kilometre with your hockey gear. And you are going to do this until I say so! I'm not putting up with this shit anymore. I've let you boy's get your own way, but to those who had nothing to do with this. You can thank the ones who spoiled it for everyone else. If anyone has anything to say Do it now. Don't forget, I brought you here; I made you what you are. I hold your transcripts; I see which club is looking at you. It's your choice, my way or the highway. It's simple as that." He signalled for the driver to leave.

Our ride into the Pas seemed long for some reason. Everyone was quiet, it was the first time I witnessed this. Usually on road trips, it's like a circus. We stopped at chicken chef for a quick bite, even yet no one was talking. Shortly after leaving, Waylon sat by me. He finished eating his snack pack before he broke the silence.

"I feel like shit," he said.

"Yah! You smell like it too." I said.

"Sorry for bringing you down with us."

"Don't worry about it, I was there too."

"Oh yeah!" He gave a little laugh. "I made a complete jack ass out of myself this morning didn't I?"

"You took the words right out of my mouth, but it was hilarious, I never laughed so hard in along time. Just looking at you makes me want to laugh!" I started to laugh.

"Well, it's nice to know I'm the village idiot." Waylon had said.

Waylon and I played some cards to pass the time. Darryl joined us after he awoke from his nap. We talked about the party. There were some great highlights of the night. Darryl said he caught Dwayne, screwing Bryden's chick in the bathroom. They didn't even lock the door. Darryl said he stood there watching for a minute, before he told them to get a room. But I think Waylon would be top dog. I don't know what card game they were playing. Darryl said he was shooting back a few Dragon's breath, and chased it with a beer. Everything was all right, until he choked or something. Beer was coming out of his mouth and nose. We laughed amongst our selves. Darryl continued with Lana. Soon the bus began to slow down.

"Okay boy's, you know the drill now." Mr. Boyle shouted.

One by one we exited the bus. Standing at the rear, we waited for Mr. Boyle as he tossed out our gear.

"What are you waiting for?" Mr. Boyle said. "Grab one!"

Quickly grabbing a bag, I made sure I hadn't grabbed Timothy's bag. It was the heaviest; He was our goalie. Running a kilometre wasn't bad but too carry all that other weight made it difficult. I was really dragging my ass it was the hardest run I had to do. Mr. Boyle gave us twenty minutes to reach the bus. The bus was getting closer, seeing some board the bus.

"I'm almost there!" I thought. The bus was a pole length away, I seen Mr. Boyle look at his watch. He then got on the bus and it slowly drove away. "No, don't go." I said in fainted voice.

I just stood there, the hockey bag slowly falling from my shoulders. I totally was feeling shitty about myself. But I did not stand there very long, hoisting the bag on my shoulders again. I took off running, sweat falling from face I pushed myself ahead. "This is for you uncle, this is what you meant by the limits." Thinking to myself. "You've once told me, when things seem dim. There is light at the end of the tunnel. Never give up; or loose faith. Keep striving for what you have worked so hard to get." With that in thought I ran to the next destination where the bus waited. Finally making it too the bus, Boyle let us have it. I knew he was still disappointed, with the whole team that is.

"Well boy's, I'm very ticked at you all. I came here to coach a team to a championship. I believed that I had the best player's, someone I can rely on. Player's that would take charge and focus on winning. If you don't give a shit! Then you don't belong here. I expect the best of you tomorrow: You either shape up, or ship out."

The next four hours were very quiet. It was a long ride that seemed forever. Nobody wanted to talk or do anything. Passing by Yorkton with out stopping my stomach growled. As did every one else I guess. Wishing for something to eat, my mouth watered as I seen a sign chicken chef next right turn. I guess we all were looking out the window as we passed it. I was glad I took my Walkman along; soon we were in Melville, Mr. Boyle took us for something to eat and then checked us in at the local hotel.

6

Game Night. February 3rd.

On the ride over to the rink, I felt butterflies in my stomach. My hands were clammy and my mouth was dry. Pulling up to the rink, the parking lot was half full. We had one hour till game time and people were already filling the arena. This team had quite a booster club, our fans where not as hockey crazy as Melville. As we walked through the rink, I could not believe how huge it was. It felt like I was walking through the Brandon Keystone Center. It even had a second level with over hanging balconies.

"Holy Toledo! What an entrance." Steve had said.

"I wish we had an arena like this, the barn looks like a barn compared to this." Waylon said.

"Jeez, were not even playing yet! And there's a crowd already." Darryl had said.

What a pressure to play under, it seemed as if the whole town was there. I've played in big arenas before, but not in front of a crowd such as this. The guy's began to pull out their gear and hanging them up. Sitting there watching, the butterflies were in my stomach. Feeling nervous I tried to stay focused, mentally preparing myself for the game. As I got ready, I taped my sticks, I also sent for my skates to be sharpened. Play-offs were weeks away, there were only twelve games remaining for me too prove that I can make the best of it; sixteen points shouldn't be too hard to reach. Trying for the scoring title would be the first time I ever come this close.

Soon as my skates were ready, I suited up and went for our pre-game skate. Walking down the hall towards the ice surface, stepping on that ice and looking around. I had this incredible urge too play, leave my mark here. My adrenaline rushing through my body, I gave a quick burst of speed and raced around our end. When everyone from the team was on the ice, we warmed up Timmy. We did the horseshoe, some breakouts and two on one drill. Once that was done, Darryl shouted for us to do a quick two laps and stretch out.

The crowd cheered as the Millionaires touched the ice; they skated by center ice looking at us, sizing us up perhaps. Farmer boys we called them, the size of some of them was unbelievable. But we were not intimidated, I watched as one by one circled center ice. Looking for him, maybe he was not playing. It was as life itself had come to a complete halt, as he appeared.

Number 27 slowly made his way to the ice, Wade McCormick. Standing 6 foot 5 with his skates, you can almost hear the ice separating as his blades cut through it. I watched his every move; the way he handled the puck, it was like it was stuck to his stick. He had soft hands for a guy his size with a quick release. I was in complete awe witnessing his talent.

"That's the guy you want to watch out for." Waylon had said.

"Huh, What?" Catching me in a daydream.

"McCormick! Man he's good isn't he? But you can take him out eh?"

"I don't know." I had said.

"Ah don't doubt yourself. Just because you're only 5' 6," he's not that much taller than you."

"5'10" and 170lbs." I said cutting him off.

"Whatever, remember that guy in Dauphin?" Waylon said.

"Oh yah! How can I forget? That was sweet; I still have his face imprint in my shoulder pads, from catching him in the trolley tracks. I really smacked him good didn't I?" I grinned from ear to ear.

"That you did," Waylon said with a smile. "I want you to do that too McCormick. Show him there's a new boss in town."

Hearing that from him psyched me up. I had more courage to play, once our skate was over, we went to the dressing room to wait for the start of the first period. Mr. Boyle's game plan was simple, rough them up and knock them around, show them we were not scared. The ref blew his whistle to signal us. "Make sure you look out for one another, I want you to rough them up. Remember we are here to play hockey, these boy's may be big. But the bigger they are the harder they fall. We can take these chumps, I believe in you. I believed in you all season, now's the time to believe in yourself. I can only lead you so far; it's up to you to go the rest of the way. So come on boys, what do you say? On three." Mr. Boyle had said.

"One two three...*MOHAWKS*!" we all shouted.

We were pumped, to see all those people made us more eager to play. Once we were on the ice we exploded, skating hard around the rink. This was the game of the century, the big game. We didn't take them too lightly, as they probably were told the same about us. The announcer was talking a mile a minute. The crowd cheered as the music man played old rock tunes. The Millionaires made there way to the ice, my game face was on. Mr. Boyle made some quick changes to our line up, putting me on the first line. "McKay get out there and stir things up, set up the plays. Clark! Don't let them get past our blue line, as for the rest of you. Do your job; now let's play some hockey." Mr. Boyle had said.

"Ladies and gentlemen, boys and girls of all ages. Welcome to the Melville Millionaires arena where the Millionaires host the Cranberry Portage Mohawks. Please rise as we play our national anthem." The announcer had said.

Once the anthem was over, the ref blew his whistle to start the game, facing off staring into my opponents eyes. Waiting for the puck to drop, losing first draw. The play was quickly in our end, chasing it in as they dumped it. They regained access of the puck, cycling it around. Forgetting to play the body, we were running around like chickens with no heads. They set up for the point shot, with Tim being screened; he still managed to block it leaving a rebound. Another shot was fired on net, ringing off the cross bar the crowd wooed; with the puck was still in play, it was dumped into the corner. Tired and my legs burning, I chased after it with my opponent coming in hard. I went for the puck once he was close I put my shoulder into his chest, knocking him to the ice. The crowd roared, soon we were breaking out of our zone, getting the puck past center we dumped it into their end and we changed lines.

"Great hit McKay! He never saw it coming." Mr. Boyle slapped me on the shoulder.

Changing on the fly, our guys played the puck well in their zone getting four shots on net. Desperately trying to get it out of their zone, wrapping it off the boards behind the net. Blaine misplayed the puck sending the opposition on a break away.

"Come on Tim, save it." Was the only thought I had as we all stood and watched. With a fake to his left, Tim committed and gave up a goal. The house erupted with a roar. The guys moaned in disbelief, the arena was filled with cheers. It was end-to-end action with both teams exchanging shots and hits.

Still down by one, late in the first period we received a break. Stealing the puck from the player he was back checking, Darryl went down on the defence, it was one on one. Taking him outside Darryl beat him with his speed, a quick head fake ringing it off the cross bar and in. We jumped up from our bench; we were back in the game. The period ended tied at one, the shots favoured the Millionaires 17-12. As we waited for the ice to be cleaned, Mr. Boyle lectured us about defensive hockey. Drawing out our plays on the chalkboard, making changes to our line up again, I had sort of drifted away for a moment. My mind started to wonder, thinking of Terry. Wishing he were here to watch, I really missed seeing him in the stands hollering. Listening too him yelling Tomahawks drafty, encouraging me to hit someone.

"Hey McKay, are you listening?" Mr. Boyle asked.

"Yes sir," I said shaking myself out of a daydream. "You wanted me to play defence."

"No! I said for you to fore check in deep and hustle back to help our defence. If you were paying attention, maybe you would understand what was going on," he said, going on about playing defensive.

Heading back out to the ice, hordes of kids were waiting for us. They were asking us for autographs, and our sticks. Being ignored by my fellow teammates, I stopped by one kid; he looked up at me with a big smile and asked for an autograph.

"Sure what's your name kid?"

"Stewart, but it's not for me. It's for my sister; she never missed a hockey game, now she's at home sick. Mom says its pneumonia." His smile now disappeared.

Feeling sorry for him, I asked for her name. Sally was his response; I signed a cap and gave him my stick for her as well. His face lit up as he stood there holding it.

"Wow thanks mister." He shouted out to me as I skated to our bench. I watched as he ran to where he sitting with his dad or something. A warm glowing feeling ran through my body, it made me smile. Grabbing for my other stick, Mr. Boyle whistled to me, catching my attention. He gave me a wink. "That was very thoughtful of you; it makes me proud to have you on my team." he said. Looking at him I just smiled. He put me on Darryl's line for the first shift. The puck dropped and the second period was under way. Winning the draw, it was dumped in their end zone. Racing for the puck, Darryl had his man beat. Looking for an open winger, he dodged a hit loosing the puck.

Reaching for it with his head down, he didn't see McCormick coming. "*Crunch*" that's what it sounded like, the arena rocked. It was a hard hit and clean. Darryl was slow at getting back to his feet, wheezing struggling for air. The play continued and was down in our end. I skated back to help the defence. I had seen my chance to get even. I watched as one of their player's go behind the net for a wrap around. I took three hard strides, catching him with his head down also; I put my shoulder down, I felt his head sink into my shoulder pad. The force of the hit pushed him into the boards as well. I can still hear that collision our equipment and the boards made.

It was complete silence when we collided. The crowd was now on there feet screaming for a penalty, the play had been stopped. The player I creamed never got up; he had lain there like he was dead. Their trainer was led to them. He was knocked unconscious; some of the Millionaires were trying to get at me. The linesmen pulled me aside leading me to the box. Mr. Boyle was furious, yelling at the ref that it was a clean hit. Pushing me into the box, I had no idea what I was getting a penalty for.

Jason our team captain was trying to talk to the ref, but he told him to go to our bench. Both the linesmen and the ref were talking amongst them selves. The player I hurt was taken off in a stretcher, now the game was changed. The tension was high; you could feel the crowd's reaction. "Mohawks penalty, to number 19: Robert McKay, a 5-minute minor for charging. Time of the penalty, 16:46." The timekeeper announced.

"Hey ref! Where did you get your certificate?" Mr. Boyle yelled. "A cracker jack box?"

Sitting in that box, people were throwing garbage on me. Some were swearing while others were calling me names. I never heard such language, facing discrimination. I was almost at tears from hearing such powerful words from a fan. I tried to block them out, but it was next to impossible. "Go back home Indian. We don't like your kind here, fucking squaw." One fan had said. "Hey Indian!" another banged on the glass behind me. "Your mom's a hooker, I know because I fucked her last night." he laughed, patting his mouth with his hand.

I turned to who said that, he leaned over the glass and swung violently at me. I slashed at him with my stick. The crowd reacted to that. The ref came to my aid. I told him what had happened. He didn't see it nor did Mr. Boyle. I still had to sit out my penalty; it was the longest 5-minutes of my life. The name calling continued I just sat there feeling angry with the crowd. I hated them for what they had said. Once my penalty was over, I jumped on the ice, instead of going to our bench. I skated into the play, feeling the rage over come me. I wanted to get rid of it. McCormick was on the ice, which made things worse. He was the one I needed to get rid of, their top player. I really wanted to hurt him. I could hear Mr. Boyle screaming for me to come off. But I couldn't, I've waited too long to face McCormick.

During my time in the box, the Millionaires scored 2-minutes into my penalty. Skating down into our end, Wade was leading the rush. Cutting through the trolley tracks, big mistake. Dropping a pass to the trailing winger, he was admiring his pass. I gave him a beautiful hip check, sending him sprawling over me into the boards. The house erupted with an uproar. My hit was clean. With the play now in our advantage, I skated into the open across center ice. Receiving a pass I led a two on one rush.

Faking a pass, the defender played my winger. Leaving the goalie and me alone, at the top of the hash marks on his left side; I let a zinger of a slap shot go, ripping it past him off the cross bar and in. Skating past their bench, I patted my cage with my glove giving a war cry. I was pumped after I scored for us also from hitting McCormick.

"What the hell were you thinking? And what in gods name was that you just did?" Mr. Boyle scolded.

"I scored didn't I?" I had said with a tone.

"What was that?" He gave a brute look. "You play my way or the highway McKay. We are here as a team not as individuals. What you did back there was completely unacceptable; I'm fuck, very upset right now. As of now you're benched until further notice."

Before the end of the second period, the Millionaires scored two more goals. The score was 4-2; the shots favoured them now 39-27. This team was good; they not only out shot us. They over powered us. Wade McCormick had added another goal to his title, point number 88; there was no way I could catch him now. There's nothing I could do from the bench, since Mr. Boyle sat me out. Once in the dressing room, I received another lecture only that I faded him out. Turning from me, he now was speaking to the team. Bringing up our mistake we made the night before. Because of that we were losing and our brains were out to lunch yet as he put in that perspective. But I cut him off.

"Mr. Boyle, if you're upset with me. Don't take it out on the team. I made a bad judgment by not coming off the ice. I was mad at the world for a moment, if you only heard what they were saying to me. They were hurtful words. Words I never heard before, all I heard were squaw thumper. Indians go home and such. My heart filled with rage, I wanted to get them back and the only way I saw it was to take out McCormick."

"Well…" Mr. Boyle searched for words.

He stood there for a minute looking at us. Then he walked toward the door calling Mr. Patterson to follow. He said he'd be right back, and then left for several minutes.

"Hey," Darryl said. "We all faced discrimination one way or another. Don't let it get the best of you, just try to ignore it. I'm getting called down out there too. I'm sure we probably all are."

"I never thought people could be so cruel." I said.

"I was told that growing up was never going to easy. We just have to get use to it. They're only words Rob, that's all I could say." Waylon had said.

Sitting there hearing what they said just astounded me. I grew up with friends of every colour and here, the boy's who were from all surrounding areas. Some were from Duck Bay, Swan Lake, and Norway House, Cross-Lake, Dauphin, Thicket Portage and a few other reserves I can't remember. These boys came here to play hockey as well as I did. I never took notice as to where they came from in the beginning. I mean they spoke to each other in their native tongue. I was never taught my language which is Swampy Cree. It was breathe taking for me. They constantly spoke to each other in their tongue. The whole school was that way; some had hard English.

I never thought of myself as being aboriginal until now. Before I was just a person to my friends, but now; now…I'm a fucking Indian or squaw what ever they called us. Soon Mr. Boyle along with Mr. Patterson came back into the dressing room.

"Ok, I talked to the referees. I told them to handle the game professionally or we walk. I'm not going to put up with this shit. All I could say is they're jealous and scared of a better team. McKay I'm sorry this had to happen to you, as for the rest of you. This world is full of cruel ignorant people. Discrimination is one of the worst words I truly hate. We must fight through this together. My colour or yours does not matter here in this dressing room. What I see are a bunch of players who came to this club, wanting to play hockey. And that's all I want us to do, this is just one of life's obstacles we all encounter some where in our lives. If you could get through this, you can do anything. So let's get out there and play hockey."

The boys raved on the thought; once the ice was ready they stormed out. I sat there thinking of undressing. Those words still bothered me that was now haunting me.

"Come on Robert, let's go!" Mr. Boyle had said.

"I'm benched any way. I might as well undress."

"You're not benched," He smiled shaking his head. "I only wanted you to know I call the shots. Show me some respect, will you; I brought you here because I believed you are good player for this club. When I watched you for the first time, I couldn't believe how much you improved in you skills. You have to cool down a little. I don't want to loose you to a suspension, I know there under your skin right now. But that's what they want, it's the only way too throw you off your game. Remember…have fun out there."

Walking down the hallway to the bench, I could hear the music playing. Already the music man was playing "Rock You" from Queen. This tingling feeling ran through my body as the crowd chanted the lyrics. Joining the team on the bench, Mr. Boyle put me on the third line. The ref blew his whistle to start the third period. The centers squared off, Darryl winning the draw; McLeod passed it across to Stephen Beardy the other defence. Faking a pass and carrying it in, throwing it across to Dwayne who was breaking hard to the net. A quick wrist shot on net, the goalie easily made a blocker save giving a rebound. Jason was all over it and scored. Our bench was on their feet. Scoring under two minutes into the third; that's all we needed to boost us up. Mr. Boyle put our line out to try too score and doing some hitting. Fore-checking we managed to keep them at center and dumped the puck out of our zone. The Millionaires caught us off guard by quickly turning the play back into our zone; we were in the middle of a line change.

While going one on one with Waylon, their winger faked going wide. Catching him off balance, the winger pushed him aside and set up a pretty play. He gave a beautiful saucer pass to the trailing center; one timing it as Tim sprawled to make the save. The crowd moaned. Later on in the period, we received a break. Jason was sent in on a one on one with their defence, with a burst of speed gunning for it taking him wide.

The Millionaires defence gave Jay a hard hip check into the boards sending the crowd onto their feet with a roar. Jason crawled around on the ice as he was in pain; the ref blew his whistle to stop the play. Mr. Patterson raced to him; he was slow to get up as he was winded. The whole game turned into a grudge match, both teams were physical wanting a victory. Which one was to win, they led by one goal and there was plenty of time to catch them. Waiting to be put on a line, I glanced at

Waylon who came off his shift. He looked over to me and patted his shoulder; not sure of what he meant, I shrugged my shoulders.

"Hit somebody when you're out there." he said.

Soon I was out with Darryl and Dwayne, the play was in our end. Breaking out from our zone, Brian threw it up the middle towards Dwayne who wasn't expecting a pass. Banking off the opposing player, Dwayne whacked at it deflecting in my direction; I received it, only it was behind me. Looking back to get it in front of me, I turned and to skate with the puck. Instead I was hit hard into the boards; all I heard was the crowd erupt into cheer. Getting back onto my skates, I raced back into play. Dwayne streaked down the left side, dropping a pass to Blaine who let a slap shot go. Ripping it over the net hitting the glass hard, Darryl was there to get the loose puck. Only to let it go by after seeing a hit coming. Chasing it in the corner, I had seen my chance to hit someone. As he was carrying it out along the boards, I put my shoulder down to hit him. Ducking my check, I hit the glass hard. I felt and heard my shoulder crunch.

I was in pain intensely. Leaving the ice I sat on the bench holding my left arm, the pain was unbearable. Mr. Patterson told me to take off the shoulder pads, he lifted my arm and I shrieked in pain. He looked over to Mr. Boyle and said, "It's not good."

"Try to relax Rob." Mr. Patterson had said.

Try to relax he says, here I was holding every little pain in just so I wouldn't scream like a girl again. After looking at my shoulder, he says to me it might have popped out of place and he will pop it back in. I asked if it was going to hurt, he looked at me, smiled and said. "Just a little."

"Now on the count of three, I'll yank your arm to snap into place. Are you ready?"

"Wait a sec, hold on…. Okay." I was hesitant.

"One. Two. (YANK) Three."

I screamed in pain.

"I thought you said on three. (SOB)"

"Can you move your arm now?" he asked.

Slowly moving it around.

"It hurts a little, not as much as before."

I looked up to see how my team was doing, just to keep my mind off the pain. The Millionaires were breaking out of their zone, catching us on a bad line change. Going down four on three, the defence trailed. It was too late for our forward to get back into play as they scored. The whole house roared. Trailing by two again, time was running out for us. Five minutes were left in the game, to make matters worse; Darryl had got a penalty for high sticking. A few seconds later, Blaine had sneaked by the defence. Receiving a break away pass from our end.

Our bench stood up and watched in silence, a quick snap shot and in. We cheered as the crowd groaned, while Blaine scored short-handed. Soon the game was minutes away from ending. We desperately wanted to tie them up, Mr. Boyle screamed for Tim to come off so we could get an extra attacker out there. With only a minute and a half remaining, our boys poured it on giving it all they had in them. Keeping the puck in their zone, letting shot after shot go. Fighting to keep it in our favour, their goalie made save after save.

With just second's left the crowd was counting down, we had a few more shots on net. Then Jason had a glorious opportunity, a rebound and an open net shooting at it. I could hear my heart beat; every thing was in slow motion. We stood up with excitement: Suddenly a glove out of nowhere catching it. The crowd cheered and the buzzer went off.

Jason looked up to the heavens in disbelief; I too could not believe the goalie made that save. I felt sorry for Jay, probably feeling he should have had that. Losing 5-4 I know we could beat these guys. But it will have to wait till Sunday.

"Boy's," Mr. Boyle said out loud. "I just want to say, you played one hell of a game out there. We had them on their toes till the very end. That's what I call a good hockey game, no guts no glory. Shower up and get on the bus."

"Hey how's the shoulder?" Waylon asked.

"Sore, what do you expect?"

"Hey lighten up; we'll get back at them on Sunday."

"Yah what ever. I'll cream that number 19." I said.

"Come on, I'll help you carry your gear out. Taking a shower first?"

"Yah I guess I should. You can come wash my balls for me."

7

"Get lost fag! Hey you guys don't drop the soap, Rob's a queer!" he shouted.

"Oh that's good, you got me there. I'll get you yet." I said as he laughed.

"Are you going to shower?" I asked.

"I'll take one at the room," he said.

"What's the matter, afraid every one will see your cunt?" The guys in the dressing room laughed. Soon after when we were done laughing and teasing, we boarded the bus back to the hotel. My shoulder wasn't bothering me as much although I preferred not to use it. Sitting there with my eyes closed trying to relax.

"You know Rob? It's been bugging me," Waylon said. "I need to know."

I turned my head to look at him.

"What do you think of Lana?" he asked.

"Nothing…Where's this going?"

"Do you think she'll give me a chance, man she's hot? Probably one of the prettiest girls I ever laid my eyes on. Well since you're chums with her I thought…you know, put a word or two in for me."

"Sure if you want me to."

"Nah! Just kidding," He laughed. "But there is one thing I like to know. Did you kiss her?"

"You are an idiot! Give it up."

"Come ooon. You can tell me, just me." He insisted.

"Can you keep a secret?" I asked looking around.

"Oh yah of coarse I can." He anxiously waited.

I leaned over to whisper in his ear.

"So can I. Now leave me alone."

"You asshole," He smirked, pointing his finger at me. "Something happened your not telling me. Huh?"

"Waylon, if I tell you. Would you let it go?"

"Of course!"

I traced back to the night of Brian's party. Where I was walking her home, she not only asked if I walk with her but to spend the night while her while parents were in the Pas. She kissed me on the cheek; we both looked into each other's eyes than began a passionate kiss. One thing led to another, undressing each other. We were grasping one another as she led me to her room. Stopping only at the foot of the bed, I picked her up and tossed her on the bed. She told me she likes it rough, with her finger she was telling me to come closer. She pulls me on the bed and began to rip off my pants, pulling my shorts with them. She then dug her nails into my chest pulling down to my stomach. Licking my wounds going down, she started to suck on my now erected cock. Asking if I had a condom, she pulled one out and slipped it on me.

Sitting on it she rode me like there was no tomorrow. I had to be dreaming, this is not happening. After she was done that she laid on her back spreading her legs. She asks me if I wanted to taste her, as she was rubbing herself. It was pink and luscious, now I know what Jason meant by (all her pink parts). She insisted I taste her, I didn't know what to do. I told her I never done this before. She said all you have to do is lick all around her here as she pointed out. Then stick your tongue inside sometimes. I licked and licked, she moaned and shivered. And she pleaded me to fuck her. So I did, harder she screamed. Until we both came, when it was over I couldn't believe what had just happened. I lay there on the bed exhausted. A few moments had past then she climbed on top of me again for another screw, where does she get all this energy I wondered. It was great. Waylon sat there with his mouth wide open imagining the whole thing.

"There I told you, now leave it at that." I had said.

"Wow what a story. That really happened?" Waylon asked.

I thought for a sec.

"Yes, that's why I kept it to myself. Don't tell anyone what I just told you. Promise me"

He promised he wouldn't tell a soul and crossed his heart. We left it at that; Waylon had sat quiet the whole time. When we had arrived at the hotel, He looked at me and smiled. Everything was going smooth, so I retired for the evening. The next morning, my shoulder was aching. The pain had awoken me. I sat on the armchair thinking it would pass. I sat there for two hours; it was around eight am when I went to see Mr. Boyle. Mr. Patterson examined me again, slowly moving my arm. Tears formed in my eyes as I tried to hold back the pain I was going through. Looking at Mr. Boyle he shook his head, suggesting we go to the hospital to be absolutely sure it wasn't fractured or severe. We waited for an hour that seemed like hours before they called me in. Mr. Patterson gave his observation of my shoulder.

"Hello Robert, I'm Dr. Solomon. I hear you have a shoulder problem, yes?"

I nodded.

"I can't move my arm."

"And what happened to cause this pain?" he asked.

I told how I tried to hit an opposing player, only that he ducked the check and I hit the boards hard. Hearing my shoulder crunch, it felt numb instantly before the pain came. The pain wasn't that bad till I had awoken with such pain.

"Why don't you take your shirt off so I can have a look see?" He smiled. Dr. Solomon sent me down to the x-ray room for a quick look to be cautious was his exact words, when the results came back they were negative. I had not broken or fractured it at all, but gave me strict orders to rest my shoulder for six weeks before I can play hockey again.

This was not good for me I pleaded for a shorter term; he said four at the most but would like me to wait six for proper healing, I maybe stretched a ligament that supports my shoulder to turn and such. He gave me a sling to use if my shoulder starts to hurt again, also prescribing me absorbing junior.

What was I to do; I couldn't lose to McCormick this way. There were only eleven games left to play. I was finished for the season, what a crummy deal I had gotten. I remained quiet on the way back to the hotel, I did not want to talk to anyone I just packed my stuff together. When Mr. Boyle heard the news he came to see me. "I heard the news; sorry you have to sit for awhile. But we have to respect his wishes."

"I can't just sit and watch; I have to play. I can't let McCormick win this way…its. It's just not fair." I put my head down in disbelief. "I still want to play regardless, I was told to never give up. Coach I'm having a dream season, I've never had this many points in the past, I can't lose this way."

Mr. Boyle stood there and shook his head with a smile.

"Sometimes I don't know about you kid, but you're a fighter. That's what I like about you. We'll see how you feel when Sunday comes, but if that shoulder is still a bit sore; you have to sit for a while. No questions asked okay! Do we have a deal?"

"Yes sir we do. You have my word on it."

I sat on the bus waiting for everyone to finish loading. I thought to myself, "I jinxed it by saying I hope not too get injured." I sat there totally feeling down, my mind was wondering and I never noticed Waylon to sit by me.

"Hey buddy why the long face?" he asked.

"My season's done. I'm supposed to wait for six weeks before I lace them up again. But I can't let this happen; I just hope I feel a little better by Sunday. Because I'm playing I can't let McCormick win the scoring race, not this way."

"Are you crazy, what if you really hurt yourself, and can't play for a long time like next year, or permanently. You got think of things like that man. I'm sure there's next season to score more goals; I'm not saying this to put you down more. I'm just looking out for you Rob, that's what friends are for. Hey Jason said he is throwing a party at his place tomorrow, why don't we go and check it out. See some girls to cheer you up you stud muffin, isn't that what Lana said. Well you know what I mean.

I still can't get over it. You're one lucky son of a bitch." Waylon had said with a wink.

"Yah sure, why not. I need some loving tender right now." I said.

"Well pucker up sugar lips, pretend I'm Lana." He smiled.

"Yuck, get lost freak!" I laughed.

"You know me; I'm always a loving guy."

Waylon had always cheered me up, although I had only known him for a short time. But we became instant friends at the tryouts and never looked back. I'd always think about him at times and use to wish to bump into him. He was a big role in my life I would never forget about him, he gave me a lot of support and some advice. He gave me that extra drive I needed; he was part of the other crew, he'd fit right in along with Bill, Lance, Jason and Joey. I miss those guys too; they were a lot of help to me in my early stage of playing hockey. They gave me that support also. We use to play a lot of outdoor hockey, just about every day after school. Sometimes we'd skip class early in the afternoon, just so we could get first cut off the fresh ice. Once every one was there from around the community, we would have a real game; Body checking and all. No mercy for the other guy if he had his head down, even if he was your best friend.

Those were the days of glory, we'd play until the lights went out and even then we just keep playing. We had enough light from the streetlights, until the guys get sick of skating for many hours. Then we would go over to seven eleven for our usual super big gulps. By then it would be two or three in the morning on a school night. I never would have to worry about getting shit because my mother at times worked a night shift. I thought about those days as we were leaving Melville. I just sat there staring out the window thinking. "I'm down for the season, how can this happen? Why now? Why couldn't be after the play-offs!"

"Hey Rob, you okay?" Waylon had said.

"Huh!"

"You okay? I lost you there for awhile, I was talking to you but you just stared right through me."

"Yah I'm fine, I was just thinking of a bunch of stuff." I said.

"Maybe you should get some rest; we have quite a trip back. I'll go sit with sickening."

"Who?" I frowned.

"Darryl," He said with a laugh. "You sound like a damn owl."

"Yah, what ever!"

"Well it's good to see you back to your old self. You cheeky son of a bitch!" He laughed.

"Oh please! Go fetch me a soda since you're closer to the fridge."

"What! Get it yourself. You hurt your shoulder not your legs." He smiled.

"Oh that was go-od. I like that one."

"I thought you might of. But you should get some rest I'll come chat with you later."

"Alright, I'll see you later then. I am kind of tired; wake me when we stop for some munchies."

I had slept for an hour before we stopped in Yorkton for a bite to eat. Of course I probably would have slept till we got to the Pas; But Waylon gave me a hell of a shake. And he also added two light slaps in the face. He laughed, as I got mad at him for ruining my beauty rest. Every one had to get their grub to go for we still had five hours to Cranberry Portage. Soon we were on the road again, Waylon, Darryl and I played cards most of the way. It wasn't long until we were back in Cranberry; we arrived around seven that evening. After we all unloaded the bus and set our gear out to dry. Most of the guy's went to the cafeteria where there was a lounge down stairs. I was too tired so I went to my room, not long there was a knock at my door. I went to open it and to my surprise, it was Lana standing there.

"Well are you just going to stand there? Or are you going to let me in?" She had said.

"What are you doing here? And how in the…"

"Wow, is that how you treat all the girls?" She said with a smile cutting me off.

"No," I smiled back. "Come in."

She had come in the room and sat on the bed. I sat on the chair at my desk, cleaning the room a bit from my papers from schoolwork. As I was tiding she looked through my scrapbook of drawings. "I didn't know you were an artist? These are pretty good. How come you didn't join the art class?" She asked. "I don't know," I shrugged my shoulders. "I was too busy with school and hockey I guess!"

"So how did the game go? Did you score any goals for me?" She looked at me with a big smile. I sat on the chair and told her how the game went; it was a rough hitting game. Both teams were like gladiators, fighting to the end for that win. I told her how the atmosphere was; she looked at me in disbelief. It was part of the game, playing with your mind and emotions. I continued to tell her, she sat there eager to hear more. Telling her I hurt my shoulder also, but never gave up. I sacrificed myself for the team. She was upset that we didn't win but came close to tying them in the dying seconds. "Wow that was some game," she said. "Don't worry you boy's can beat them on Sunday. It's called home ice advantage. Our crowd would be there for the Mohawks."

I smiled at her; I couldn't resist that pretty face. She had always made me smile; she was a good friend to have around. Lana seemed to go out of her way to make me feel comfortable in any situation. We sat there and talked what seemed like hours, chatting about school, hockey and where I'm from. I talked about my days in Elmwood, I told her about my little gang of booster boy's. She laughed when I told her what Bill and the boy's did for me when they found out I was leaving. I even told her about Lori Chartrand, but have no memory of it at all. Lana sat there giggling shaking her head at me. She then began to tell me her adventures into Winnipeg. How a bunch of her and friends get together and use fake Id's to get into the nightclubs. She go on and tell me story after the other, I would just sit there and smile. She was so interesting to listen to. Everything was so calm; I was able to talk with out feeling jittery. She then asked if I would walk her home again. I smiled and said I was scared to get lost in this big town of hers again.

She looked at me and laughed.

"You're serious, it's a small town."

"Well I don't wonder around and look. I'm here most of the time on campus."

"Hmm, I'll take you on a tour then, tomorrow afternoon." She had said.

"Sure, I would love that."

"Great," she smiled. "It's a date then. After that we can go to my house and watch a movie."

We walked down the street towards town, as we walked past the cafeteria; Lisa confronted us. She tried to get mad, but I put my arm out towards her to stop her from trying to fight Lana.

"What's the matter with you?" I asked.

"Are you with her now?" Lisa blurted. "What about us?"

"There is no us, what are you talking about? We broke up!"

"So you're just going to ditch me for this tramp?"

"Lisa, stop it! Just drop the subject; you're embarrassing yourself. She is not a tramp. She's my friend. What ever, no wait. What am I doing, I don't need to explain myself to you. Come on Lana let's go"

Turning my back to her was a huge mistake on my behalf. Lunging at me she began to pull at my hair and hit me. She was screaming hysterically; turning to Lana she attacked her. I tried to help Lana but the two guy's Lisa was with stopped me. Trying to fight my way to help, one of them punched me in the stomach. There was nothing I could do, I could only watch in despair. Man they went at it, I never seen girl's fight like boys before. I thought this was a treat. But I really felt bad for what was happening. What was only seconds seemed like minutes! Soon the fight was over, the two guy's Lisa was with; Hollered that she creamed her good.

The two separated calling one another down. Lisa turned to look at me; she had an awful smile I can't describe. Then she had walked toward the cafeteria with her friends. Standing there watching her walk away, I hated for what she had just done to me. Turning to Lana to ask if she was okay, but she had already walked away. Calling out to her, she ignored me or didn't hear at all. Running after her I called to her once more, she turned to look but kept on walking. Pleading for her stop, she stood under the street lamp. I can see she was bleeding from her nose. Standing before her, I said that I was sorry for what happened. I told her that Lisa had no right to do that to her, telling her we broke up. Lana Looked at me for a sec then turned away.

"Maybe you should leave me alone," She had said. "I'm probably better off without you."

"What is that suppose to mean?" I asked.

"It's obvious you're not over her," She looked at me. "Tell me, are you over her?"

"What do you mean? Of course...We broke up last week.

"What do you think of me?" She asked.

I stood there staring at her. I had no clue to what to say, I just shrugged my shoulders. She growled in frustration turning away from me, she began to walk, but much faster now. I chased after her, grabbing her arm. I asked her what was wrong, why was she getting mad after questioning me.

"You have no fucking clue do you?" She had said, pushing my hand away. "You don't see that I like you. I've practically thrown myself at you and you don't get a hint."

"Well I...I." I was stuck for words.

"Ooh," Throwing her arms in the air. "Just forget it. I like you, but I don't need to put up with shit like this. So just let it go. If this is what I have to go through day after day, forget it. It's not worth it."

"Wait a minute, what are you saying? Us? What..." Sighing. "You don't understand," Searching for words in my head. "I...I aaaaah, it's complicated."

I wanted to tell her what I've been through. I was afraid she wouldn't understand. All those agonizing thoughts filled my head. She stood there waiting for an answer, an honest answer. But I could not speak; my foot was in my mouth.

"Well say something!" Tears were forming in her eyes. "To be honest, I don't want to fight on a daily basis. So please let me be, I just need to be alone right now." Wiping her eyes. Her blue eyes stared deeply into mine. I felt her pain; her emotions tore me up inside. I stepped toward her to give a hug. We embraced for what seemed like a minute. Sobbing on my shoulder, I held her tight. She then pulled away from me, with one hand against my chest. I was going to tell her, but she put her hand on my mouth. Nodding that I say nothing, she turned to walk away. I watched as she strolled down the street. Hoping she would turn to look at me. If she were to look at me one last time, I would run to her.

8

I could throw myself at her feet and beg forgiveness. But she didn't, she disappeared around the corner. Feeling alienated, I stood there thinking of everything that had happened, and it was so fast I didn't know what to think. Rubbing my face, I never knew she had taken a like to me, all I thought she was; we, we were friends. I really don't think I wanted to jump into a relationship, not after what I had experienced with Candice. Oh how I so much wanted to tell her, but I had a career I was chasing. Dreams of glory, I felt hopeless standing there. I eventually made my way back to the dorms.

The next day I had kept to myself. Lying on my bed, my roommate had asked if I was feeling well. I told him what happened the day before. He sat there and listened, Gerald. That was his name. He and I really never spoke to each other, I mean share our emotions. If something was bothering me, he usually left me alone. This was the first time we actually communicated; I was opening up to him. Sitting there he asked if I liked Lana as well, stating the way I was talking about her. It seemed I liked her too. I said that all I thought was; she was my friend. I then sat there for a moment; Did I like Lana more than a friend, or was those feelings for Candice.

I thanked Gerald for listening, but sat back on my bed. The more I thought about it, the more Candice circled around in my head. What was happening, why am I feeling this way? I was beginning to feel resentment.

Candice hurt me big time, yet I wanted her. "Why am I fucking thinking of her?" I thought. I mean she shattered my heart; she knew how much I liked her. But she led me so far, I was mad with her. Starting to feel lost again, I wanted to go to her. Frustrated and hurt, I wrote a letter to her. I told her how I felt like quitting and that I wanted to go home. I explained how she made me feel, expressing my emotions. Tears filled my eyes as I wrote; how I couldn't function or think at all. My school and hockey were filtering away; they became second to what I was going through.

Why would she do this to me? If she knew how far she was, claiming it was mine, she destroyed my trust, our friendship, and my dignity; she had taken away my world from under me. After writing it I put in an envelope. Looking at it one last time, the feeling I had was confusion. Going down the hall to the post office, I stopped along the phones. Fear sank in my head, Should I phone or mail it. With a deep sigh, I put in the mail before I changed my mind.

"Hey buddy," Waylon called to me. "What's new?"

"Nothing much, sending a letter home." I tried to hold a smile.

"What's wrong?" he asked.

"Nothing! Just tired, that's all."

"A few of us are going to the Pas. Were going to eat and maybe see a show, want to come?" He had asked.

"Nah! I'm broke. Maybe next time!"

"That's okay, I'll treat you. Come on; let's get off campus for the day." Waylon put his arm around me.

"You sure, I mean. I don't want you to go out of your way and all." Frowning at me, he gave a smile and shrugged his shoulders.

"Of course, what are friends for? Look here's my money." He opened up his wallet. "Here take twenty, give me back later or something. But let's go, Jason and Crystal is waiting for us outside."

On the ride into the Pas, I thought about Lana. How hurt she was, I sat there quiet for a bit. Staring out the window, I thought about what to say to her if I had seen her again. Leaning up against the front seat, I asked Crystal if she had spoken to Lana. She turned to look at me, saying she was a bit upset. But she never said anything. Sitting back, chewing my nails. "You know," Crystal looked at me. "She does talk about you quit a bit.

She likes you, I can tell. When were talking among friends, if your name comes up. She lights up and sort of brags about you. It makes me wonder…" Looking me up and down.

"Hey, what are doing? Hey. I'm right here, hello." Jason had said, taking a quick look at Crystal.

"Don't take it personal Jay," She smiled. "Tell me, do you like her?" She asked me.

"I'm not sure, I mean…I just think of us as friends. Well I did until she told me how she felt towards me. This is frustrating; I don't want to lose her friendship. What am I to do?"

"Just talk to her, be yourself." Crystal had said.

"She told me to leave her alone. She doesn't want anything to do with me."

"Just talk to her, she's coming over tonight," she said.

"Over where?"

"The party!" Waylon slapped me on the arm. "I told you yesterday. On the way back, remember?"

"You are coming aren't you?" Crystal asked.

"Uh…Yah, of course I am."

I had totally forgotten about it. It was the least of things on my mind. Arriving in the Pas, Crystal had said she needed to pick up some stuff at the mall. I asked Jay, if he was going to pick some liquor. Looking at me from the rear view mirror, he smiled and said it was already taken care of. When we got to the mall, we all went to the food court. After eating we separated for an hour. Wondering around the mall, Waylon and I went to play some pool. The afternoon had gone by fast, not noticing the time. We missed supper back at the collegiate; Jason and Crystal came looking for us. Jason wanted to get back to set up; Waylon asked if he had some booze in the car. Crystal smiled at him, giving him thumbs up. Waylon's face lit with joy. On the ride back, Crystal had pulled out vodka coolers.

Waylon took a big shot, handing it to me. But I refused; Crystal grabbed it and took a sip. Jason said he would wait till the party. Dropping us off at the dorms, Waylon said we would see them later. Waylon had wanted to go see the guy's at the lounge. To look for Darryl, there wasn't too much happening. Playing some ping-pong, to kill some time, Waylon was reminding every one about the party. Seemed to me no one learned a lesson from the other day. I tried not to think about it, just have some fun with the guy's here. Soon the lounge was packed, music playing. Some were playing cards; others were talking about the big party. Melville would be here tomorrow, sitting back looking at the boy's. All that was on their minds was Jay's party and girl's. I stayed for a little bit, I told Waylon I wanted to shower for the party. When I had got back to the dorms, I passed the phones. I stopped for a second or two.

Grabbing the receiver, I thought for a moment. I decided to phone Terry, maybe get some advice for the game and such. I was glad he was home; I spoke to my auntie Jean for a word or two. But wanted to talk to my uncle, when he came on, I said hello. As I talked my voice started to tremble, tears were in my eyes. I cried on the phone, saying it was too hard. I wanted to quit the team, along with school and go home. I couldn't cope with all the things going on in my life, everything was happening too fast.

"Every once in awhile, we come to some obstacles along the road we travel. We some times think it's impossible to over come, we shouldn't give up, Life is a journey; the road may at times seem endless. You at times may feel alone and lost, we tend to forget, the love ones who support us through thick and thin. We are all there, spiritually supporting you. When you hurt, we feel your pain as well. Even when you cry, we shed a tear too. Right now, you are only home sick. These emotions are understandable, being a man isn't easy, but what you're doing makes me proud. Moving away from home, for the first time has it's up's and down's. Hang in there; you are doing what you do best. And that is hockey. Listen to your heart my boy, and follow your dreams." He gave me a word of encouragement.

After speaking with him, made me feel a whole lot better. What he had said was what I needed to hear. It was awhile since I heard his voice; I guess I was only homesick like he said. Now feeling better, I went back to my room. I had got into the shower, thinking of what to say to Lana. Another party, man these guy's put Bill and the crew to shame. Bill and the guy's were party animals, but nothing like these dudes here. Getting ready I wondered what to wear, I caught myself standing there. What was I thinking; here I was trying to look good for Lana. Shrugging off the thought, I picked out some good clothes, a nice pair of slacks. A casual dress shirt to match my blue slacks; Slipped into some oxfords, combed my hair styling it to the side a little. Looped a belt around my waist, squirted on some Polo cologne; I stood in front of the mirror, Thinking of Lana.

"I'm going to rock your world." I said looking at myself.

Knocking on the door, Waylon let himself in.

"Wow, what's with the duds?" he asked.

"Just want to look good for the party." I said brushing my teeth.

"Or Lana?" He smiled.

I looked at him through the mirror. As I was rinsing

"Do you think it's a little too much?"

"The shirt is fine, but you could lose the pants!" He looked at my shoes. "And those hideous things." he said laughing

"What's wrong with what I'm wearing?"

"Nothing at all…If you were going to church that is." He grinned. "Throw on some jeans and let's go."

Like a trained dog, I listen to him. Grabbing my coat. Waylon held the door open. We headed down the hall to the exit. Laughing he said I looked like a nerd. He couldn't resist teasing me along the way. Meeting up with Darryl in the link way, he asked what was so funny. Waylon felt he had to tell him; He took a quick glance at me. His smile he had was now ear to ear. Closing my eyes, with a deep sigh, I thought. "Here we go again." He didn't have to say it; I knew what he was thinking. His face was practically glowing, he was dying to say something but he held it in.

"Why don't you say what you want to say?" I said.

"What!" He looked at me. "There's nothing to say." He smiled.

The suspense was killing me; I knew Darryl would like to know about Lana. Why else would he question me before? But now, he's not saying a word. It was bugging the hell out of me. Why is he not so interested in Lana now? Why isn't he bugging to know the details of my every move? What ever he was doing, it was working. I tried not to let this bother me; I didn't want to go to Jay's over worked. Darryl looked over at me, asked "Why the long face?" Shaking my head, I said it was nothing. Changing the subject, I talked about the game on Sunday. Waylon slapped me on the shoulder, saying no one was going to get stupid. Besides they had the whole day to sleep it off.

Jason's house was starting to liven up; you can hear music down the street. Most of the music was the beat of drums. Every now and then you can hear an electric guitar. We walked right in. The people before us had helped themselves; taking off our shoes, we heard Jason in the kitchen. Some of these people I haven't seen. Going into the kitchen, the guy's wanted a beer.

"Hey guys," Seeing us come in. "Help your-self, beers are in the fridge. I'm making a punch, if you want some." Jason had said.

"Is Lana here?" I asked.

"Not yet, she's coming with Crystal."

"What kind of music are you listening to?" Waylon had asked.

"Oh that! That's my brother. He and his buddies are jamming here tonight. Thought you guys might like it. Come on let's go up stairs."

Following behind him, there were quit a few already in the room. Especially girls "Wow." I thought I had seen the entire girl's from school. I started to talk to one of them; I asked her what her name was. "Tanisha." She had said. Smiling I said that was a beautiful name. Darryl tugged at my coat, and shook his head. Reading his lips, he said "Lana." I smiled and chuckled to myself. Here I was, looking good for one girl. And already I was hitting on another. Well it wasn't really hitting on, more like chatting to feel comfy. Jason's brother really rocked on the drums. It sort of reminded me of Terry; he played the drums as well. I walked around, after watching those guy's play some old AC/ DC tunes. I looked for Lana, I seen Crystal. I asked if Lana was here at the party. She said soon, I must have waited for what seemed like a couple of hours, she hadn't shown up, Soon I was beginning to get bored, I didn't feel like drinking or even go too the party for that matter. I only went, so I could talk to Lana.

9

I sat on the couch thinking. "What was I doing here?" I said to myself. Then all these thoughts ran threw my head. Candice, Lisa, Lana and even Lori were in my thoughts. I was having mixed emotions. Feeling aggravated, I decided to leave. I didn't feel like watching every one get drunk again. Leaving Jay's, I thought it was right thing to do. I mean too try and talk to Lana, while she may have been drinking. It might set off a different mood. Who knows what she might have said to me, or I might have said the wrong thing, she may have miss under stood me. When I was in my room, Gerald had stopped by for a sweater. He asked why I wasn't at the party. I told him I wasn't feeling well, that my bones were aching. Lying too him; He said he was going to a party of his own and left.

Sitting there worrying for nothing, these emotions I felt were just my guilty conscience. What was I feeling guilty for? Then Candice floated around in my head. Thinking about the fun times we shared, that moment of passion. Everything about her raced through my mind, almost like a roller coaster. Was it ever going to stop? This wild ride of emotions, was I losing it? What was happening to me? Then it hit me. Maybe I was in love. My heart raced at the very thought of her. No I couldn't. It will never be the same between Candice and me. The way I felt about her, she wouldn't feel the same way about me. I felt like screaming, God help me. Closing my eyes, trying hard not to think about everything that was bothering me. Then suddenly, I was standing in the spot light.

Laughter was all around me. Faces would appear in the light, changing ever so constantly. Candice telling me it's not Todd's, Mr. Boyle saying how disappointed he was. Lisa saying, "I hate you." And Lana with tears, strange faces calling me names. I was turning away from one face to another. Spinning faster and faster, getting dizzy.

I woke up screaming. Now sitting up in bed, I looked around to see where I was. I rubbed my face with my hands. Letting out a big sigh, what a nightmare. I fell asleep so fast with out realizing it. I looked over to Gerald; to see if I had awoke him. He was snoring. I let out a little chuckle, and then went to the washroom.

Still a bit woozy from my dream, I splashed water in my face. I looked into the mirror. As beads of water dripped from my face, I wondered what came over me. Feeling sick, I splashed some more water in my face, to wake up. I felt butterflies in my stomach.

"What is happening to me?" I thought. (I looked in the mirror.) "Do I love her? Why can't I forget her, get her out of my head. I need to stay focused." I went back to my room. I tried to sleep, but I couldn't. Never feeling like this before, I thought maybe it was something I ate the night before. I couldn't shake it, was I coming down with something? I can't explain the way I felt. As much as I wanted to go back to bed, I decided to take a walk. I wasn't sure what time it was, but the sun was rising. Leaving our dormitory, Paul our supervisor, had stopped me, wondering were I was going so early. I told him I was going for a walk around the track.

Walking out into the cold crisp air, it had taken my breath away for a second. Stretching out my muscles, I noticed the sun rise. The sky was a pale pink on the horizon, with some fluffy clouds in a distance. Feeling a warm glow, it surged through my entire body. It was beautiful. I jogged around the track four or fives times. During that jog, I thought about what Terry had said. It brought a smile onto my face, making me feel energetic and positive. When I was done jogging, I walked back to the dorms. I stood outside the doors, and took one last big breathe of fresh air. Feeling great about myself, I knew I was ready for the game that evening. After showering, I was beginning to get hungry. I wondered about Darryl and Waylon, how their night was. Sitting around in the TV room, I debated on whether to wake them, too go for breakfast. Then I remembered when they woke me up, with that horrible mask. Knocking on their door, I heard some one stumbling around.

"Good morning!" I said to Darryl, as he wiped his eyes.

"What's so good about it?" He said while yawning and lying back down.

"Come on get up, let's go eat."

"What time is it?" Waylon's voice was croaky.

"Its time to eat. Hurry up; I'll wait for you guys in the lobby. Then you can tell me how the party went."

"Yah by the way, what happen to you?" Darryl asked.

"Nothing," I paused. "Just got bored that's all."

"Did she shoot you down?" Waylon asked.

"Tss, no. She wasn't…Ah forget about it. Just hurry up, let's go I'm hungry." I said, leaving their room.

Waiting in the lobby, I stared out the window. The snow had sparkled from the sun; smoke sifting in the air. The sky was a perfect blue. The scene of it was so spectacular. I stepped outside; I love the smell of burning wood. It reminded me of home. A peaceful feeling over whelmed me. "McKay…You ass! It's only eight o'clock." Darryl had said, coming through the doors.

I turned around, smiled and shrugged my shoulders.

"Wipe that smile off your face," He said, "Before I knock it off."

"Man, you're a grouch. Didn't get it last night or what?" I asked.

"Ah quit your squabbling," he said yawning, "It's too early for me. Let's just go eat, I'm starving." Waylon had said.

"How about we go into town? And eat at the bus depot." I suggested.

"What's wrong with the cafeteria?" Darryl asked.

"Just something different, that's all." I had said.

They agreed and so we went into town. Entering the depot, we were laughing loudly. The people, who were there, stopped and looked at us, we snickered after realizing how loud we were. We sat at a booth near the door where we came in. Hardly having a chance to look at the menu, the waitress asked us what we were having. I asked for juice, for the three of us. And I said to give us a minute. She stood there for a brief moment, chewing her gum with her mouth open, her lips smacking. She rolled her eyes at me, and then left.

"What's with her?" I said under my breath.

"Mm, you see that," Darryl had said. "I'll give you something to chew on baby."

Sitting there, the guy's began to talk about the party. The stories they told seemed unlikely to happen. I was biting my bottom lip to hold back my laugh. But I couldn't hold it in any longer; I burst out laughing. Darryl said some chick threw up on Tim, while she was giving him a blowjob. The more they told; I wished I had stayed longer. My stomach was sore from laughing, I laughed at Waylon and Darryl. Getting our breakfast, we finally calmed down a bit. But we still had a few chuckles here and there.

"So, what do you guy's want to do after we eat?" I asked.

"I think I'll just go back to bed." Waylon had said with a yawn.

"Yah me too, lay around. It's too early for me." Darryl had said.

After we ate, Waylon and Darryl went back to the dorms. I decided to take a walk down to the lake. When I got to the end of the street, I walked towards the dock. I stood there and gazed across the frozen lake. I was in a daze, thinking of everything. "What if Candice was still pregnant? What was I to say to my mother? No. She said she had an abortion, but still. I could've been a father. What if she is lying? What if she still is? I can't think like that." I thought to myself. Just then I heard an eagle. It was flying in circles high above me. The very sight of it brought me to ease. A smile was now on my face. I watched it for a short time, until it vanished in a distance. As its scream faded away with it, I walked back to the collegiate

From there I went over to the hanger. I wanted to tape my sticks, a pre game tradition. Instead I cut down a couple of new sticks. I taped the handle the way Terry had done. Spinning the tape, wrapping it around with ridges. I don't know what made me do this, but I did it anyway. Next I lit the torch, and put a heel curve on the blade. Looking at my sticks, just the way Terry like's them. He said it was easier to give saucer passes, also great for wrist shot's. After doing what I wanted, I went back to my room. I was lying on the bed, trying to imagine the game, picturing myself scoring. Then Candice came to mind. Thinking of her, wondering how she was doing. I thought of phoning her, "She wouldn't get my letter till next week." I thought. Without any hesitation, I hurried to the phone. Feeling excited I grabbed the receiver. I stood there for a moment, with the phone to my ear.

"What if she doesn't want to talk too me? Oh she would, wouldn't she? She would be happy to hear from me. I think!" These questions circled in my head.

Suddenly, the very thought of Lana dissipated those questions. Hanging up the phone, I remembered that moment. Seeing her standing there under the street lamp, I can still see the pain in her eyes. Tears streamed down her cheeks, waiting for an answer. I really liked her too. But only as a friend, If only she could understand, what painful decisions I face. My heart felt heavy, I felt that I should tell her the truth. No more hiding, maybe she would understand. I had too tell her how I truly feel about her. I went back to my room, quickly put my shoes on. I grabbed my coat on the way out the door. I thought about what to say, as I walked down the path to the street. As I neared her house, my heart began to beat faster.

A lump was in my throat. Turning to walk away I stopped myself. I had to let her know what was happening to me. Debating with myself, whether I should tell her, or chicken out. It wasn't too late to run away. But I'm tired of running. Pacing back and forth, who knows how long I did this. Feeling frustrated and confused.

"Ah forget it, she wouldn't understand." I said aloud without knowing.

"Understand what?"

I turned to see who said that. There was Lana standing on her porch. Bundled up in her father's winter coat; Feeling embarrassed and speechless at first. I then asked her how long she had been standing there. She smiled and said, long enough to enjoy watching me argue with myself.

"So…" She looked at me with a bright smile. "Who won?"

Now feeling good, that she was able to joke with me. I walked to the bottom of her stairway. Still wondering, how to be open with her. She asked me, what made me go see her that morning. I stood blank for a moment, telling myself to hurry up and say something.

"I just wanted to see your beautiful face." Oops, wrong choice of words. I thought to myself. Here I was, going to say I want to remain friends. And I stuck my foot in my mouth. Now feeling hopelessly lost for the right words too say. I had quickly said, we needed to talk; Smiling she asked about what. When she looked into my eyes, her smile disappeared. I needed too and wanted to tell her about Candice. How it was eating me up inside. She turned away from me. I reached for her hand and she glanced into my eyes.

"Please listen." I pleaded.

She stared deeply into my eyes, and then led me in the house. She asked if I cared for a cup of hot chocolate. I smiled and said yes. I took my shoes off and waited in the living room. As I was taking my coat off, her mother came in the room talking about something. Not seeing me there, she asked me something about bingo. Her eyes fixed on buttoning up her cuffs; on the blouse she was wearing. When I spoke to answer her, she looked up startled. Blushing, she gave me a smile. She then called Lana into the room. When she came, she was holding two cups of hot chocolate. Her mother leaned toward her and was whispering. Judging by the way she was looking at me, I figured she was asking who I was. Before she left, she kissed Lana in a fashionably way. Both of them bent towards one another, their cheeks touching, and kissed the air. I found it strange; I had never seen any one kiss like that in my life.

I couldn't wait for her mother to leave; I really needed to get this weight off my chest. I wondered how to explain it to her, without her getting the wrong impression.

Searching for the right words to say how was I able to talk to her about Candice? Lana sat in the comforter beside mine. Handing me my cup, I looked away for a second. I eagerly wanted to talk. My mouth was getting dry. That lump was back in my throat again. I can feel that my hands were getting clammy, I felt suddenly hot. The longer I waited; the anticipation was building up in me.

10

"Lana," I said. "I have something too tell you." My voice trembled. Sitting there, I felt emotional. Tears began to form in my eyes, my hands trembling as they rest on my forehead. I was afraid to speak, the fear of saying something wrong. She then came and sat beside me. She put her hand under my chin, lifted my face up. Then gently touching my face, she wiped away a tear. Feeling my lips quiver; I tried to hold it in. She held me in her arms for a moment. Her warm tender hug sent a vibe through my body. All my anger, fear, frustration and loneliness poured out onto her shoulders. I grasped her tightly as I cried. Once I calmed down, I sat back and gathered my thoughts.

I stared into her beautiful blue eyes; I held her hand in mine. And told her how I was grateful for her friendship, how it meant so much too me. I told her how I could trust her, and that she was the only one I can be honest with. Slowly I began to tell her what I had been through. That I was still struggling, again the tears were there. But she sat and listened to what I had to say. I let it all out, even the thought of quitting school along with hockey. I felt that I was at the end of my rope. I valued our friendship, and didn't want to lose it. If things did not work out the way she expected, our friendship would no longer be there. Lana hugged me again and assured me, that nothing would come between us. She said she would stand beside me, and not to give up so easily. She would be my friend and nothing more. She apologized, for adding more pressure.

But I said it was okay, I said I was sorry for leading her on. Sniffling, I smiled at her.

I felt a lot lighter, to express my feelings like that. It was though a weight was lifted off my shoulders. It was the first time I shared my most inner fears, the thing's I was hiding from the world. Everything was good. My feelings were restored. I felt more confident than I ever did. I was myself again, and not putting on a mask. We had another cup of hot chocolate, sat and chatted for a while. After realizing the time, I then said I had to go. To mentally prepare for the game; She walked me to the door, and gave one last hug. She smiled and said "Good luck." I thanked her for listening, and then left.

When I got back to the dorm's, I sat in the link way. It seemed like everyone was still sleeping, not a soul in sight. It was complete silence. I remember thinking, how the game was going to be. Imagining the rink, the sound of music playing. Blaring the song I like, from AC/DC. If you want blood, you got it. The crowd on their feet screaming, the clashing of the boards when bodies hit into it. The puck ringing off the post, echoing through out the arena. Picturing myself scoring the winning goal, and the crowd roars with excitement. Then I snap out of it, from laughter coming down the hall. This was Darryl and Waylon. I sat there and waited for them to approach. Yapping away amongst them selves, and giggling. Hearing them laugh with their tongues hanging out, I couldn't help but laugh also. I found that funny. Waylon waved at me to follow them. Joining them, Darryl asked what I did all morning. I told them I hung out at the hanger, cut some new sticks for the game. We talked about the game in Melville, saying we were not going to lose this time.

Approaching the cafeteria, we hung out in the lounge down stairs. We played table soccer to pass up the time. Soon the place began to fill up, music was playing. It started to get louder and louder. The tunes were blasting, students were letting loose. It felt like I was at a dance. Soon the other guy's from the team showed up. We all played table soccer and screamed whenever someone scored. I was having fun again, no worries, no thoughts. I finally fit in; I had found peace with a new gang and myself. I had found that I have friends here, and not recognized it before. It wasn't that I did not miss my friends back home; they'd always be there.

I became a lot closer to my new friends that day. I was having fun, and relaxed. I wanted to enjoy the day, before game time.

One hour before game time, 6: PM Sunday, February 6th.

Entering the locker room, I had this incredible rush of adrenaline. I was full of energy; it hit me like a wave. Now feeling pumped and ready to play, I could hardly wait. Our equipment was already put into our stalls. All the sticks on the rack, each one with names on the shaft or butt end of the stick. Mine had nothing on them yet. I had grabbed my two sticks and drew my number on the shaft. While we dressed for our pre game skate, my heart began to race with excitement. There were no butterflies this time. It felt like I was only out there to skate. I mean, as if I were back home. There would be a bunch of us, playing out door hockey and it was fun just fooling around. This is how I felt, like I was playing out door hockey.

As I looked around the room, everyone getting ready, laughing and teasing one another. It was a total different atmosphere; you could sense it in the room. Sitting there, I couldn't help but smile. This was my time to shine; I could feel it within me. With no urge to get on the ice, I had taken my time to get ready. Eventually I made my way to the ice, stepping on it and hearing the ice crack as I skate around. My mood had changed; I now had the urge to play invincible. To play with no fear and no feelings, I had set out to take my prize. And with that I said to myself, "McCormick! Tonight's my night. My crowd, I'm going to outshine you." We did our usual warm up on Tim. We had done the horseshoe, one on one's, then two on ones then breakaways. The time on the clock was running out for our pre skate.

The Melville Millionaires had not shown up yet. With a few minutes left, Mr. Boyle called us off the ice. As everyone made their way to the dressing room, the first thought that came to mind was; they were not coming, I hadn't even got the chance to blow McCormick away. The chickens! After what they did to us, they had better be scared. The weather that evening was horrible, the snowfall was quite thick. It was hypnotizing if you stared at it long enough. "This is great, just great. I was at my peak, ready to be the center of attention. Now, they probably won't make it. I wanted to show McCormick my skills, how the crowd roared for me. I am god here." I had said thinking to myself.

Mr. Boyle called out to us to pay attention for a minute. Going over some play's we had practiced. Drawing them out on the chalkboard, he went through them. As he explained who was to go where they were positioned, he was interrupted by a knock on the door. Mr. Patterson had opened it, and the head official came in the room. "Jamie," He had said. "We may have a problem. Melville has not shown up, it's been twenty minutes past game time. What do you want too do?"

"Well…I'm sure they'll be here soon," Mr. Boyle sounded positive. "We'll wait a few more minutes Patrick! Don't forget, it's snowing!"

Looking at his watch, he gave Mr. Boyle a meek smile. The guy's had already started to take off some of their equipment. Mr. Boyle had told us to stay dressed. Some of the guy's complained that it too hot to sit there and wait. So Mr. Boyle said to remain half dressed, keeping only our pants, skates and shin pads on. The time was winding down, and the crowd was beginning to get irritated. Soon Beverly, Mr. Boyle's wife, came into the dressing room. She had informed him that the Melville Millionaires had arrived. Mr. Boyle along with Mr. Patterson was called outside the room. The coach from the other team and the officials were discussing, why they were late I suppose. But it wasn't long before they came back into the room.

"Okay boys," He clapped his hands to get our attention. "The Millionaires are finally here. So let's give this crowd a good game eh! They were patient and waited too see how the Millionaires are. We gave them a run the last time, so let's beat them this time. Remember one thing out there; hockey is not just a game. It's passion, desire, credibility; it's what dreams are made of. Play with heart and soul. Get the rest of your thing's on and let's go." Once the guy's were fully dressed, one by one we exited the dressing room. Jason was standing by the door, and patted us on the shoulder as we passed by. I was the last one out of the room; Jason and I bump our gloves together. Following behind him, I stared down the hall. Looking through the door at the end.

I can see the boards and Plexiglas; the crowd cheering as the boy's touched the ice. I was feeling tense; I rolled my head around to loosen up.

My heart pounding like a drum, the closer I had gotten to the door; the faster it had pounded. Getting louder by the second and drowning out the crowd. Stepping into sight, the sound of the crowd came back. A tingling feeling rippled through my body, making the hair on the back of my neck stand up. With a burst of speed, I skated around the rink. Now feeling anxious, I skated to the bench. I searched for one of my old sticks, to use on Tim as we warmed him up for the game. The Millionaires headed for their bench, I looked for McCormick; thinking he hadn't come along.

My thoughts were erased as he came through the doors to the rink. He stood at the door for a sec, and then gave a wave to someone in the stands. I seen some girl wave at him, and thought to myself. "Uh…Isn't that cute, he brought his girlfriend." But not noticing myself at same time, I was being envious. Wishing some one close to me was here to watch as well.

The timekeeper buzzed the horn, to signal the start of the period. Jason was out there with Darryl and Blaine, while Brian McLeod and Ryan Smith on defence. My heart was beating intensely; it felt as though it would pound right out of my chest. I could hear nothing; Mr. Boyle was saying something to us. I seen his lips moving, all I can hear was the sound of my heart. Thumping as we waited for the puck to drop. Then like a loud clap, the puck hit the ice. Jason won the draw, and Blaine tied up his man. Receiving the puck, Brian pivoted back then skated behind our net. Setting up the play, Darryl hustled to take the puck. Taking three quick strides up the ice, he left the puck for Brian. Jason was cutting across at center; Brian gave him a hard pass.

Skating to the blue line he dumped it in. Giving chase was Blaine, he and his opposing winger had a foot race. Darryl had gone to aid Blaine who was now fighting for the puck. Body checks were thrown as they fought for it. Jason coasted into the slot, trying to elude his man. Blaine maintained the puck, skated behind their net quickly as he could. He spotted Jay and passed it to him, going for a one timer. It was there, a perfect set up, all alone. Before he could get any wood on it, his man lifted his stick.

The crowd was on their feet, and moaned when Jay fanned the shot. Brian had kept the puck in play, quickly passing it across to Ryan who one timed the shot. Hitting a body in front of the net, Jason picked up the loose puck. He then cycled around the hash marks, looking for an open man. Stick handling around one player he coasted in a bit, and then let a quick wrist shot go. Ringing off the post, the crowd groaned again. The Millionaires now had possession of the puck.

Desperately trying to get out of their zone, Dwayne had caught a winger looking back. Receiving the puck, he only had a chance to shoot it away. Dwayne hammered him good, knocking his helmet off as he went down. The house rocked, and cheered frantically. With that hit it changed the atmosphere of the game. Jason too was playing his heart out. That line was forcing the Millionaires at every point. They checked their wingers, pinning them against the boards. While Ryan kept the puck in play, again shooting it towards the net. A few times Jay picked up the loose puck, and shot it from every angle when he had the chance.

Not being able to control his rebounds, their goalie was making save after save. That line alone already had ten shots on net. With only the defence line changing, Jay's line was beginning to tire out. This goalie was like a wall. Nothing was getting by him. Finally he froze the puck, and got a whistle. As both lines on the ice changed, you can see the exhaustion in them. Slumped over coasting to the benches. Shift after shift, our boy's changed on the fly. Jumping over the boards to get into play, exchanging hits to satisfy the crowd. It was still scoreless half way through the period, and I haven't yet to get a shift. Shot after shot, they made their goalie look unbeatable. The clock was beginning to run out. And with five minutes remaining, the Millionaires received a break, catching us on bad line change. McCormick jumped on the ice, as they were capitalizing a two on one rush. The six-foot, five giant was trailing behind the play. He yelled for a pass as he coasted into the slot.

With a feather like pass, he ripped one hell of a slap shot. It was like a bullet, zipping by Tim as it rang off the inside post. The crowd groaned and we did as well. Skating by their bench. They all were getting high five's. They celebrated the goal. Our boy's slowly changed up; Wade had taken some light out of us. "Millionaires goal; scored by number 27. Wade McCormick. Assisted by number 19, Jamie Houda, and number 8, Blake Stevenson. The time of the goal, 4:32. McCormick from Houda, and Stevenson at 4:32." The timekeeper had announced.

"Come on ladies, don't look so glum! It's only the first period. There's a lot of game left. It's only one goal, let's get it back." Mr. Boyle had said.

Sitting there listening to him, he was right. We were acting like we lost, already giving up the way it seemed. But our boy's played hard; giving it they're all. The problem was; how are we going to get the puck past their goalie. There has to be a weak spot, some how score on him. But Rapaport was solid in net. He was on top of his game. Sharp as a tack, the reflex's of a fly. "He's good, but he isn't that good," Jason had said watching him. "I'll score on that fucker! You just watch."

The first period had come to an end, with Melville up one goal. The shots on net favoured us. Looking at the scoreboard hurt like hell. One nothing for them; their goalie was like a wall. He had stood strong in net. Heading to the dressing room, I wondered if I was going to play at all. Anger was beginning to sink into my thoughts, shaking it off I knew inside I was going to play. It was just the matter of when. As I entered the room, Mr. Boyle was drawing some plays on the chalkboard. He mostly talked about defensive plays, and what we were doing wrong. I sort of drifted off, thinking about my situation.

"Am I going to play, or just sit on the bench; like a bump on a log? I wasted my time even coming here, I should've watched from the stands." I thought to myself.

Watching as he instructed us what to do, but I wasn't really listening. My mind was somewhere else, in a fantasy world. The clap of his hands brought me out of that state of mind. As he finished, he asked if we had any questions. Sitting there biting my tongue. "I have a question for you!" I thought, "Why aren't I playing?" I so desperately wanted to say that, it was killing me just to sit there. Anger was burning within me; I couldn't sit still at that moment. The ref blew his whistle, to let us know that the ice was ready. One by one the boy's exited the dressing room. I waited to be the last one out; I figured since I'm not playing, why bother to race out. Taking my time, Mr. Boyle called to me.

11

"How are you feeling?" he asked.

"I feel fine." I held back what I wanted to say.

"How's the shoulder?"

"It's okay! It doesn't hurt." I said.

"I'm just making sure; I don't want you to get hurt. So when you get out there, take it easy."

"Yah I know, I'm fine. Really! I am." I assured him.

Walking out to the ice, I thought about what he said. "Was I ready?" I only wanted to play. I had nothing to be afraid of; this was my one and only chance to prove to mysel. That I can do this, to get through this game, and out shine McCormick. Skating to the bench, I thought about Candice again.

Sitting there, I wondered and wished that she were here to watch me play. She was one of my good friends, although I had crush on her. We were close; she at one point was someone I can trust. Then all of a sudden, my dreams came true. I desperately wanted to sleep with her, and I did. You think I'd be happy and get on with my life. I felt our friendship had become distant now, over one night of intimacy. I still didn't know if she was lying to me, or trying to scare me. I should have finished reading her letter, but instead I threw it away. It started to bug me now, what else did she have to say.

"Oh no, I wrote her a letter. I forgot what I had written in it. What if

I wrote something to hurt her with? What is she going to think? What will she say?" I thought as I scrunched my face.

"McKay! Are you ready or what?" Mr. Boyle had said.

"Huh, yah…" He snapped me out of my daydream.

"Well get out there."

Skating out to Charlie Oigg's wing, as Ronald Malcolm on the right. I tried to shake off those thoughts. Feeling not all there, the puck dropped. My man I supposed to watch knocked me to the ice as the puck slid our way. Stumbling to get back up, the noise of the crowd now filled my head. Feeling a little embarrassed, but I also laughed at myself. That's what you get for not paying attention. I quickly skated back into play.

The Millionaires had dumped and chased it in our zone. I skated hard to get to my man, who was acting as defence. While they controlled it in our zone, I rubbed out my man as the puck came to him and slid across the blue line. As Charlie scrambled to get to the loose puck, he skated up ice with it.

Taking it wide, he went behind the net. Setting up a shot in front, Ron had got robbed by the goalie. Their player's tried to shoot it out, by banking it off the boards. I managed to keep it in play, but paid a price for it. I was slammed into the boards hard, the sound of our equipment clashing echoed. The crowd roared, as the level of the game was beginning to get tense. The Millionaires picked up their offence; Tim was faced with shot after shot. We were starting to play sloppy in our end. Melville looked like they were on a power play, as one of their defences received a pass. With all the time he had, coasting in waiting for the right opportunity. Then he wound up and took a slap shot just outside the hash marks.

Tim barely saved it, as he was being screened. The shot had nearly knocked him over, as he must have seen it at the last second. My line desperately tried to get the puck out of our zone; my legs along with my lungs were burning. My line mates and I were on the too long, we tried to dump or shoot the puck out. I can hear Mr. Boyle scream for us to get a whistle. The Millionaires played keep away with us, as we were scrambling out there. Tim was sprawling around making one save after the other.

Finally he was able to hold it to stop play. The house erupted into a cheer to applause Tim for his effort.

Sitting on the bench, I removed my helmet, to run my hand through my hair. My head was soaked from sweating; this team sure knows how to pick up the pace. I was completely drained, gasping for air. My lungs burned at every breath, I wasn't playing the way I should have. I needed to get it together, forget about Candice and worry about how to score on this guy. Having time to rest and get my wind back, our line was back out there. My plan was simple, just stay with my man. Where he goes, I go. I skated along a side of him, not letting him out of my reach. I shadowed him good; he never touched the puck while I watched him like a hawk.

The puck was in our end, when Waylon seized the puck. Breaking out from behind the net, I coasted high in the neutral zone. Sneaking by their defence, I skated across the ice to the other side. Waylon had seen me and gave a nice hard pass; receiving it I was now on a break away. Skating in hard, making sure no one can catch me. I was going in on Rapaport's right side. Faking a shot on my fore hand, I faked him to his left. Then put on the brakes, switching to my backhand then slid it pass him.

The crowd roared, while my teammates gathered around me, to congratulate me. The feeling I had was unbelievable. It was like scoring for the very first time, I was now pumped. Changing the lines, Mr. Boyle patted me on the back. Putting us on the scoreboard and hearing my name announced, had sent shivers up my spine. The wall had crumbled, finally getting one by him. As the game went on, Melville started to take the body more. Trying to intimidate us, with their height. But our boy's stood up to them, both teams' exchanging hit after hit.

The crowd loved it; the whole place was in an up roar. We were like warriors, fighting until one gives up. The goalies stole most of the show, dazzling the crowd with some impossible saves. It was hockey night in Cranberry; both teams playing from different divisions, both at the top of the standings, almost like playing for the Holy Grail. The house was now packed, as some had come in after the first period. Sitting on the bench, the boy's were excited. The score was now 1-1.

Sitting on the bench, I glanced around the rink. Seeing all those people there, and hearing them cheer us on. It built up our confidence. Then I spotted Lana behind their net. I stood up and asked to be put out there. I wanted to play good for her, sort of show off I guess. I pleaded to Mr. Boyle; he looked at me and said. "Go then, get out there!" Without any hesitation, I leaped over the boards on the next line change. Jason had already carried the puck into their zone. Crossing over the blue line, he then cut across to delay the play a little. Waiting for help on offence. Leaving the puck there, as Brian was late going in. I quickly skated into the front of the net, trying to screen their goalie.

Brian then took a low slap shot; Melville's goalie easily stopped that. Jason picked up the rebound; again Rapaport robbed us. Giving another rebound, this time Jay passed it to me. Deflecting it pass him this time. The house rocked with cheers. Giving a fist pump, being surrounded once more. I looked into the stands for Lana; she was cheering along with the crowd, she then gave me a little wave. With a big smile on my face, I waved back. We were now leading 2-1. At face off my adrenaline was flowing and my heart racing. The sound of the crowd roaring in my head, winning the draw Jason had bolted ahead. Brian pivoted back, and then passed it ahead to Darryl who tipped up to Jason as he broke in on the right side. Fighting his attacker off, crashing the net he still managed to get a shot off. Easily stopping it, Rapaport deflected it to the corner. I skated in after it, my man checked me into the boards. Fighting for the puck I picked pocketed him, as I tried to go behind the net to set up a play.

Another forward hammered me into the boards, a sharp pain stretched across my chest. Falling to the ice, I tried to swing my stick to regain the puck. Another pain occurred, this time down my arm. Clenching my teeth I forced myself up. The agony I was in, thinking I popped my shoulder or worse. Trying to hide my pain, as I skated back to the bench. But the puck some how had gotten caught in my skates. I looked down to see, big mistake. Again I was drilled, sending me to the ice only this time I didn't get up. The pain was so intense; tears had formed in my eyes. The ref blew his whistle to stop the play.

The crowd was silent as Mr. Patterson ran out to me. Biting my bottom lip as I tried holding back the pain, Mr. Patterson had asked if I injured my shoulder again. I quickly responded with "No! I'm only woozy from being creamed." Slowly I arose to my feet, coasting back to the bench.

The crowd cheered to give their support. Mr. Boyle asked me if I was okay, looking at him I nodded. There was no way I was going to leave this game; I've come too far not to let McCormick win. We were up one goal and the Millionaire's wall had been broken.

The game went on; I had decided to sit for a while. Till the pain had gone away, during that time McCormick took charge of the game. He dazzled the crowd, setting up plays and he even walked right through our defence. Like they weren't there at all, just him and our goalie. Tim skated forward a little, all ready for McCormick. As he skated in on Tim, he attacked from Tim's left side. With little stick work, Wade stuck the puck between his legs along with his stick. Shooting on Tim who was unprepared, we watched as the puck hit the back of the net and adding Goal 45 for the goliath, and his 89th point.

Their crowd and bench cheered with excitement. We were now tied 2-2, as the period had come to the end. The shots on net were almost even; it was 24-22 for us. Still hurting, I had followed into the dressing room. Taking off my helmet, I sat back in my stall. Little beads of sweat rolled down my face, struggling to hold in the pain. I had put a towel over my head to hide.

"Something wrong McKay?" Mr. Boyle had asked.

"No, I'm just beat from getting hammered out there." I said.

Sitting up I removed the towel. Waylon was next to me, whispering he asked if I was okay to play. I looked at him and smiled. As Mr. Boyle was talking about some play's Waylon just kept asking if I had got hurt badly. I didn't want him to know my situation.

"You should just sit out, save yourself for play-offs or something." He murmured.

"Waylon! I see you're not listening, care to share with us how to beat this team...Mm we are waiting Mr. Clarke." Mr. Boyle was steamed.

"I'm sorry, I was only asking if he..." Mr. Boyle had cut him off.

"If there's one thing I can't stand is someone like you not listening. What was it Mr. Clarke was asking you McKay?"

"Uh, he was asking if I uh...Hurt my shoulder again. I said no, I was only sore from being rocked. That I was dizzy."

"Well maybe you should sit for a while, Mr. Patterson will have a look at it." Now turning his attention away from me.

He drew some plays on the chalkboard; I looked over to Waylon and shook my head in disbelief. I was filled with anger, he knew this game meant a lot to me and yet he gets me benched.

"What was that?" he said whispering. "Look I'm sorry, I was only trying to look out for you."

Focusing on Mr. Boyle I continued my argument, I was so mad. I can feel the blood rush to my head. I never let him have a chance to explain, I was so peeved I quit talking to him. But before I did that, I looked at him. I wanted say something to him but it came out differently. "Mr. Boyle, why should I get benched? You know how much this game means to me. I can't just sit and watch McCormick win this way. I need this, if you're not going to stand beside me. I'll do it alone; I've come too far to quit now. I'm playing whether you like it or not. It's a sacrifice I'm willing to take. No guts, no glory. I want to play."The room was quiet; Mr. Boyle had given me a long hard stare. Eventually he gave a warm comforting smile. Jotting his finger at me.

"That's what like about you kid, you got spirit. Ha, ha, Well team, I hope you got what Rob here has. It's for the love of the game, that he is willing to sacrifice all just for the win. What do you say that we follow his example? Go out there and give our all."

With that being said, the boys looked at each nodding their heads. Minutes later the ref blew his whistle to start the third period. I put on my helmet; Waylon tapped me in the shin pads. Giving me a smile, I put out my glove for him to bump it. The other guys were pumped for the third. As I walked down the hall towards the ice, a chill went down my spine. When I heard the crowd cheering us, as we one by one stepped out onto the ice. I was having the game of my life. Having already scored twice, I wanted it to be a hat trick. This was my night, my moment of glory.

I had to let McCormick know that I wasn't too far behind. It was a rough game, but they beat us on their home turf. We needed this win on our turf. Once that puck drops, we become warriors of the rink. Fight until the end not giving up anything, gladiators once again. The two centers squared off, waiting for the puck to drop. Melville wins the draw;

their defence passed it back and forth, then up the side to a forward. Who in turn had dumped it into our zone; Waylon gave chase to get to it first. Shooting it off the boards behind the net, he received a hit. Brian had taken the puck, banking it off the boards, to Blaine as he cut up ice. Looking for a helper, he carried it to center. Passing it across ice to Charlie, one of the Millionaires intercepted the pass. Creating a turn over, their lines changed on the fly.

Houda yelled for a pass in the neutral zone. Receiving the pass he delayed the play in our end. Skating across ice he left the puck for McCormick, who then carried it in far as the hash marks. Passing it back to Stevenson, who quickly passed it to Houda, then back to McCormick. Tim double stacked his pads. But McCormick read him perfectly; he passed it back to Stevenson who put it in the empty side. That was one hell of a tic tac toe play, their bench roared with excitement.

12

Melville was up one goal on us now, another point for Wade. I wasn't about to give up; this was one battle I was not going to lose. Changing our lines, Mr. Boyle patted me on the shoulder to get out there. My heart raced with anticipation, I only had one goal in mind. I needed to score the first hat trick out of the two of us. Wade probably should have had it first, but he had chosen to share his glory. I skated out to Jay's right wing. Dwayne was on his left. Facing off against Melville's top line. McCormick gave me a look, before staring into Jason's eyes for face off. It was a look of intimidation, but it never affected me. I gave a smirk, "What ever." I thought.

"You boy's are going down, this is one game you should have sat out." Houda had said to me facing off.

"Like your mom. Going down on me bitch." I quickly responded.

"Oh you're going down! You can count on it." Anger was now in his voice.

I only smiled knowing I agitated him. Getting him upset made me feel I don't know, good I guess. Cussing and cursing me I only waited for the puck to drop. When it did Jay had won the draw, tipping it past McCormick. He quickly passed it to Dwayne, who carried it in their zone. Houda slashed me in the ankle. I fell to ice, the crowd screamed for a penalty. But the ref had seen nothing, so he couldn't do anything. Taken the pain I forced myself into the play. I was going to get Jamie back for that; my chance will come.

The pain was too much, barely making it back to the bench. I shouted for a line change. Mr. Boyle had screamed for the ref to watch the game. There were two teams out there to watch not only one. The fans were screaming the exact same thing. This game was turning ugly, both teams fighting for that top spot. We were down by only one goal, and there was a lot of game left. I sure was taking a beating just to get the attention I deserve. Especially when Lana was here to watch me play, it was kind of embarrassing for me, for her to see me get hammered out there. My ankle along with my shoulder was aching. The score now 3-2, the Millionaires were not taking prisoners. They kept on with the hard hitting; we rolled with the punches and hit back. The house was in an uproar with excitement.

I sat there debating whether I should punish myself any further, my body was sore and I wasn't sure if I could take it. But this game had meant so much to me, I wanted play as if though Uncle Terry were here in the stands watching and witnessing my feat. Then all of a sudden I had felt a warm feeling surge through my body. It was like a warm wind had came out of nowhere, but the feeling I had it was unbelievable. I no longer had any pain or what so ever. I felt completely fine and energized; I stood up waiting for next line change. Mr. Boyle screamed for a line change, I looked at him and patted my chest signalling I'm ready. As soon as he nodded I was gone with the next line change. Darryl was on my line, with his speed and my passing skills. We combined for what seemed like a dream team.

Breaking out of our zone I gave him a break away pass up the middle, right on the tape. He poured on his speed, splitting their defence, all alone with Rapaport. Our bench was on there feet rooting for Darryl, with little stick handling. Faking going with his backhand, he switched back and let a quick wrist shot go. It rang of the cross bar and trickled across the line. The ref had already seen it before Rapaport pulled it back. The house roared with cheers, congratulating him on his goal. Darryl screamed with excitement, it was a new game now. One goal away from a win, as time was winding down. Melville had called for a time out; Mr. Boyle had called us in as well. He quickly drew some plays and briefly explained how to play. He wanted us to play in the neutral area, not letting them pass that point.

The crowd was cheering, my body felt tingly all over. The crowd was getting me all riled up, as for the rest of my teammates they probably felt the same way. Soon the ref blew his whistle, our boys centered off. It was though we were playing in the play-offs, the tension was so high in that rink. McCormick stood waiting for a line change, screaming for his teammates to pick it up a bit. Then as luck would have it, we had got a penalty. Dwayne had gotten 2-minutes for hooking. The Millionaires were now on a power play. I stood and hoped that our boys can hold them off for those two long minutes. We scrambled around there for a bit, Wade was on his feet waiting for a change, screaming for teammates to change up. Soon he was on the ice, skated in to the play. Receiving a pass on the right side, he skated so far and took a slap shot on Tim. It's McCormick's way of dumping it in.

McCormick had one hell of a shot. We certainly didn't want that one to sneak in. Waylon pick up the loose puck and fired it out back down to their end. As the Millionaires were breaking out, Wade skated to center. As his line switched positions, McCormick hollered for a pass up the boards. Dwayne's penalty had expired, just stepping out of the box. McCormick hadn't seen him, Dwayne put his shoulder into the giant, catching him dead square in the chest. Bouncing him off the boards, the house rocked again. This had pumped us up, changing on the fly. I was on the ice; I skated along with the winger I was to watch. We were in the neutral zone, when the Millionaires had a bad line change, stranding their defence for themselves.

We capitalized on it. Again Darryl and I were together. Jason led the rush on the right side. I was on the left; Jason carried it in then passed it back to Darryl as he was trailing. He coasted in then turned towards Jason, drawing the defence to that side. He gave me a beautiful backhand saucer pass. I stepped into that one; I didn't even feel it hit my stick. I rifled it pass Rapaport as he tried to get across in time. Again the house roared with cheers, I dropped to my knees sliding, giving a fist pump. With only a couple minutes left on the clock, I felt as though I scored an over time goal.

To hear that house roar and to feel the adrenaline along with all the excitement was a good feeling. I was pumped, forgetting I had scored a hat trick. I was having the game of my life. Glancing at the clock, the score now 4-3 for us. I was. I mean we were pumped. Just play these last few minutes with heart and keep the win.

"Let's keep it up boys. We got them worried now." Jason had shouted. Facing off I still had those chills. I had shown Wade I was a warrior too, and I wasn't going to give up. My uncle had always said. "It's not over till the fat lady sings." I haven't heard her sing yet, so we still had a battle to fight. Winning the draw Jason held up McCormick, which threw him off a little. He gave Jay a good whack across the back of his legs, breaking his stick. Which in turn the ref gave him a penalty, sitting him out for the rest of the game.

Angry at the call he turned towards Waylon who must have said something, and started fighting him. He was only making the call worse, adding a 5-minute major for fighting and misconduct. He swore at the ref, which wasn't good. Wade received a game misconduct. That's a twenty-seven minute penalty right there.

At this point, it was good for us we had a man advantage. With Waylon serving a fighting major, it was 4 on 3. But I guess the fat lady had just sung. With all the commotion I forgot about Jay who was lying on the ice. Mr. Patterson was there checking on him, Jason was slow to get up. Darryl helped Mr. Patterson with Jay back to the bench. Squaring off at center again, as Darryl took over being center. Dwayne joined our line filling in for Waylon on defence. Brian was on the opposite side. Darryl won the draw. Dwayne took control and skated back behind our net, to kill some time. Waiting for Melville to make a mistake, finally one forward gave chase. Setting up the play Dwayne passed up to Darryl who led the three on two rush.

Brian was a little too far ahead but managed to keep on side, this drew one defence to him. Darryl went one on one I was behind. I yelled to him, and he left it there for me to pick up. Now I was all alone. Only Rapaport and me. Skating in on him hard, not wanting to give him time to set up. I faked a wrist shot, with my feet still moving. I pulled it to my backhand; I could hear my heart beat.

Life seemed to have come to almost a stand still. I watched as the puck left my stick. Slowly it passed by Rapaport's right shoulder and in. I had tripped over his pads and slid into the end boards slamming into them. I quickly jumped to my feet, to celebrate another goal. The whole arena was crazy, with only seconds left on the clock. I looked into the stands behind the net. And there she stood, Lana cheering along with the crowd. There was only seconds left on the clock, Melville's coach had signalled to run it out. When the buzzer went, our bench cleared to surround Tim and celebrate the win. The house was filled with cheers; we beat them on our turf. Our meetings were now tied and it was the last time we meet. Or till play-offs, if either one of us makes it to the finals. Winning the game 5-3 and I had scored 4 goals and one assist. Making it 38 goals and 39 assists for 77 points.

This was truly the game of my life; I had thought of Terry and wished he were here also. But I felt a warm glow inside of me, as if though he was here. And then thoughts of me actually coming here was because of him, he inspired me. I wouldn't have come here if he never gave me that talk about setting out for my dreams, and when I felt like quitting he gave me words of encouragement. I smiled to myself as I thought of him.

"This game was for you uncle. I sure wish you were here to see me score those goals." I thought to myself. This was the most celebrated victory we had done. Melville was the highly favourite team in the SHSL (Saskatchewan high school league). We were playing triple AAA midget. But Melville was the best team in the western division, these boys played well.

As I headed back to the dressing room, I had thought of calling Terry and tell him about the game. Our dressing room was noisy, and the boys were excited. It seemed we already won the centennial cup. The feeling I had is unspeakable, I can't describe with words. But it was something I haven't experienced before. I just wish Terry were there to watch me score the most important goals in my life. We didn't get out of the dressing room for quit some time, at least an hour. To my surprise Lana had waited for me to come out. She came towards me and gave me a hug to congratulate me.

And then without any hesitation she planted me with a kiss. Being caught off guard, I had totally forgotten I wanted to phone Terry. She then asked if had liked to join her, along with some girl friend's for something to eat at the depot. I sure didn't waste any time to say yes, but I wanted Waylon to join as well. They nodded and didn't seem to mind Waylon.

"What? I can't come or what?" Darryl had scolded.

"I, well..." I searched for words. "It's not like that."

"What then, seems to me you guy's always leave me out, when it comes to the ladies."

"It's not that way at all, you're getting the wrong idea."

"Waylon is the only one that can go?" he persisted.

"Why do you have to be so pessimistic?" Waylon added.

Standing there arguing, Lana had gotten upset waiting. She and her friends walked toward us. And had asked what the hold up was. I stood there and shook my head at Darryl; he couldn't act polite around the girls. I was a little embarrassed but I hoped to god Lana wouldn't say something rude. It would only make matters worse.

"Uh, Darryl wants to know if he can come too." I had said.

"Sure, why not. He can come, if only if he can buy the sodas?" Lana looked at him.

"Really," with a cough, "I mean yah of course." Darryl had said.

The girls giggled to Darryl's response. I looked over to Waylon, we both smiled. Whew I thought Darryl would have said something cheeky. But it was fine; we headed to the depot for a bite to eat. For those few moments as we walked down the street, I noticed no one had mentioned the game. For that short time it seemed nice to talk to the girls about life in general. Something other than hockey, we were away from hockey just for a minute. But then that silence was broke, when Melanie asked if it hurt when we had gotten hit along the boards or open ice. Darryl quickly answered that, he said only if we didn't expect it. Then the girls asked Darryl a lot of questions about hockey. The girls seemed to enjoy themselves, I was a little worried for this was the first time Waylon and Darryl had actually sat with what they called chic's. I hoped they would not mention that word at all during our time out with the girls. We were along with local girls, probably the prettiest ones in school. But my sights were on Lana, I found her very beautiful. When I was with her, I seemed to forget my past problems. Candice and Lisa were not there in my head. When I look back to those days, I sometimes think I was actually in love with Lana.

13

But I mostly thought it was mixed feelings between someone else. I felt totally different around her. I was comfortable. I was myself; I need not to pretend to be someone I'm not. Besides I told her I only wanted us to be friends. I sat there and watched her eat, and talk. I was in awe with her beauty. We sat there and chatted for sometime, I hadn't realized the time. It was nearly eleven, close to our curfew. So we had to cut it short, the boys and I chipped in for the meals. Since that what boy's were suppose to do. Before leaving Lana had called out to me. I turned to her; she slid out from the booth and approached me.

"Aren't you forgetting something handsome?" She had said.

"What's that?" I asked.

"Don't you want a good night's kiss?" She grabbed me and planted one on me.

I heard a bunch of woos from her friends, which made me blush. Now feeling shy I stood there blank for a sec. I didn't know what to do. I thought we made it clear that we were to be friends. Lana moved her lips. I read them and she said good night with a smile. I smiled back no longer feeling shy, and turned to leave. As I got outside, Waylon and Darryl were on my ass about that simple little kiss. But I had the hugest smile I ever had.

"Are you two a couple now?" Waylon had asked.

"I don't know, I thought we were just friends." I said.

"Oh come on now," Darryl jumped in. "She likes you, and if you can't tell by that, you are one dumb mother fucker."

"I just don't want to rush it guys." I had said.

"Oh come on Robbie, you have got to like her don't you?" Waylon had asked.

"Well yah, I do but…" I only smiled feeling lost for words. "She is pretty hot."

"Well duh." Waylon had said.

"Forget Lisa man, when you can have something like that. Wow, you'd be stupid if you don't. And she likes you Rob." Darryl added.

With him saying that, I thought for a moment. Thinking back to earlier that day, what I had said to Lana. What I had shared with her, I mean I cried on her shoulder. I opened up to her expressing my most inner fears. Maybe in that moment of despair, we had come closer. Now she was changing all the rules, but then again I shouldn't have let her do that to me. But I liked it, was I starting to like her back. She was one hot broad, but I said I wanted us just to be friends. Was I stupid, no wait here I am leading her on again. "What am I thinking?" I thought to myself. Wait a minute; I wasn't doing any thing out of the ordinary. She was the one flirting with me, and I was doing the same. The more I thought about it, Darryl was right. I'd be crazy if I let her walk away. I have to ask her out, she's just waiting for me to ask I know it. Besides it's just a date, it was the least I can do. After all she did fight Lisa over me.

Thinking it over, whether I should ask her out or not. I forgot Waylon and Darryl were even there, they were rambling on about who knows what. I wasn't paying any attention to them; I was in my own world. Before I knew it we were back at the dorms. It was then I remembered I had wanted to phone my uncle Terry. I dug into my pocket when I was nearing the phones. But I didn't have any change; I certainly didn't want to call collect.

Uncle wouldn't mind he would want to hear from me. He would want to hear how the game went and who had won. I asked the boys if they had spare change, so that I can make my call. To my disappointment, they spent it. So I decided to call collect, as I waited for the operator to connect me. I noticed Lisa coming down the hallway. I was hoping someone was there to answer, so I wouldn't have to talk to her, but as my luck was turning into a disaster. The line was busy. She stopped by me waiting. I had told the operator that I would try again later. I only glanced at her, and watched as Waylon and Darryl deserted me. With a big sigh, I felt that I had to talk to her. She said hi as I hung up the phone, she also asked how I was doing. Not understanding why she was here.

"Why are you talking to me all of a sudden?" I asked her.

"I only wanted to see how you are." She had said.

I shook my head, feeling that I don't have to talk to her. I had got up and started to walk down the hall away from her. She chased after me; I wanted nothing to do with her. She pleaded for me to stop, and begged for me to listen.

"Okay, alright. I missed you. I need you. Is that what you wanted to hear?"

"Lisa, we broke up. It's hard to talk to you right now, especially what you had done the other day. I'm a little upset. It's something I can never forgive you for."

"Rob, please…I'm sorry. I forgive you for cheating, why can't you forgive me for this?"

"Humph, that's not the point Lisa. Its over, why can't you see that."

Turning from her, she had grabbed my shoulder. And pleaded for me to stay there a little longer. But I had no intensions to hear what she had to say. I continued to walk down the hall. I then heard a sob from her, but she was trying to keep it to herself. I stopped for a second, thinking maybe I should just hear her out. Maybe she wants to try being friends, but that was impossible. Fighting my emotions I only wanted to get to my room.

"Robert, please." she sobbed. "I'm sorry."

I stood there feeling a lump in my throat. What was this feeling? Was it that I was beginning to feel sorry, or guilty about the whole situation? I heard her footsteps coming; I looked up to the ceiling closing my eyes wondering, "What am I to do?" I shook my head to get myself together. I didn't want to look at her and if I did, who knows what would happen.

I only wanted out of that moment in time; I never would want to live to regret knowing if I looked at her once. I would fall into her spell, saying the right words and knowing how to touch me. The only thing I could do was to keep walking. Then from what were walking steps turned into running ones. At that moment, my heart raced with fear, not expecting her to do what she had just done. She grabbed me from behind, throwing her head on my shoulders and sobbed. I didn't know whether to hold her, but I felt that I owed it to her. We did start dating two months after my arrival; it seemed appropriate at the moment.

Recollections raced through my head at that moment as well. I actually turned to face her, and looked her straight in the eyes. I wiped away her tears with my thumbs as I grasped her face. Feeling her tremble, I did the unthinkable. I kissed her without passion; I only wanted her to feel my lips one last time. I lifted her chin up with my index finger, to look up at me. I had to tell her good-bye, but it wasn't going to be easy.

"Lisa…Lisa, I'm so sorry."

"I'm sorry too." She had said as she grasped me.

"No Lisa, you don't understand!"

"Oh but I do Robert." She continued to hold me.

"No you don't. I'm sorry but we're through. Good-bye Lisa."

She stood there frozen like as tears again formed in her eyes. Her lips quivered as she tried to speak. I felt as though I wanted to cry, feeling that lump in my throat. Just then Paul came into the hallway. He called out to me and said it was curfew. I looked over to Lisa and said I had to go. She slowly walked down the hallway, her head down. I could hear her breathe of sobs, I watched, as I was now feeling bad. I took a deep breath and headed to my room. Paul asked if everything was all right, I glanced at him. And said things were fine. Lying there in my bed, I was staring up at the ceiling; Gerald was still up but was reading. He had his lamp on, so it wasn't really that bright in the room. I couldn't help but think about what I had done just now. I probably destroyed her by breaking up. But we broke up a month ago; I just had to let her know I had no feelings for her any more. It was time to move on, I choose too, why couldn't she? Man I couldn't stop thinking about her.

Watching her cry as she walked away, it had been a month since the bedroom scene. Here I am having feelings for some one else, and it felt good. I mean I no longer had Candice on my mind; I was only starting to get past what we shared. It was fun and exciting, nothing bad there. But the whole Candice ordeal was that she claimed to be pregnant, still I don't know. I really should have finished reading the letter, oh well! I was young, we all were. Still in high school, we had our entire lives to live for. With that in mind, I began to think of Lana.

Thinking to myself, should I ask her out on a date? And I would do it in the morning before classes. So I planned on how and where to do it. I could barley sleep, I was too anxious. Oh I know she would say yes, except that part of me thought she wouldn't. As the night wore on, I finally fell asleep. The next morning, Gerald had to wake me up. I did not hear the morning buzzer. Good thing he had forgot some papers, or I would slept through the day. That's how tired I was; I had only fifteen minutes to get ready before the second buzzer. I rushed around because I wanted to see Lana before classes started. But as usual, luck was not on my side. I missed her. During the first class I figure I'd write her a letter, at first I thought it was lame. I mean what guy in his right mind would even think of writing a letter, that's chic stuff. Man! Now I'm starting to sound like Darryl.

I didn't write it till second class. Mr. McDowell's Native Studies class, I spent the whole period writing my letter to Lana than I did on my essay. It was to be done for the next class, which was the next day. I really do know how to put myself in a jam.

I didn't pay any attention to his speech on Louis Riel, something on metis rights. I read the letter to make sure I made sense; I ended up writing it three times before I was satisfied. After class I strolled down to Waylon's locker feeling good. When I seen him, I asked to give Lana my letter. He stood and looked at me; I stood there with an idiotic smile.

"A letter?" he said holding it.

"I'm going for it man."

"Why don't you just go up to her and ask her yourself." Waylon had said.

"It's just easier this way."

He tried to argue with me, but I pleaded for him to just give her the letter. Finally he agreed, I said I would meet him at his locker after the next class. Before we go to the cafeteria. As I went to my class, I was kind of excited. Okay I was extremely excited. When lunch had rolled around, I practically ran down to Waylon's locker. As I veered around the corner, I came to a halt. Lana was standing there with Waylon. "Hey you," Lana had said. "Waylon says you have something to ask me?" I had just stood there feeling a little embarrassed. I tried to smile.

"Uh, Mm. You're such a kidder."

"Come off it Rob, I know what you want to ask me. And Waylon never said a word."

I looked over to Waylon, he gestured that he had never said nor gave her the letter. Now I was completely lost for words. She stood there with a cute smile, I had felt hot in the face, and I could feel myself turning red. She gave a little laugh.

"Well, I'm waiting."

"I was wondering uh…" I grunted to clear my throat. I took a deep breath and then asked her. "Would you like to go humph?" I covered my mouth with my hand mumbling.

"What?" She asked with a giggle.

"Would you like to out with me?" Gesturing with my hands.

She leaped forward and gave me a big hug and kiss. She had practically knocked me over; I caught Waylon giving me thumbs up. I gave him thumbs up back with a smile.

"Does this mean yes?"

"What?" she said leaning back.

"I'm just kidding." I said with a laugh.

"Rob, you're a goofball," she said smiling. "That's what I like about you."

"So, where you two love birds going for your first date?" Waylon asked.

"How about that movie date you promised me?" Lana suggested.

"Movie date!" I lifted one brow.

"I asked you the first time you walked me home. Remember?"

"Oh, that…Right, I remember now." I lied.

"Can you come over and watch one tonight?"

"Yah sure, say about 8 o'clock?"

"Great, I'll make some brownies and cookies." She added.

We sat together at the cafeteria; Waylon joined us, as did Darryl. We all sat and talked about class subjects. Who was best at what and who had got the most homework? Suddenly Mr. Penner was added to the conversation. We had him for English, and man he loaded the homework. We should have had a bet on which teacher gave the most work, even on holidays, he took the cake. It wasn't long before Lisa walked into the cafeteria. She was along with Melanie; she stood at the doorway for a moment. She stared right at us, Lana did not see this nor the guys they were to busy blabbing. I pretended I had not seen her, I could see the anger in her eyes. They were lit with fire, and she glared at Lana.

She had probably wanted blood, but I told her straight that it was over between her and I. After lunch, Lana and I went for a walk, we had gone to the track. We walked around a few times to kill time as we talked. We held hands at times and then out of the blue, she asked if I was going to stay here Cranberry. I looked at her not knowing what she had meant. "Of course." Was my only response. She told me she had a dream that I was there one minute then gone the next. I assured her it was only a bad dream. She stopped me and gave me a warm hug. This sent chills down my spine but it was good. We stood there for a while holding each other. I wasn't sure of what was happening, but in that same moment, I never thought my life would take a change of direction.

14

It was during second class after dinner, when the secretary's voice came over the intercom. She had asked Mr. Mc Cloud if I was in class. I was asked to go down to the office, the class teased as if I was in trouble. I wasn't sure why I was summoned. My marks were great. Maybe not the greatest, but they were passing marks. I hoped that I passed. A lot of things circled my head, mainly about my marks. That was the only thing that was making me sweat. If I fail, then I can't play. If that was the case, I would be lost. Putting aside my shoulder injury, play-offs were around the corner. I'd play hurt, I was going to be there playing no matter what. The closer I got to the office, the more I became afraid. Hockey is my life, it's all I think, do and dream it. If it were a meal I'd probably eat it. My hands became clammy and I had cold sweats. "What's wrong with me, it's nothing. Nothing at all," I thought. "There was no way they would just let me go, that would be insane. They know I'm the team leader. I'm behind McCormick in the scoring race."

As I approached the office, I stood at the door. With a big sigh I went in. all I remember thinking was "Please god, I don't want to fail. I can't fail, oh please I just can't."

"Hello Robert," Kathy, the secretary had said. "They're expecting you."

"They?" That thought ripped through my head like a pinball machine.

There was no way I was leaving the team; the board was in there. I just know it, waiting to tell me I can no longer be on the team. McCormick has already won; I was no longer a player. "I'm just getting my self worked for nothing. It's nothing; I don't know who really is in there." I thought. When I entered Mr. Smith's office, Mr. Boyle was there, this brought fear in me. What was going on here, am I in trouble? My heart began to beat faster. My mouth suddenly felt dry, I felt as though I was losing my breath. Panic was now setting in. "Mr. McKay," Mr. Smith had said. "I'm afraid I have some bad news. You better sit down." I sat and tried be calm about what was going to be said. Were my marks low? That I might have to sit out? Although I had too doctor's order. But I still played; it's in my blood. I was born to play hockey.

"Son! I'm really sorry," Mr. Smith said with concern. "But there's no other way I can put this." He then got up rubbing his face. Turning his back to me.

I wondered why was he so upset, was it that he knew I was a good player, that it bothered him too sit me a while. Then Mr. Boyle sat beside me. His hands clamped together resting on his knees. He sat there shaking them; he seemed he wanted to say something.

"Robert!" Mr. Boyle had said. "Your grandmother phoned this morning."

"She said your grandfather was on his way to pick you up." Mr. Smith cut in.

"Why is he coming to get me?" I asked.

With a deep sigh Mr. Smith rested against his desk. One arm half folded, with his face buried in his hand. Pondering what to say.

"It's your mother Robert."

"What's wrong with her?" I stood up. "Is she sick? What is it?" I was frantic.

"Robert please," Mr. Boyle had said. "Sit down please; I know this is very uncomfortable for you right now. But listen to me. This is not easy for us to say this; we find it hard as well. Your mother, she was in a car accident. We don't know how badly, your grandmother just said for you to come home. That's all we know."

I froze for a moment, the feeling I had was like my entire body fell asleep. It seemed numb from head to toe. I couldn't speak. The room at that time, had went dim, I felt dizzy and nauseous. I dropped back in my chair and the room fell black. It was like my life flashed before my eyes. Those vivid memories of my mother came floating back, from when I was little. I can see her in her favourite dress, the one she wore to church. It had pink flowers and it was red. When she wore it, she looked radiant. It came up to her knees, with just a shoulder strap baring her arms. She was beautiful. She always wore red lipstick, her wavy brunette hair hung to her shoulders. This was my last memory of her, what I can remember. It was in the back of my head any way. Why would I only remember those times? I seen her over the holiday; maybe that's the only time I can remember her being happy. I don't know. When I came too, Mr. Boyle was fanning me. He asked if I was okay. I nodded and Mr. Smith was standing over me as well.

"Robert," He had said. "Take all the time you want. What ever you decide, meaning education wise. If you decide to stay home its fine, I only want you to be happy. Mr. Boyle and I discussed that you would remain on the roster until you let us know, if you desire to play in the city just to be close to home. We are behind you. We give our deepest regards to you and your family. Our doors will always be open to you." My fate, my future all seemed so small compared to what I was going through. I was terrified; I didn't want to lose my mother. She had meant more to me than hockey, I knew right then and there I had to leave; I need to be by her side. She needed me and I needed her in my life. She was my only family. The very thought of losing her, brought tears to my eyes. My emotions were high; my dreams of glory were now put on hold.

I had to push the very thing that kept me going, put my dreams away for now. I banished the word and pictures of hockey from my mind. Tears rolled down my cheeks. But those pictures kept coming back, my moment of glory I had the night before. It seemed so wrong; I was having the game of my life.

"God please! Don't do this to me. Not now...not now!" I thought.

But god wasn't the blame, and it was horrible for me to think that. I took a moment to gather some thought. Both Mr. Boyle and Mr. Smith sat there with me, quiet but it was assuring. Then I asked if I could be excused to get my things together. I walked out of the office, and on the right was the trophy case. There were a number of trophies through out the years. In every sport the school was involved in. Basketballs, soccer, track meets, lacrosse, football, swimming, cross-country running, there were many. And even ones for hockey, but the last banner and trophy were two years ago.

I stood there staring at the trophy, looking at their picture holding the banner and the prize right in front where every one can see. I was lost within it; I can't remember what was going through my head. But I remember walking away with tears blurring my sight. I desperately wanted that same trophy. The Centennial cup and I wanted to beat McCormick. I stopped and looked back at that case, my heart felt heavy. Either it was the news of my mother or the thought of quitting the team. I knew I wouldn't be back; I couldn't leave her side again. Not this time.

I packed my clothes, lost in my thoughts. I sat there on the bed, my head down. I fought to hold back the tears, that hard lump in my throat hurt when I swallowed. Feeling my eyes swell, I looked at my hands and they were shaky. My chest felt like it would explode, and it was sore from the pain, my heart was broken. Part of me wanted to stay, and part of me was letting go. Those dreams were now drifting away, and then there was a knock at the door.

I hollered for them to wait, I scramble around the room. Wiping my eyes to hold my composure. I opened the door, and with out warning I burst into tears. It was my grandpa; he put his arms out to me and I wept on his shoulders. Mr. Boyle was behind him to show where I would be. He shook my hand before leaving, and gave me a warm smile. For some reason, this time it felt different. I guess we both knew that this was it. I turned to pops, that's what I called my grandfather. I was so glad to see him, for I haven't seen him or my grandmother for quite some time. The same time he sat me down, sitting next to me.

"My boy," He said. "I know this must be hard for you right now. Your mother is fine at the moment."

"What do you mean? At the moment." I asked.

"She's in a coma."

"She is going to be fine? Isn't she?"

"The thing is, that uncle Terry was with her."

"What happened? Is he okay?"

"I'm sorry son…He didn't make it."

My body had got a jolt, and I felt weird, it wasn't the same when I learned the news of my mother. "No, this can not be real. I'm imagining this; it's only a dream. Some sort of nightmare." I thought to myself. From what seemed like a dream come true, everything I worked so hard to accomplish, one moment I was having the time of my life; living what every boy dreams of. A fantasy. High hopes of playing in the big leagues. Then in a blink of an eye, reality jumps in shattering those dreams. Destroying my self-confidence, flushing my hopes, dreams and happiness away. To make things worse, I had to go to the hanger to get the rest of my things. Pops drove over to it, I watched as it came into sight through the trees. Getting closer and closer. My head filled with memories. Remembering all those times, from the games we lost and the ones we had won. I really did not want to go in, but I had too. I turned to look at pops; he put his hand on my shoulder, and gave a little squeeze. I knew he wanted to say something, but the look he gave was more than enough.

I slowly entered the place, I looked around and my emotions were a little choked. I can almost hear the laughter of the guy's, echoing through my head. As I approached my stall with all my equipment, there staring back at me was a picture. It was one with Darryl, Waylon and I. In the background was Brian's place; I totally forgot we had our picture taken that night. Holding it in my hand, I turned and sat in my stall. Looking at it, tears began to roll down my cheek. But I smiled as well remembering that party. "I'm sure going to miss you guy's…who knows, maybe I'll see you soon." I said to myself.

I then took a good look around the place. Banners from recent years hung from the rafters. Ghost figures now seemed to come into view. I can see them all. Past hero's the ones that led them to a championship. They were real team leaders, which I wanted to be apart of. I only dreamed of winning that cup, since my arrival I planned on holding it and drinking from it. I didn't know what my fate was. Was my journey only beginning or was it ending. My friends, who became my family, would be nothing but a memory now.

I began to pack my gear into my bag; I didn't realize I would take the team bag. My eyes watered as I packed, stopping from time to time. Keeping myself from falling apart. When I zipped up my bag, I stared down at it. My number and the team emblem stared right back. Was this it? My fate, what would the future hold for me. I had gone into a state of confusion. Everything that had happened had to have happened for a reason. I remembered my mother once said that very quote.

I began to wonder, and was beginning to lose myself in my very thoughts. Memories took over, things that had gone wrong from my past now appeared with a vengeance. Candice popped up and everything else that went with her. It was haunting my memories, was I losing it? Was I going crazy? I screamed in fear tossing things around. The pregnancy had haunted me with out even knowing it did. Was it his or mine? Everything that bothered me came all together. Ganging up on me, when it hit me.

It hurt big time. I couldn't handle this. Dealing with the fact, of my mother in a hospital bed; not knowing what to expect. And all these other things involved in my life. With even Uncle Terry's death, it was all too much for a seventeen year old to handle. I had no more father figure, no one to give that extra push.

Then with out warning, I fell on one knee and broke out into tears. Now sitting with my back against the wall, I bawled and let it all out. All my anger, all my hurt and everything else I just let them go. My knees bent and against my chest, my arms around them with my head buried as I cried. I didn't want to leave, not like this. But I had no choice. If there was a slight chance of returning I would, but I couldn't answer that. I didn't know what my future held. I finally had the strength to get up off the floor and grab my gear. I walked outside; pops got out and opened the trunk. He put my gear in for me. I turned and looked one last time at the hanger, my eyes fixed on it, as I was lost for a moment.

"Come on son, we have a long ride." Pops put his hand on my shoulder.

A warm glow flowed through my body after he said that. It was comforting; I no longer felt the way I did. Getting in the car I began to feel different. We were driving down the road, when I remembered Lana; I needed to say good-bye at least. I asked pops to stop near the school, which I needed to talk to a friend before we left. He never questioned me; he had only stopped by the school entrance. School was out; students were beginning to come out of the doors. I had got out of the car, I waited for Lana to come out, and when she did. She stopped in her tracks for a second or two, and then came to me. I was afraid to tell her what was going on. But she started to cry; in some way she knew I guess. She held me, which seemed like forever. She looked up at me, and her eyes seemed a darker shade of blue. She then said something about her dream. She had dreamt this, which I was leaving. In her dreams she didn't know what it had meant, but now she understood.

"I don't want to go. I never wanted to leave; hockey is my only way of living. I never wanted to give up…" I paused as tears now rolled down my cheeks. "I'm sorry for leaving you like this, it's only for the time being. I'm sure of it, but it's something I have to do right now. Put away my dreams."

"Don't say that don't ever say that." she sobbed.

"Lana…I have to go now."

"Robert, I'm so sorry. But please don't give up on your dreams."

She held me tighter and didn't want to let me go. I wasn't sure of what to do, so I held her also. We embraced for a minute. Then I said good-bye, Crystal had to sort of pull her away from me. She sobbed, and before she let go. I wiped away the tears from her cheeks, and I said to her that I'd be back. Was I lying? I didn't know. I had said what had come to mind, probably something to calm and comfort her. "I love you," She looked me with watery eyes. "I love you with all my heart."

With that being said, I was awe struck. I couldn't speak; the only thing I did was bend towards her. And pressed my lips against hers and hold her for what seemed endless. It was the first time I heard a girl say that to me, it was something I never experienced. It was a good feeling; I felt tears streaming down my cheek. I never wanted to let her go, but I had too. I kissed her on the forehead and said one last good-bye. She stood and watched me get in the car. I Looked out the window at her, as we drove away I gave one last wave which was all I could do. The feeling I had was guilt and sorrow, thinking that McCormick now had it easy. No one to worry about, he already won the scoring race.

15

That guilty feeling was because I was leaving Lana, after me asking her out steady. And the sorrow feeling was because I really never wanted to leave this place. I felt as though I was already home, as my emotions began to act up again. The thought of quitting really brought me down, I wasn't sure of what was to happen. With eleven games remaining I figured I'd miss three games at the most, at least I hoped I did. When we had got out of town, I was quiet till we were in the Pas. But during that ride, I thought of Lana. She made me happy when she was around. She helped me through my troubled time, dealing with the fact that I was going to be a father.

She was there to help me emotionally; she listened to me and let me get my feelings out. A way a true friend would be. I think if it weren't for her I'd go insane. Then out of the blue I asked pops.

"How do you know pops?"

"Know what, son?"

"How do you know when you're in love?"

"Ah son, you shouldn't worry about that. You're young and free; you have all the time in the world for that," He looked at me briefly and sighed. "Only time will tell, you'll know. Believe me, you'll know. Now get some rest, we still have quite a ways to go." Then he smiled at me.

Smiling back, I glanced out the window. Then I looked at him and asked when was the first time he knew when he was in love with grams.

He just kept staring forward, and he was quiet. I felt odd at the moment bringing that up. He'd give me a brief look as though he were saying "Close your ears, you're too young for this stuff kid." That was the look he always gave me when I was little. But this time was different. He gave a sigh.

"I guess you're a man now," he paused.

"How old were you then?" I asked.

"I was your age I think, sixteen maybe to be exact," He said smiling. "Your grandmother was fifteen years of age. And boy she was beautiful. I remember asking one of the boys I was working with, who was this angel of light walking past the shop. He told me that was old' McDougal's daughter. And I said that's the women I'm going to marry. It was love at first sight, and when we started dating, we'd go into the woods for a picnic. Then after we ate, we would have a piece of tail if you know what I mean!" Now laughing.

"Ewe, I don't want to hear that." I had said with a smile.

After we settled down, I told him that I think I was in love with Lana the girl I was hugging before we left. Again he told me I was too young to be chasing girls. Then I said to him that he was the same age, when he said he was in love. Without any hesitation he said times were different then. That he had it hard growing up and it was during the war. He told me he was in the war, that he was seventeen the time he left, and that he had lied about his age to join. When he left to go over sea's he said he thought he would never see Beatrice again, my grams. But then he shut down from there. I never knew he was part of the war, nobody mentioned that to me. But he really kept to himself my mother always told me. I had no idea what she meant till now. But he was happy to be a grandpa; always giving us money for treats when we were growing up. "But when you love something, if you let it go and it comes back. It was meant to be. And if it doesn't, then I guess it wasn't love at all." he said. "Pops, I love the game and I really think I'm in love. Reason being…." I pondered whether to share with him the way I did with Lana. "I think I should be honest with you, but don't tell mom or grams."

"Son we're two men sharing our thoughts and emotions. Do you think

I want to share with grams? There are things I don't even tell her. This is between you and me, and I promise you that."

I felt as though I wanted to cry, but I tried to hold back the tears. I was afraid he would think different of me. But I spilled the beans and told him everything; right from day one till the very moment we were sitting in the car. I cried and I said I was sorry for doing the things I did. I expressed how things were taking a toll on me as I was in school, and the way it affected me in my games. I was an emotional wreck and I thought I was going to go crazy the way things were going. I even mentioned that I was thinking stupid like taking my own life. I felt alone up here I told him and I was missing home. I thought I only had friends back home, but soon I adapted to this place and made friends like they were family. And soon after I said that, I stopped and thought about everyone and everything I was leaving. Then I started to cry asking if my mom was going to be fine, so good that I can come back to my home. I sobbed and began telling my dreams of glory, on how I wanted to play in the big league. How I was going to look after the family. But now my dreams were shattered, I lost all hope and my faith.

"What did I do to deserve this? Why is god punishing me?" I wept some more.

"Son, don't be so hard on yourself."

Then it hit me; it was the other night when I was waiting for McCormick. I remember thinking "I am God here." Is this his way of saying it was wrong for me to think that? Adding myself as an idol, the way people treated me as if I were? Thou shall not put any other gods before me. I remember that commandment. I then prayed to god in my head, pleading for forgiveness. I never meant it in that way; just to mean I was also good as McCormick. Feeling down, I thought of everything. Then this time Lana popped in my head, I wondered about her. How she was doing and hopefully she would wait for me.

Then I thought am I falling for this girl. I mean she was there when I needed someone. She was one person I can trust. I then thought about her for a while, taking those other thoughts off my mind. I actually didn't know for sure, if I was falling for Lana. But those feeling I was having for her were real. I hadn't experienced this, it's hard to say the way I felt and thought. Man I couldn't get her out of my head. Or was it mixed emotions about what was going on in my life. I had a lot on my mind, adding another thing to it. I fell asleep while I was thinking of everything. Before I knew it, pops awoke me in Portage La Prairie.

We stopped at Mc Donald's for a bite to eat. It was there that I had asked how was I to know love from fear of losing someone. Because I really didn't know if I was falling for Lana, or was this fear of what might become of my mother. Pop's had looked at me, and gave me a meek smile. I had put him on the spot where he had no answers to that question. I knew then not to say any thing more; and pops must have been tired. After all he must have traveled early to get to Cranberry from Winnipeg. Soon we were on the road again and once again I thought of Lana, was this good that I wasn't worrying about my mother? But in some ways it helped me to cope. I must have dozed, because when I awoke we were already in Winnipeg. Feeling hungry I asked if he could take me to McDonald's before I went home. He had asked if I wanted to go to the General Hospital, I wanted too, I really did but I felt I needed more time for it to sink in.

I refused to believe that my uncle and mentor had died in a car crash, and yet he was along with my mother. Was my mother next to pass on, just thinking about it had brought tears to my eyes. I couldn't lose her. Tears rolled down my cheek, I tried to hold them back. The back of my mouth was burning, I wanted to cry but be strong the same time.

"Is she going to die?" I blurted out.

"Don't think like that son, she's just sleeping right now."

"Why? Why now? When I 'm having the best time of my life." Tears streamed down my cheeks.

"You know...Things happen you can't explain," Pop's looked at me. "But right now, let's think positive."

I looked out the window in tears, and asked him to drop me off at home. I only wanted to be alone. He only smiled and took me home, he also asked if I needed any thing I should just call him. My mind was blank as I hauled my stuff up to my apartment. We stayed on the third floor, before I opened my door. Our next-door neighbour said hello to me. He asked how I was doing in Cranberry. I said it was terrific, and I was home for a short visit. But I told him I was in a hurry, and needed to get ready for a supper with the family. He wished me luck in the rest of my season and then left. When I got into my apartment, my hockey bag slid from my shoulders. I just dropped every thing right there and wondered into the living room. I sat there with no thought, and then it hit me. I tried to hold back, but it was useless. I buried my face into the cushion and balled my eyes out. The very thought of losing my mother had gotten the best of me. I pleaded with God not to take her. Then I thought of Terry, at the same time I stopped crying. I felt completely ashamed; here I was feeling sorry for myself. Yet I couldn't imagine what my cousin's were going through.

They had lost their father, and my aunt lost her husband. My mother lay in a hospital bed, still here with me. "I should be there right now." I thought to myself. I really didn't know what to do, part of me wanted to go there and be with her. The other half wanted to stay home, because I was afraid to look at her. For a long time I sat there motionless, and for some reason I picked up the phone. On instinct I dialled the number; it rang three times before some one answered.

"Hello," Candace's voice. "Hello…"

I didn't answer; I was lost within myself and really didn't realize I called her number. I was shocked and scared to talk.

"Robert, is this you?" She asked. "Where are you?"

I tried to talk, but instead I sniffed on the phone as my eyes again filled with tears. I thought she would hang up on me, but she knew it was I. She asked if I was home, I so much wanted to talk. But I don't what came over me, why couldn't I speak.

"Candice," I finally said with my voice crackling.

"What's wrong?" She had asked.

"I need to talk. Can you come over?"

I really don't know why I had asked her to come; in retrospect I think I needed some one close to me there. She and I were close at one time, but I let things change just for lust. I sat there thinking of what we had. Friendship could still be there for us, but maybe I needed to find out about her pregnancy. Was she lying to me or was it for real, I began to wonder and that haunted me.

At that time I think I needed a hug from a close friend of the opposite sex, and I chose Candice. She agreed to come and see me; I thought I would be excited. All I thought about was my mother; I was scared to death of losing her. I waited patiently for her; I tried to keep myself occupied by flipping through the channels with the remote. When I had gotten up to use the washroom, I stopped and looked at my hockey bag. Memories started to flood back into my head. I became an emotional wreck. Forgetting I needed the washroom, I grabbed my gear and went through it. When I opened the bag, right there staring at me was the picture of the boys and me. I thought I had left it behind. I forgot about them being in there, I sat on the couch staring at them. For a moment I glanced outside and thought of returning.

But in harsh reality I knew I could not, as much as I wanted too. My mother came first before any other decisions. I then put the pictures on the end table, and tried to call Candice back. I just wanted her to know that I had decided to go to the hospital instead. But was too late in my decision, she had already left. I had gone down to the lobby to wait for her; it wasn't long before she arrived. She had come along with Melissa, which is why I never noticed her in the car. I was expecting her to come alone by walking. I went over to the door to open it for her, and she gave me a hug to welcome me home. I couldn't help but smile from this unexpected smile from her when she had seen me.

"What was wrong?" she asked. "You sounded upset when you phoned."

I looked her straight in the eye and I told her what was wrong. Candice didn't know how to respond at first, but gave me some encouragement. She asked what she could do to help. I didn't mean to say it but it just came out. I asked her to tell me the truth about her pregnancy. She stood blank for a long time, shocked at the way I asked her in my state of mind I guess. Why I blurted that out, I will never know.

"This is not the time, nor place to talk about it," She put one hand on my face. "I will tell you, but…" Tears now formed in her eyes.

"Look I'm sorry; I didn't mean to say that. It just came out; I didn't know what I was thinking. There's a lot going through my mind right now."

"That's okay." She smiled wiping her eyes. "I understand."

She gave me a hug and said were things were fine between us. But not to think that we still had a bond. She then gave me a kiss on the cheek, and asked if she could give me a ride anywhere. But also asked if we were still friends, I was going to say yeah; but I remembered the letter. Oh I'm going to get it for this, but I can explain. I mean she hurt me. She had broken my heart and yet here I am talking to her, which has got to stand for something. Doesn't it? I so wanted to ask her about her letter, and then tell her about the one I wrote back. But I just needed to see my mother. Pops asked but I wasn't sure, but now I was.

I asked Candice if she and Melissa could give me a ride. She looked at me and said it would be all right. So I jumped in, and we went. The funny thing is that; I wasn't worried. I was calm. I thought I would be different from the way I was acting at home. Before I knew it we were at the hospital, as I got out she asked if I needed her for anything. I looked at her for a moment, and in that moment I saw Lana. With a big smile I said "I couldn't do this with out you." Not realizing what I had said to Candace.

But I was so absorbed with her beauty, those bright blue eyes, and the way she spoke. It was as if she was there with me. Forgetting whom I was actually talking too. I think it was meant for me to be with Lana. Why else would I think of her in this drastic time? When I really did see whom I was talking too, I thought with a smile. And then thanked her for her hospitality and the ride over.

16

She stood for a moment or two, and asked if I was feeling all right. I just looked at her and said, "Never better, thanks for asking." Through my time in despair Lana was the one to help me. I immediately wanted to phone her and tell her how she meant so much too me, even though my time of loneliness, how she is keeping me strong. I never knew how much of an impact she had on me. She was the one person keeping me alive inside. I could honestly say she was a true friend. She held my heart, and she always will. If it weren't for her, I'd probably be insane and be in a nut house. Whenever I thought of her, it brought a smile to my face.

But going back to that hospital, it really was my dark time. I must have experienced those times over and over, a nightmare really where I was afraid to face reality. As I walked down the corridor, to find I.C.U where my mother's room was. You could smell the sickness in the air and a faint smell of death. When I was approaching her area but it was that smell we all hate, it wasn't pleasant. Some family members were out in the hallway as some were in the waiting room. When I seen them my eyes watered as I had gotten closer. I was scared to go in and see her, as they pushed me mentally. I pushed the button to go in; when they let me in I slowly made my way to where she laid. And when I got to a desk I mumbled my mother's name. They pointed to where she was; I stood by the doorway for a sec, looking at her.

There was this machine hooked up to her, nothing but tubes running in and out of her body. There was a bag that filled up with air and then it would pump out. And another machine that kept her heart rate, seeing this I thought I would break down. But for some strange reason I was sensible. Just looking at her, she seemed so peaceful. With all those cuts and bruises, I had seen nothing but beauty. The way she was, the way she had always looked. And in that instant, I cried. Holding on to her hand, I said what she always told me when me when I was sick. "I know it hurts, but it will pass. Mind over matter." And then I clenched her hand. Feeling and knowing she was still here with me made me happy inside. I wanted to cry even more, and inside my head I begged her not to leave me. I held it in as much as I could. The back of my mouth burning, my lip quivering and tears strolled down my face. I really don't know how to explain the feeling, but I was shaky and weak.

But as time went by, some more family members and friends had come and went. Before I knew it; visiting hours was over. But I wanted to stay with my mother. Grandma insisted I go home and get some proper rest. I was fine, and I told her I was, but she wouldn't cave to my pleas. Grandpa looked at me and said he would take me home. That I should really stay at their house, I was in no condition to stay alone. That he'd worry about me. With out any negotiation's I went. I couldn't sleep at all, my mind was wondering. I was thinking of everything, from school to hockey and my future. I had it all planned out; hockey was my way into college. I only dreamed to play for North Dakota: The fighting Sioux. What was I to do if I don't go to college? But the more I thought of my education, the more I began to realize the long road I traveled. I worked really hard to get the marks just to stay on a hockey team. It wasn't just about hockey. My schooling had played a big roll; it was my ticket to college. My life spiralled around hockey. I thought it as the only thing. These thoughts bounced around my head that night. The next thing I knew it was morning.

It would be a couple of more days, before I phoned any of my close friends. I just needed to be alone. Candice would call and check to see how I was doing, I ask her not to mention to any one that I was home. I just couldn't talk too her after awhile, I was too afraid of what I had wrote. Guess she didn't receive the letter yet. The only one I'd rather talk too was

Andy. He'd write to me in Cranberry but I never responded. I never hung out when I was home visiting; and he only lived across the river. We grew up together in the north end. We went to Norquay elementary school. We were inseparable; always together we made that oath like all kids do. Best friends forever and even shook on it promising till the end of time.

When we entered high school, I went to Elmwood and he too River Heights. Still we call each other and hang out down town. Those times were the best especially when we'd take our girlfriends to the show at the Town Cinema. He was like a brother, my best friend. We'd reminisce about growing up and those crazy things we done when we were kids. Everything was great. Until he broke my heart, when he stole my girl from me. I was so mad and hurt. I told him I'd never forgive him. I would never speak to him nor think of him, he betrayed me and I would hate him forever. And yet, he is the only one I turn too.

Despite what he had done, how angry I was. No matter what feud we had. I only thought of that oath we made. Brothers no matter what, best friends will always be by your side. As I spoke to him on the phone, he asked what was wrong. That he heard it in my voice. I explained to him what had happened and how scared I was. He listened and gave his condolences about my uncle and asked where I was so he can come over.

One thing I learned about friendship, they will always stand by your side. In my time of need Andy was there. It wasn't long when he arrived at my grand parents. He came inside with his father. Who was concerned about me? And talked to grandpa. His father looked towards me and said. "If there was anything that we could do to help, just ask." Andy's family was like family to us. Since we only lived across the street from each other, when we were younger. As his father sat with grandpa, we went outside on the veranda. We sat and talked about other things, as he was only trying to take my mind off the situation.

"Andy?" I said with my voice trembling. "I'm afraid to go back."

"You don't have too; I'll stay with you if you don't."

"Thanks bud," I looked at him. "You don't know how much that means to me. I also want you to know. About Elaine..."

"Hey man, don't..."

"Just listen to me. I'm not mad any more. That's small potatoes right now. I forgive you," Tears formed in my eyes. "I'm just glad to have…a friend like you. With all this shit going on and everything we've been through. You still came."

"What else are friends for? Besides a kick in the balls." Andy smiled.

"But you're all arse." We laughed at that.

We sat there for hours chatting and teasing. Good thing grandpa had a heater out there. We'd probably freeze. Then when we got to talk about hockey, I then told him how my season was going. Then I just stopped for a moment; then I filled him in on everything right from the beginning. He just sat and listened as I told him from Lisa to Lana and how Candice made me think I got her pregnant. I laid it on thick and he just sat there like a true friend would. I talked all night right up to what had happened to my family. I asked if it was wrong for me not to go to uncle's funeral.Everything was passing by so fast; I just couldn't accept the fact that he was gone. It's like I'm still waiting for him to have come right through that door, to comfort me about mom. As I began to cry again, Andy just put his hand on my shoulder. I was filled with gratitude he was there; I had no one else. No one but…Lana! Then I felt remorse I guess, because I just left her. Then I told Andy about her and how she helped me through those difficult moments.

"I'm in love with her, but I never told her. Not even when I was leaving, when I found out."

"Maybe you should call her. Tell her how you feel towards her." Andy had said.

"I can't."

"Why not?"

"I don't think…I could go back." I sobbed.

"You should phone her, she's probably worried about you."

"I can't." I shook my head.

"You must. You owe her that much."

I looked at Andy with tears streaming down my face. I smiled as wiped them away and thanked him, that I would call her. How I needed her as much as she needed me. So I did, I called her and he was right. She did worry, but I told her everything was fine. She said she would come in to be with me, I was a little taken off guard.

"You'd do that for me?" I asked.

"I'd go to the ends of the world for you. I love you."

"I love you..." I was choked up. "I just don't want you to miss school over me."

"Everyone feels for you, your friends know. Your team knows. We all want you back. I want you back."

"I know. As much as you want to be here, you don't realize you are. In my heart helping me cope. I love you...wait for me?"

"I will," she sobbed. "I will. See you when you get back?"

"Yes." Then she hung up.

I sat there looking at the ceiling thinking was I lying? Am I going back? Would my heart let me? But now she knows. I have too go back for her. She blew me away what she had said. It made me feel invincible. Andy came in and asked what happened, I just smiled and said he was right.

"You see," He jabbed me in the shoulder. "I'm always right."

"Let's go to 7-11 or something, get out of here for awhile." I smiled.

"There's the ole' Robbie I know. I'm wishing for a big gulp too."

A few more days have passed, which lead to a week. Soon it would be a month that I was home. Andy stayed with me that whole time. His dad dropped some clothes for him the other day. Getting up that after noon, since we stayed up nearly all night. Forgetting what day it was; I turned on the television. Tuning to the weather channel, to see what day and time it was. Feeling hungry I went to the fridge. Instead of food, I grabbed a can of soda. Breakfast of champions Andy and I would always say. Sitting there watching the tube, the phone rang. It gave me a start, I answered and it was Grandma saying I should be down there. They were having a family meeting; I wondered why I had to be there. I woke up Andy, telling him I had to go to the hospital. He got up to get ready, but I told him I had to go alone this time. As I made my way down the hall to conference room, I over heard the doctor asking if everyone was here. I heard everyone chatter, and then poked my head inside. Grandpa motioned to me to go sit down.

The doctor began saying why he had asked for us to be there. He gave his diagnosis of my mother. Telling us what stage she was in, saying something like the swelling had got worse. He carried on, with few questions here and there from the family. But I didn't understand what was happening. Then I heard him say, "Pull the plug." What does he mean? I thought. Then he said the decision was theirs to make. Those machines were the only things keeping her alive. She'd be a vegetable, or let her go. "LET HER GO?" that thought raced with my heart. "Their decision? What about mine." Tears formed as my heart pounded.

"NO." I screamed.

The doctor tried to explain, but I refused to listen.

"You mustn't."

"Son." Grandpa grabbed me.

"No! She's my mother." I was frantic.

"Son, listen…" He struggled with me.

"You can't take her." I sobbed

"Robert William James McKay! " Pops shouted.

I stopped fighting, tears in my eyes. My throat burning, my heart pounding so hard I can feel it in my head. I shook my head, pleading with my eyes. Pops now had tears running down his face. "Robert, listen to me," He said as he wiped his cheeks off. "I know it's hard for you to understand, but if we let mom stay. Just her body will be here, not her soul. She's already gone son…I'm sorry. So sorry." My head rested on his chest and again I cried. Only this time it was my soul weeping for her. Trembling I sat down, and then both grandma and pops were beside me to comfort me as much as they can. It was hard for me to except it as I wept, the room was silent I could only hear myself. The rest didn't know how to console me. It was probably the most difficult decision grandma and pops had to make in front of me. It's hard to let go of some one when you never had the chance to say good-bye.

My mother's funeral was held back home in Scanturbury; it was a small church. But it was where she wanted to be when her time had come. I stood outside with the others for a bit before the service started. I then wondered to look for my uncle's grave. Strolling along with no thought at all, I then came to his burial site. It was just a white cross bearing his name, stuck into the frozen ground. My eyes swelled with tears, I felt ashamed of myself. For not being here when they had buried him, I mean after all he was that father figure I never had. All those talks and lectures, about how he was turning me into a man, but I didn't feel like one at that moment. My heart felt heavy and sore. "I'm sorry." I thought. I then remembered our talks and his encouraging words. "Life is a journey and we all face obstacles we sometimes feel that we cannot over come. When life seems dark, there is always light at the end of the tunnel." And it all came flooding back. It gave me strength and courage to go inside.

I sat in front with my aunt and family. The pastor began his service, and then we all recited the Lord's Prayer. As he went on talking about how a wonderful person my mother was. I sort of drifted into my own peace of mind. I was lost for those moments, staring blankly at her coffin with no emotion. A sudden feeling of sadness and loneliness fell upon me. And I had pictures of her in my head. Seeing old memories brought tears to my eyes, and I tried to hold in the tears to keep myself from falling apart. But as time went by nearing the end I heard the pastor ask if there was anyone who would want to share a few words, that the pupil was open. And there were friends of hers who shared how my mother affected their lives and made them feel good. They thanked her as some kissed her on the fore head. Others, their hands and then touched her casket. Then after everyone, had finished sharing, his or her fond memories of my mother. The pastor gave his last condolences and the last viewing began.

One by one they lined up, and they were many. As they viewed her, some were in tears and others held it in. They had come to us now and gave us handshakes, as others gave us a hug. Then soon it was our turn to view her; I had felt funny and scared. As I was beginning to get closer, the back of my throat began to burn. The closer I got my lips quivered as I fought not to cry. But she didn't look like my mother; she had looked like a totally different person. Then I burst into tears as I looked over her. I broke down and found myself bawling, feeling weak I fell to my knees. I had lost it and was crying like a baby, crying hard as I finally realized. This would be the last time I will see, and touch her. I didn't want to let go, it wasn't time to let go; it just wasn't fair. It would be awhile before I had settled down.

As time passed; moments I don't remember. We were around her burial site. And as I recall there were a lot, I had not noticed till later. Cars were lined up down the road; I didn't know my mother knew so much people. She had many friends who loved her as I did. The pastor began reading scriptures from the bible. Then he asked. "What brings us together in a time like this," He then looked around with a smile. "Love…love brings us together, as we remember Sylvia as she was. And she was loved dearly, which is why we are here today; not only to say good bye…but to remember those beautiful things about her, how she made us smile and made us laugh." He flipped through his bible.

"I would like you all to gather around for moment, Let us recite the 23 Psalm of David."

The lord is my Shepard;
I shall not want.
He maketh me lie down in green pastures;
He leadeth me beside the still waters.
He restoreth my soul;
He leadeth me in the path of righteousness for his namesake.
Yea thou I walk through the valley of shadow of death,
I will fear no evil; for thy rod and thy staff they comfort me.
Thou preparest a table before me in the presence of mine enemies;
Thou anointest my head with oil,
My cup runneth over.
Surely goodness and mercy shall follow me all the days of my life;
And I will dwell in the house of the lord forever. Amen."

I then went up to her casket and placed a rose on it, as did the others. I watched as her casket was lowered into the ground. Tears formed in my eyes, but I tried to hold a smile. For I should be happy as she is now with Jesus, as I stood there I felt someone's hand on my shoulder. I fought not to cry, as the back of my mouth burned. It was pops hand on me, and then he turned me towards him for me to cry. That it was okay to cry, crying is a way to let go. And so I cried. When it was time to leave, granny held onto me as we went to the car. We then proceeded to my late uncle's house. Where Aunt Jean prepared snacks for everyone. It was a time to share memories as some looked at photos, and others laughed telling stories.

I was not ready for that just yet. I wanted to be alone, so I disappeared into the bedroom. As I sat there I noticed some pictures with uncle. One particular, it was when his team won the championship. There beside him was me, and Lil' Terry on the other side. It brought tears to my eyes, but tears of joy. I don't remember that day, but it made me feel good inside. Auntie Jean then came into the room looking for me. She asked if I was okay, I nodded as I held onto the picture. She sat on the bed beside me, and gave me a hug.

"You know, uncle loved you and was very proud of you playing hockey. He would talk about you to his friends; he was excited for you. Remember when you phoned when you were lonesome? When he got off the phone, he just said you're a warrior. Warriors never quit, and I'm sure he would have liked to see that you finish what you've started."

17

I hugged her tight and cried some more. And the same time I thought she was right and it was just like him to say that, maybe he did through her. I just held on to her and wept, and maybe I was weeping for uncle also since I never really had the chance. She then said I can have that picture and that uncle had something for me, that it was special. She then pulled out this shoebox from the closet and put it on the bed. She opened it, gently put her hands in, and then she unwrapped it. It was a Dream Catcher, which he had made for me. It was special; I held it and thought of him. Auntie said he was planning on giving me when I had come home for spring break. It catches all my bad dreams, and lets through all the good ones. "Follow your dreams." I remember his words vividly, from when I had spoken to him for what was the last time. Follow my dreams, which is why he probably made me this Dream Catcher. He knew how much hockey meant to me. It was all I did, my dream to play in the National Hockey League. From that moment on, I knew what I had to do.

The next day, when I awoke I lay in my bed at grams. I rolled over to face towards the dresser, and my Dream Catcher on it. I thought of his words, "Follow your dreams." And the same time tears rolled from eye to eye and then on the bed. I closed my eyes for a moment. My nose running now I got up to blow it. I took a deep breath and let it out. I slowly got dressed, and staggered into the washroom. Still tired I washed my face and brushed my teeth. While brushing a memory of Waylon flashed. As

I was gargling to rinse, I choked. I remembered that moment he lay in the snow gargling. I laughed and choked the same time.

Pops came to ask if I was okay. I looked at him and smiled. "Yes." I said. But I guess that's what made me change my mind about quitting. I needed that laughter and it cleared my mind. Man I started to miss them, Darryl and Waylon that is. Looking at the clock, I went into the living room. Pops told me my lunch was on the table. So I went in there to eat. As I sat there eating, Pops was reading the free press in the den. I asked if he could drop me off at the drop-in when I was done. I felt like being with my friends. I knew that's where they would be; it's the only place we ever hung out. When I got there, I guess school was still in place. No one was there. I really never paid attention to the time, but an hour wouldn't be long; I went in the entrance on Talbot Street. I went upstairs to see Mark one of the workers. He was surprised to see me walk through the doors. He stood up from his desk, and came to shake my hand. He asked how I was doing, and that he missed seeing me around the place. Then Kim and Val, other youth workers, came to hug me and say hello. This made me feel great, and I was happy to see them.

When Mark had asked how my hockey was going, I tried to hold my smile and shook my head no. I then had tears streaming down my face. "My mother passed…" I was chocked up. Kim gave me a hug along with Val. "I…I quit hockey." Was all I had said. What was I saying? But I just blurted it out on a spur of the moment. Then Mark led me to a room where we could talk. Mark was a really nice person. With red hair that looked like shaggy and he was slim. He was very tall, taller than McCormick. I guess you could say I really looked up to him. We talked about what I was going through; he explained to me that he too had faced losing someone close to him. Life is full of surprises and we cannot change what had happened. We can only try to move on, which doesn't mean forget. He told me this one line, and he said his late father told him. "It either makes us, or it breaks us. Which one you choose it's up to you." I alone had to make a choice. Makes sense I wondered; we talked for a while. And we talked about times that made us laugh. I couldn't help but remember this one time.

He was walking with us from 7-11, Me, Lance, Joey, Bill and Jason. It was summer and dark out already. We were going back to the drop-in, when a big Rotty strolled onto the street. Mark stretched out his long arms to stop us. This dog was only meters from us; like say two streetlights away. We stood behind Mark; he said, "Don't run." But already we split, running for my life I was the fastest of the guy's. Then suddenly Mark zoomed by me; I just saw these long legs zip by. I nearly pissed myself.

He leaped over this fence like a hurdle. It was a tall fence one that I had to climb. But I just kept running, laughing the same time. I had to stop; I looked back the dog was gone, and my stomach hurt from laughing.

The guys disappeared, and I went to see Mark. I called out for him, his head poked over the fence. I burst out laughing more. Not that his head veered over the fence, I saw a sign that read Beware of Dog. We all met up at the drop-in, we scattered when the dog gave little chase. Sitting there I laughed as I remembered. And told him what I was thinking, he just gave a chuckle. "I told you guy's not to run. But when I looked back to you; no one was there." He snorted. "Forget this I said, and I took off right after you." I laughed as he was telling me.

Having a little laugh, made me forget about mom for a bit. Kim, Val and Mark were very supportive. I mean to me it seemed like they too didn't want me to give up. Then I thought about my dream catcher, everything good was flowing already. Feeling down the way I did. I never had seen it until now. My friends, family were edging me forward little by little. When I thought I would never get past the point of defeat. It was them that sort of carried me, guiding in some way. And I thought of Mark's quote.

As I waited for Bill and the gang, the more I thought, the more I thought of returning. I thought about everyone and everything, what I started needed to be finished. This was an obstacle and I was sitting in the dark; and was slowly being led to the light at the end of the tunnel. Thinking I was alone in my life and I didn't realize I had a big family. My family of friends was there in my time of need. When Bill finally strolled in, when he had seen me, he came and gave me a handshake. And said he was sorry to hear about my loss. I just gave a small smile and thanked him. We then played some ping-pong, to pass up the time. And too sort of take my mind off of things.

I figured I'd spend some time with them before I go back. And I spent time worthwhile, as we had a great time. Jay and they really never said anything to me, for I guess they didn't want to upset me. But with them not saying anything was word of... What's that word, they need not to say. But I knew what they were thinking. My mind was made up, and I wasn't going to let myself get lost. "Follow your dreams." This thought had flashed in my head. The same time Lana appeared in my thoughts as well, which had made me smile, because I was going back to her. She was my anchor she kept me together. I was in love with her.

My heart swelled with excitement when I thought of her, I was nothing without her. And what she said to me earlier, "To the ends of the world for me." I knew I had to go back. Not just for her, or for my friends. I had to go back for myself, to collect the other half of me. My heart, for I had left part of it and that half was set on hockey, it was all I did. My world, my life; it all revolved around it. It was my destiny. For my journey was only beginning. "It either makes you, or it breaks you." Marks words now rippled through my head. I chose that it makes me, life wasn't going give me anything if I just sat there; wallowing in what was self-pity. I had to pick myself up and continue on. Mr. Boyle's words were also on my mind, "We all face obstacles, if you can get past it. You can do anything."

That night at home, I told Pops I was going to go back, to finish school; and to complete my dreams hoping it wasn't too late. I would also call Mr. Boyle to let him know I was going back. He was thrilled; you can hear it in his voice when he spoke to me. And the good news was that we still were in the play-offs. My teammates had made it their mission to go the distance, for me. They said they owed it to me, he said they would kneel before every game; give a little prayer for me, and set out in hopes I would return to lead them. He told me he would let it be a surprise to them when I get back. We were in the third round, playing against the Neepawa Natives. We easily swept the Dauphin Kings in the first round. Then barely beat Flin Flon Jr. Bombers in the second, taking it to game seven. But we were tied 3-3 again to Neepawa in the series. With me returning for game seven, just in time and hopefully we can go to the cup final. We were to play the following evening. I couldn't wait to lace them up again, for I had rested my shoulder long enough. I was glad that we were still playing hockey.

Further more I found happiness in it. I was born to play hockey, and I was going to play hockey. Excitement over whelmed me as I sat there listening to Mr. Boyle tell me everything. But I cut him off by asking where Melville sat; I don't know why I asked. I should already know. They steamed rolled their competition in the west, hammering Yorkton Greyhounds in the first. Slaughtered Battlefords North Stars in the second; but they had encountered a roadblock with the Weyburn Warriors.

That series deadlocked at three a piece as well. Oh man I was getting the goose bumps, I found myself rooting for the Millionaires. After speaking with Mr. Boyle, I told him that I would be there the next day. I just sat there on the couch feeling anxious to get back. Wanting to leave that moment I told Pops I was ready to go. I just wanted to play again, since it's been five weeks that I have skated. I went to get my clothes ready for my departure. As I was packing, I thought of those games. Ones where Mr. Boyle told me my teammates gave a little prayer for me. Kind of makes me think, was I that important to them. I just thought of myself as a player at that moment, not a leader. All I ever cared about was being top scorer, but that all went down the drain.

I bowed out to McCormick, I didn't want too. But I had too; he was a true leader to his team, now they face elimination against Weyburn, as we did. And in the back of my head I had wanted the Millionaires to win their series so that we can play them in the finals. Already thinking that we were waiting for them, we had to beat the Natives first. Pops would drive me to Neepawa, where Mr. Boyle and the rest of my teammates would be for game seven. I looked at my hockey bag; I just stared at the emblem. Our symbol and colours were that of the Chicago Black hawks. Staring at it, I thought of them. I would go and try to lead them. And I would don the sweater with honour, and glory. Win or lose I was proud to be a Mohawk.

That evening I thought I wouldn't be able to sleep, with all the excitement I was going through. But I slept good, well rested for the game I guess. But before leaving that morning I thought I'd give Andy a call and tell him I was leaving for Neepawa to help my team and try to get to the finals. And thank him for his support; also I was glad that we mended our wounds. I called Bill as well, telling him I was going back. My team needs me in this time of need. I said I would go and win game seven for him and the boy's. He just said to call when we win game seven. Give some words of encouragement I suppose; take over where uncle had left. But I said I would.

We would arrive in Neepawa around four, two hours before game time. And now those butterflies were in my stomach, already nervous, was it for the game or was it that I was going to see my friends again, my teammates. Pops would pull into chicken chef for a bite to eat. He had chicken. I ate pasta. I needed that energy for the game. Soon we went to the arena. Pops waited with me till my team arrived. So I could load my bag of clothes on the bus. I was anxiously waiting sitting there on the bench in the canteen area, I starting reminiscing about Waylon and Darryl. About those parties, man I probably missed a bunch. With a smile on my face I thought back to our games over the season. How much I missed the sound of my blades cutting into the ice. Anticipation was building up within me; I so desperately wanted to play.

Pops had handed me a drink, taking me out of my daydream. And said they were downstairs, "Must have came in through the side entrance." I jumped to my feet and threw my bag over my shoulders. Pops put his hand on my shoulder, taking a sip with other. He looked at me for a moment. Then he gave me smile, a warm comforting one. I knew he was proud of me. And then he turned me slightly and patted me on the back to go. I turned to look at him as I was walking for the door. He just stood there smiling, and gave a salute. Like see you later kind of thing.

When I reached the bottom of the stairs, I stopped for a moment. A tingle ran down my spine, I opened the door to the hallway. Biting my bottom lip, I took a deep breath and let it out. My heart racing as I walked down the hall. This feeling I had, was it for the game or for my friends. As I reached the door, one more deep breathe. I looked up to the ceiling, closing my eyes. I stood there, and you can hear them all. They were laughing and getting ready. Slowly I walked through the doors, not knowing what to expect. When they had seen me, some with their heads looking up from what they were doing. Then with a big cheer "Hey…Robby." they ran to hug me. Surrounding me they patted me on the back, some with force so hard pushing me. This brought a smile to my face, so hard it hurt to smile. Excitement filled the room, and it had a positive glow. One called out, "They're done now. We're in the finals." And then they cheered. I looked towards where my sweater hung with number and name faced us. I was lost for words.

"That was my idea," Waylon had said standing with me. "Sort of like a monument." I had tears in my eyes now.

"Thanks…" I wiped my eyes. "Now let's go waste these fucker's!"

The room filled with cheers, they were happy I was back, happy to hear me say that; it gave them energy. The hair on the back of my neck stood up. I was so excited and ready to play. I stared at my sweater for a moment, and thought of my family. Fighting what seemed like tears. My throat had a lump in it, and then I made a small number. I would put uncle's number on my upper right side of my sweater. Number five stood out with our crest. Then I slowly slid it on, and dedicated this game to him.

When we were ready one by one, we exited towards the rink. Waylon was at the door bumping gloves, when I reached him he stopped me. Putting our helmets together almost like head butting. "This game, we play for mom and for number five," he said. And then he patted me on the back. It energized me and gave me confidence. I missed him, and I was glad to hear him say something like that. It didn't matter if I scored or not. I loved hockey I just wanted to play.

18

Walking towards the rink, the music was playing, echoing through out the arena. My heart raced with anticipation, thumping like a drum. I looked around before I touched the ice. It felt good, feeling my blades cut into the ice. I almost forgot what it felt like. The crowd cheering the Native's as they skated around the rink. Usually I too skated to get the blood flowing. But I had stood along our bench my blood; my adrenaline was already flowing. I was hungry, and I was going to eat them up. A different kind of feeling ran through my body, my game somehow felt strange. It wasn't that feeling I use to get, excited. This was beyond that I was raring to go. "Good evening ladies and gentlemen. Boys and girls, once again welcome to Neepawa. Our Natives play host to the Mohawks of Cranberry Portage for game seven. And be sure to pick up your fifty-fifty draw to support our Peewee's. Please stand as we play the national anthem." The announcer said loudly.

I stood in our bench with my helmet at my side. Staring at our nation's flag, no thoughts. No fear, my heart was racing while we waited for it to be over. And when it was the crowd cheered. It's show time. Our booster of fans cheered as our first line was out there, Jason, Darryl and Dwayne along with Brian and Waylon on defence. Jay looked around to see if everyone was ready. Then he coasted in to center to face off. The puck drops and the Natives win the draw. Skating in so far they dump it. Giving chase they seized the puck in the corner. As they were fighting to get the puck, the Native's stole the puck from Waylon. With a quick pass across and one timing the shot, Tim slid and made the save. The crowd moaned. Giving up a rebound, they would shoot it again. Tim would make the save. Later on picking up the loose puck Darryl skated up ice.

He criss-crossed with Jay at their Blue line, Jay now carrying it in, he tight turned at the hash marks. Looking for helpers, he then made a sweet toe drag around their player. And then leaned into a slap shot; our forwards were in front. Dwayne deflected it; it catches the goalie by a hair. Then it trickled slowly by the goal. Desperately searching their goalie looking around, Darryl jams it in. we jump to our feet with a cheer. Our fans cheer we were up one goal now. I waited for my cue to get out there, waiting for a line change, but when? Mr. Boyle never really gave me a look. Then with out warning he yells for me to get on the ice. I leap over the boards chasing the play in our end. I skated in to help our defence. I turned to the player, who now had the puck. He slid the puck past me, as he tried to go around but I put all my weight into him. He wasn't getting by me; I slammed him into the boards. The house rocks and the play went down to their end. I hung back as Waylon now was playing forward. I can hear fans calling my name, cheering for me. I felt great, I felt invincible.

As I coasted so far, my line mates again scored. Our bench was frenzy. Was it because of me they were flying? They were high with that goal. I changed up as did the other's our bench was frantic. Mr. Boyle patted me on the back and said it was a good hit. Cheering on the other line he looked at me.

"Great to have you back." He smiled.

Goal was being announced over the loud speaker.

"Where did that come from?" Jay asked. "It's not like you to take the body."

I turned to him, and shrugged my shoulders with a smile.

"It was awesome…" He grinned.

During the first period my team was thrashing them out there with hits that send the crowd to their feet. Later on in the period I was to get a shift out there again. I was chasing their forward down to our end. It was speed against speed, but I would catch up. I pretended to poke at the puck. He pushed the puck past, and tried to leap over me. Only I would turn into him with a hip check, sending him airborne through the air. The crowd and my bench roared banging their sticks on the boards. Where was this coming from, I don't know? But I was a different player. I wanted to hit more than I had wanted to score. And it felt good.

This would ignite my teammates to play harder, and Tim was making save after save. He was robbing their forwards with a quick glove hand, and doing the butterfly beautifully. It was late in the period where they caught a break. The Native's broke out of their zone, sending a winger in on a break away. With a pump fake, he pulled out Tim. A tuck into his skates and kicked it back to his stick. He scores. "Wow" I thought what a move. The arena roared with cheers, and that horn blaring. This team was not much of a hitting team, not like Melville. They were more finesse, and quick. They would soon adapt to us, sticking to their game. Using their speed, with quick passing they changed it up on us. Changing lines on the fly, my team would try to hold them up at the neutral zone. We were up one goal, but facing elimination. It was do or die we needed this win.

There was a minute remaining in the period; Neepawa would catch us on a bad line change. Going in four on three, playing the diamond, we tried to block one shot. But it was a fake as he now walked around one player, stick handling this set up an opening. *TIC TAC…TOE* it was in. The arena was now louder than their horn. And then the buzzer goes to end the period. The score now tied at two. Heading back to the dressing room, a little tired from my shifts but they were big ones. Sitting in my stall I sat back looking up at the ceiling, with no thought at all. Waylon slaps me on the shin with his stick.

"Big hit out there," He smiled. "Keep it up."

I only smile. I had nothing to say at all, my mind was blank. I sat there rubbing my face with both hands now, pushing my hair back. Mr. Boyle draws out plays on the board. Telling us we were not executing the plays they practiced. I had no idea what he was talking about, but I made my own game plan. After Mr. Boyle finished speaking, there was silence. "Let's go guys. Pick it up a notch," I said. "Play their game, have only two guy's in with the third hanging back with the defence. Enough of this running around, we can beat them. Its do or die this period, play it like it's our last."

The boys shook their heads agreeing, making a positive note. I only wanted to go out and win, try to score for my team. Carry them on my shoulder's it was up to me to make things happen. Now adding pressure, my heart raced, as I was eager to get going.

The whistle blows, I jump up and head out first. If I were going to lead them to victory, I would be the first one out. Walking to the rink, the song Crazy train was playing. And that's how I felt that moment, "Crazy." My spine tingled and my heart racing. I wanted blood and I would try harder this period. Dazzle them with my skills.

Sitting on the bench patiently waiting, the puck drops to start the second period. Jay loses the draw, but they forced them into their end. Trying to set up their break out, one of their defence gets hammered into the boards. The house roars with excitement, driving down to our end they pass off quickly and set up a shot. Tim steers into the corner, where the Natives pick it up. Cycling they made two quick passes, across to the other defence one touch pass down low. And a quick wind up and rips one at Tim, hitting him dead square in the head. Knocking him over, he sprawls to get to his knees. The crowd roars, wooing when Tim makes another impossible save. Down and out he stretched out with his stick he makes the save. There's a scramble in front Tim gives up a rebound, with a quick snap shot from their player. Tim gloves it stopping the play.

There is applause from the crowd as they're enjoying the show. Changing the lines, I would skate out to Dwayne's right side. Darryl was on the left, pulling my elbow pad adjusting it. I glance at Waylon on defence and he pats his shoulder. I knew what he meant this time, and we square off. Dwayne wins it, I skated ahead switching positions with Darryl. The puck is dumped, and we chase it in. Darryl gets there first, fighting the opposition. Dwayne skates in to help slamming the player into the boards. I cycled around the slot, waiting for an opening. Then Darryl has the puck, he sees me. Giving a hard pass, I one time it. My knee dragging as I shoot, hitting the post it echoes the crowd woes.

Then the play quickly advances to our end, three on two. Going wide their winger winds up and drills a low shot. Tim goes down blocking the shot. It trickles through, and slowly slides past the goal line. The crowd screams in excitement, Tim puts his glove behind him thinking he has it.

Waylon holds up his man, and keeps him from getting the loose puck. We try to dump it out, but they keep it in play. My legs and lungs burning, I skate towards their defence. And slide to block a pass as he drags it around me. I swing my stick, but he jumps over and passes it into the corner. I fight my exhaustion to get up. "Get up Rob..." I tell myself. We scramble and Waylon throws another hit, it knocks his player down. The crowd roars, Waylon is dead tired. He hangs on to a player along the boards. Waiting for a whistle, but there is none. The ref calls out to play it.

I skate in to help and dig it out. I fight off checkers as I desperately help Waylon who now gets knocked to the ice. The house is in an uproar. I lose the puck. I hook and slash at him, to try to stop him. I see the refs arm go up, "Touch the puck," I yell. But no one does; they set up with an extra attacker. Darryl lay in the corner fighting to get up. He gets to one knee, they shoot into a screen. Tim barely saves it as he whacks it away. The ref blows his whistle; I slump over coasting to the box. I serve two minutes for slashing, but it was a good penalty. I kept him from shooting. The music man plays a bad guy theme. Mr. Boyle yells for me to come straight to the bench, when I was done. I nodded, this time I'd better listen.

The crowd cheering on the Natives, I just hoped that they could hold them off for two minutes. Flying down to our end, they were fast and they turned on their jets. They made three quick passes and then a quick shot on net. Tim makes the save sliding across stacking the pads. Deflecting it into the corner, another play is set up. Another rocket of a shot, Tim saves it doing the splits now. There's a rebound, blocker save. The crowd is on there feet screaming with excitement.

Man I swear that wasn't Tim, he was just inhuman making impossible saves. But keeping us in the game, we had better help. If it weren't for him we would be down at least five goals. Neepawa was all over us; we have yet to set a play. Confused our players started to clutch and grab, losing what I had said in the dressing room. Time was winding down, the boys kept them at bay. My penalty was over I raced to the bench. Jay leaps into play. Screaming for a pass, he skates low then turns towards their end. Receiving the pass he drags one leg at the red line to keep on side. Now he pours on his speed, their defenders chasing him one stride behind.

He catches up but Jason fights to keep the puck. Like workhorse he carries their defender on his back. Were on our feet watching, hoping…the goalie dives to poke check, Jay lifts the puck and falls with their defender. He's sliding on his knees, the puck past their goalie. The crowd roars, he sweeps at the puck. It bounces and rolls slowly towards the net, the crowd along with us is hysterically screaming. Their forward's dive to try to keep it from rolling in. it hits the post, rolls in and their forward knocks the net off flying into it. We celebrate the goal the crowd boos. But the ref waves it no goal, we are furious. Waylon is in the refs face clearly it was in…Jay indicates a penalty shot. Mr. Boyle is screaming mad. He slams a stick on the boards. The house is crazy; both refs now are at the timekeeper box. Jason is there and Waylon. Their captain stands calmly agreeing with the ref.

Then the ref turns, signals "No Goal." The crowd cheers.

"What…Open your fucking eyes," Mr. Boyle screams

The ref comes to our bench to explain. Mr. Boyle stares him down; the look he gave, sent shivers down my spine. I was scared. Scolding the ref he seen it go in, he was just as far as he was. Pointing at the net he disagreed with the ref, he then puts his hands over his eyes impersonating him. Then the ref warns Mr. Boyle, if he gives another out rage he was done. Mr. Boyle's eyes were ripping him apart, as Mr. Patterson pulls him to distract him. Forgetting we were there, he throws a water bottle down splashing us. He was mad; we just kept quiet looking forward. I dare not look back. Swearing he just kept mumbling. Mr. Patterson took over changing our lines.

The period comes to an end, still tied at two. We should have been up one goal, which was a bad call. Walking into the dressing room, Mr. Boyle strolls in furious. He paces back and forth yelling at us, we were sloppy out there I know. He kicks the garbage can over and demands we get it together. I sat there, sweat rolling down my forehead. I was lost for words, or I was afraid to talk. No one says anything, we just watched him as he yelled at us. Wishing the ice was ready, I only wanted out that dressing room. As did the others I guess, but we did need a scolding. I forgot how intense he was he pushed us. But maybe sometimes it was a little too far. But right now we needed that extra push. We were facing elimination.

This was our time; we were the school's last hope for a banner. Our fans were out there rooting for us. We mustn't let them down, they traveled three hours to watch us play.

19

Mr. Boyle leaves the room to cool down…I hope. Mr. Patterson draws up some plays and Waylon talks out his game plan. Speaking for Mr. Patterson he tells which lines are going to be used out there. This was crucial no one disagrees. Waylon was our assistant captain; he stood tall and gave us orders. If he benched me I would sit with out complaints. Going with three lines, the forth gave up their spots. Playing defence more, he tells Dwayne to drop back. Giving up one spot for forward, he tells me to step up. Feeling jittery I asked if he was sure, I was dead tired. Without a doubt he exclaims. More weight on my shoulders now. Dwayne slaps my shin guards with his stick.

"Its all up to you squirt!" I hated when he called me that.

"Come on guys…" I quickly searched for words. "Our fans are out there. They came along ways to watch us…I came along ways, I am not about to sit back and watch them win. We wear this sweater for honour, pride and glory. We do it for them." Pointing outside. "We do it for school…most importantly, we do it for ourselves."

Feeling charged up, the boys were anxious to get out on the ice. Darryl tells us all hands in. "For honour, and glory…" He says. "*MOHAWKS*." We all shout. Standing we waited for that whistle, some rolling their heads, others shaking their arms to loosen up.

My helmet cage, rest on my forehead. Then the signal, we charge out of the dressing room. I drop my helmet in place, and do up my chinstrap.

Heading out you can hear old songs from the eighties, blaring as they played. I was feeling excited, we were pumped. Skating around before the period starts, this one rock song sent a vibe through me as it played. Being put on the first line, I wasn't sure of myself at first. It had been five weeks, I felt sluggish. My lungs couldn't keep up to my legs, or I was just afraid to mess up. Someone else deserved to shine I was feeling weak. I was feeling discouraged in myself, no butterflies this time. What was happening to me, I use to thirst for this moment, and would grind it out. This game wasn't me, who was I and why now.

Then as we strolled out to the rink, Lana appeared in my thoughts. I remember her smile, those cute dimples. My heart filled with anticipation, as I was getting back what I had lost for a short time. It was for the love of the game, and my desire to win at no cost. She hung onto my dreams of glory, the more I thought of her. The more I wanted to play, and it was no mistake for me to step up. In some ways I led the team with my choice of words, I would say all the right things to motivate them. Now it was my turn to motivate myself. I stood along the bench, waiting as the team skated around. Tim was striding back and forth in his crease, readying his area his office. I closed my eyes for a moment, and then I had thought of uncle. Seeing him he looked at me with a smile holding my dream catcher. I felt my eyes swell along with my heart. He was encouraging me, "Never give up." He once told me. Feeling more enthusiastic I put my hand on his number above my heart. "This is for you uncle." I said to myself. And then went for a little skate before the puck dropped.

The whistle blows; the third period is under way. I play left wing this time, for it's the best angle to shoot from. Besides I was right handed and it would work perfectly for those quick one timers. Facing off Jay wins the draw; Darryl grabs the puck and passes it back quickly. Waylon pivots back then passes to Blaine who carries it in. We strive for the net, as he lets one mean slap shot go. Its low and it hits the goalie hard, his pads echoed as it rebounds in front. I scramble to it, as did Darryl. We skate by as their defenders hold us up. Jay streaks in and lets a snap shot go, and their goalie gloves it. The crowd's roar was tantalizing.

Face off was in their end on the right. I stood in the slot behind Jay waiting for the shot. Waylon stood in my wing. Jay wins it and I wind up for the shot. I lean into it and hit the post, it echoes loudly, their goalie didn't move. I blistered that one he didn't even see it. But now it was going down to our end. With my shot deflecting off the post it would create a two on one rush. Blaine pivoted backwards; they went down to our end strong. Flying in on Blaine, he took the player with the puck. Passing it through Blaine's legs, Blaine finished the check, sending both sprawling into the air. The crowd cheers and is screaming as their player now alone on a break away. He fakes a slap shot, Tim commits. Their player pulls to the left, Tim sprawls then rolls on his back, his legs in the air, stopping a for sure goal. The house roars, their horn blaring. It nearly brings the house down it was electrifying. Big save on a big move, Tim was a wall. The bench bang's their stick on the boards. As the play was still in our end, we dump it. Icing the puck the play stops.

Changing up the lines, our guy's bump their gloves as they exchange. Mr. Boyle made some changes to our lines, still using the three forward lines. The defence had more ice time than we did. We only stayed out there for thirty seconds, enough time for a quick shot on net. Mr. Boyle was only trying to mix it up, confuse them. We would have shots on net, as did they. There was hardly any hitting in the third; it was speed and skill out there. My teammates managed to keep up with them. Hard to believe this team was a sixth place team. The crowd enjoys the game; there are saves from both goalies that have the arena on their toes. Fighting for that goal, the next one would break a team. But which one both is skating hard, both are playing good. But Neepawa has us in their clutches. They just kept coming at us with their speed. Tim was breaking barriers with his spectacular saves. He marvelled the Natives, as they couldn't figure him out.

Mr. Boyle keeps reminding us Tim is keeping us alive, we have to win for his sake. Give him the glory and we could move on to the finals. It wasn't easy for us. My heart pounded as I was winded, as were the others; there was a stitch in my side. I would change up when we would go down to their end. I just couldn't go, my lungs burned at every breath I took, that stitch was there to remind me and my legs felt weak. I pushed myself though I have to try harder. "Never give up." I thought. It seemed we only went with two lines now because I wasn't able to keep up. Sweat poured from head, as I was tired. We would get little wind back in our sails before we changed on the fly again.

Snow was beginning to build up on the ice. We sure cut it up; the puck seemed to drag from it. And we were not able to catch a break. Then as we were caught in a middle of line change, a Neepawa forward carried the puck in making a pass. It would stop dead, I had just got on the ice I seen Ryan go for the loose puck. I curled waiting for it he took a slap shot, but a low one passing it to me. Making sure it doesn't stop like it did, I was now in alone. I poured it on what I had left; I came in on him faking a shot on the opposite foot I pulled him out. Way out and I had nothing but net, the crowd was roaring. I shot towards the net and curled away with my arms up. The puck slid to a stop in front of the goal line, the arena was louder than horn, and it was a mad house. Their goalie pounces on it; I look up to the heaven's clutching my helmet with both hands, in disbelief. I had it. It was in. Damn snow, I skated to the bench.

My teammates patted my shoulder. It wasn't my fault. The ice played a big roll now; it gave us the advantage and then it had taken it away from us. Mr. Boyle patted my helmet. "Don't worry about it," I looked at him. "It'll come." He now smiled. I felt good to hear that from him. I reached for a water bottle; I then took off my helmet and squirted myself to cool off. And quickly put my helmet back on. My eyes burned from my sweat and I tried to ignore that stitch, it hurt but I battled it. I gave my all and I wasn't going to sit. I wanted back so bad, now I have to fight for it. The third period would end still tied at two; we were going into over time. As we headed back to the dressing room, the crowd cheered to applause their team. When I walked into the room, players were slapping each other on the shins with their sticks. Little cheers from here and there, encouraging Tim to keep it up. But we were tired, sweat poured from some. I sat back in my stall closing my eyes as there were burning.

I had taken off my sweater and shoulder pads, to cool down. Mr. Boyle then came in with a plate of oranges. They were cut up; he gave us to reboot our energy. I needed all the power I could get so I ate some. Mr. Boyle didn't say a word this time, he just let us rest. He would go over some plays with Mr. Patterson, over looking them on his sheet. They would joke among themselves, this brought light into the room. Not feeling so tense the boys started to chat a little.

"Oh man…I had it. It was in; I just can't get over it. It'll haunt me forever." I mumbled.

"It just wasn't meant to be…" Waylon said slapping my pants. "You're meant for bigger and better ones."

Nodding my head, I just put my fist out. He bumped it with his.

"I missed you guys," I smiled. "Thanks."

"For what?" he asked.

"For being a good friend."

"Yah, I missed you too," He looked around. "Don't tell anyone I said that."

"What?"

"Its sounds funny that's all, to say that to a guy."

I gave a chuckle and punched him in the arm.

"Queer."

We laughed, and got ready for the next period. I was feeling normal again, it was great to be back and joke with old friends. I felt at ease, Waylon was such a goofball. I guess it was safe to say he was my sidekick. A real friend he was. I just smiled as I glanced at him putting on my sweater. The boys were getting antsy as they waited. My heart rest on my shoulders, we needed this win. School pride was on everyone's shoulders, as we wanted to be remembered. If we were to lose, we would be lost. We were brought here to go the distance, as long as we made the finals. People would remember us as we were. We can't lose; we can't let the school down.

Once the ice was ready, the boys headed to the ice. Jay bumping gloves with everyone as we exited the room. Strolling down towards the rink, I just had one goal in mind. To win this thing, it's all that mattered to me. Winning was everything, it was the only thing. If we were to go out and to be eliminated from the Natives, I choose to go out in a blaze of glory. I traveled so far with the team; you are only led up to a certain point. The team now resting on my shoulders, I stood at the fork in the road. One road was to a memory. The other led to glory. When my foot touched the ice, I felt completely energized. My body was ready for war. This was it, the final battle. As we strapped on the equipment, it was our armour. Our sticks were our swords. Our skates were our horses. Going into battle, I became a warrior. Warriors never quit, never give up. Never…back down. We fight for our pride, our hearts. We fight for glory.

The ref blows his whistle to start the period. Ten minutes was on the clock. I coasted to my wing on the right. Jay took one last look to see if everyone was in place. Just like in slow motion the puck dropped, I had seen it slowly flipping and falling. The two centers whacking at it to win the draw. Neepawa wins it; they cycle it around in their end. Setting up their break out, they fly around as they switched positions. I skated along side my forward I was to watch. He tried eluding me but I wasn't letting him go. They skated past center, and drilled a shot in. Waylon gave chase; Tim stopped it behind the net. Waylon banked it off the boards as he was checked. I stopped it and gave a quick look, to see who was open. I dangled around my forward, and took off up ice.

A quick pass to the other side, Darryl was breaking in. The Natives defence, poke checked it away. Setting up to their little advantage, it was a quick give and go through the neutral zone. Their winger streaked down the left side, going one on one with Waylon. He winds up, and Waylon braces for the shot. It was a fake, as he went by him. The winger then dangles Ryan as he cuts to the net. The house roars, as he's now alone but knocked off balance a little from Ryan as he tucked it by him. Tim comes out of his net; the Neepwa forward then falling tips it pass Tim as he was challenging him. Everyone is on his or her feet, "Is this the end." I thought. Their forward loses his footing. Almost a duplicate to Jay's chance, but this guy misses the puck. It's a mad scramble to the loose puck, and Waylon fires it off the boards.

I skate in too help, as the play is still in our end. I hammer a forward as we both skated for the loose puck. The crowd roars, and I get it out. Tired I skate off for a line change. The game had changed, from once was a finesse game, turned into a physical one. I sat on the bench gasping holding my side. My head down, I told myself. "Sit out one shift." Mr. Boyle patted my shoulder to go. I nodded "No." as he must of seen my face. I was in pain. He then shouted to Dwayne to take my spot. Was I out from now on, I only wanted to rest my side. It stung at every breath, I sat there grinding my teeth; it hurt so badly.

Shift after shift, my teammates changed. The crowd was like a giant fan whirling. It was so loud. Players making moves, setting up plays, and the goalies stood on their heads. I cheered on Tim as he robbed players after players. As time was nearing the end, with three minutes left to play. I had felt fine; I took in a few deep breaths and let it out. To see if it still hurt, so I stood waiting for the next line change. As the play was coming down to our end, a forward was changing. I leaped over the boards putting myself back with Darryl and Jay. Mr. Boyle called my name only once and it wasn't quit a yell, I guess he knew. So I skated into our end to help. Ryan seen me coming back, he passed it to me before I curled. I passed it behind me, between my legs to Darryl as he was going down hard. He passed it up to Jay who now carried it into the zone.

Jay passed it back to Darryl, who then passed it back to Jay. I skated in behind the play; Jason was in low in the corner, he put on the brakes and threw it back to Darryl. As Darryl was winding up to shoot the one timer, I hollered to him. Skating in high in the slot, he let it go through he is legs to me, faking out the goalie as I was trailing. The goalie had committed to Darryl. The crowd screaming, I was alone and I shot it for the open side. Their goalie stretched to get back, but he looked up in disgust; it slid through his five hole. I was now running on the ice, Darryl jumped on me against the boards as did Jay, and then the whole bench followed. The guys, as the piled onto each other, smothered me. I forgot I had scored the game winner; it only sunk in when they swarmed me.

There's nothing like that feeling when you score the most important goal. Especially in over time, I was on cloud nine. And to hear my name being called one last time, it sent shivers down my spine. I was ecstatic, what a play. Who would have thought it was to end this way. It was probably the best play of the game. A play, which would be remembered; by all who had witnessed it. We were now in the finals; we celebrated on the ice for a while. We congratulated Tim, for he was the star of the game. With out him we wouldn't be here. Our dressing room was now alive, different from the period before. Everyone was screaming, Mr. Boyle had bought us all sodas, and we were spaying them like it was Champagne.

20

Mr. Boyle ruffled my hair and patted my shoulder, and said he was glad to have me back. His smile comfort me, I couldn't help but smile along with tears in my eyes. When we were done packing our stuff, I remembered about Pops. I had forgotten he was here, and he had the rest of my stuff. I quickly got my gear together and raced up stairs to him. And he stood by the canteen stirring his coffee. I walked towards him and when he seen me, he just smiled.

"There's my star player," He boasted. "Do you want anything to eat before you leave?"

I only smile, and shook my head that I didn't want anything.

"Thanks Poppa."

"I haven't heard you say that, since you were little," He now rested his hand on my shoulder. "But it was nice to see you play again. That sure was heart felt game, had me on my toes." He smiled.

"Thanks. I just need the rest of my stuff." I had said.

"You sure you don't want me to drive…"

"I'm sure pops." I cut him off. "I only want to be with my friends. Besides, you've done a lot already. And you have to travel back; I don't want you to be tired."

And then he nodded his head and smiled. He was proud of me, happy to see me happy. For I loved the game again, I played with my heart and soul. I won it for mom I won it for uncle. And I won my heart back. I was happy to be back, for it was where I belonged. I was home, along with my friends, they were my family.

Getting on the bus I had the goose bumps, the boys were noisy from talking. Danny our driver gave me a handshake and welcomed me back. This brought a smile to my face. Waylon called out to me, he saved my seat along the window. We stopped at chicken delight for a bite, after that we headed for home. Waylon sat there filling his face; I laughed and told him to chew. He looked at me with grease all around his mouth, "Lick me." I laughed even more. I continued to watch ignoring my meal. He bounced as the bus drove on; he sucked on his finger moaning. I couldn't resist it. "I'll give you something to suck on." He elbowed me and we laughed. Yah I sure missed the guy, the village idiot as he said it. As much as I remember, the next few hours passed and we arrived back in Cranberry around midnight. As we pulled into the Collegiate, there was a crowd waiting for us. There was a banner that had my name and number on it. I felt funny at first, but was surprised. How did they know I was back?

They cheered as we drove by to the hanger. We were like celebrities; I was more shocked at how they knew. When we got off the bus, some of the guy's girl friends ran to hug them. Others were getting hugs from girl's they didn't know. Even Waylon received a hug and kiss. Students were welcoming me back; I even heard some one call out "The protocol son returns." I stood there lost in a dream like, somewhat emotional. As I watch some hug their girl friends, I wished Lana were there. I would have to wait till morning, while we unpacked our gear. Lana was in my thoughts; I couldn't wait to see her. How do I approach her? Waylon and I were leaving the hanger, and I then asked him how Lana was doing, if he talked to her.

He smiled at me, and pointed.

"Why don't you ask her yourself?"

And there she stood along side a tree, just out of the lamps light. My heart pounded, I was anxious as it felt like it. Waylon pushed me to go to her, I walked towards her, and she to me. We stopped about a foot away from each other, to sort of look into each other's eyes. Her hair was different. It was shorter and wavier, which brought out her eyes.

She was more beautiful than ever. Her eyes where watery now, as we stood there I put out my finger under her chin and grazed along her jaw line to her hair. She closed her eyes and tilted her head, her hand on mine as tears rolled down her cheek. I smiled at here. "Hey beautiful." I said. And she grasped me tightly, sobbing she now brought tears to my eyes; I hugged her too. And we held onto each other for what seemed like an eternity. I never wanted to let her go. I just held her close to me; I was over whelmed by her presence.

Then she looked up at me, without any thought I kissed her, and she kissed me back. It was one of those kinds you normally see in movies, but this one was passionate and it was real. I loved her, and she loved me. I thought I would never see her again; I was lost within myself for a while. She held on to my heart and it was just like what pops said. "If you let it go and if it comes back. It was meant to be." Only it would be her that let me go. And somehow I made my way back to her. I would walk her home, and as we walked I had asked how in the world some students knew I was back. She smiled at me and said our game was broadcasted on WPLN AM radio. And that's how come she was at the hanger. She said when she heard my name over the radio; she was shocked and then cried. It was a good game she had said, her and her mom almost fell on the floor when my chance to get a goal stopped dead. Even the announcer was right into the game; he was frantic on every play.

It was sort of, what's that word. Well it made me feel good inside. "Wow." was the word we were on the radio. I wished I could've heard it, soon we were at her house, and we would kiss again. Only that it was just a good night one, but really I wanted to stay with her, I just wanted her close to me, and so I again watched as she walked up her stairs, she looked back and blew a kiss. I stood there for a moment smiling as I was stuck beaming, finally I headed back and I would spend the evening at Mr. Boyles.

I barely slept; the next day I had only wanted to go see Lana. When I had awoken, it was nine-AM I quickly dressed and forgot about eating breakfast. Sleeping in, I raced to the school, ran like it was the hundred meter dash. She was everything and I wanted to see her beauty. She was my sunshine, the way a ray of light touches you. It has a warm glow and makes you smile. That…was Lana; it was how she made me feel. And when she smiled, she had cute little dimples that took my breath away. Her blue eyes and now wavy dirty blonde hair, it made my heart race and I was animate. I went to my locker first, but I had forgotten. I had none I packed all my stuff. Waylon was at his locker; I had asked if I could borrow some paper and pencils. He looked at me and said I was late, he told me that morning classes were cancelled, that we all had to go to the gym, for service.

I looked at him with confusion, "Assembly you mean?" I asked. He scratched his head. "No. Something else." He gestured with his hands. "You mean rally?" I said to him. He looked at me with a smirk, and slapped the side of his head. "Yah, that's it." I laughed and called him a goof. I followed him towards the gym; the guy's were standing outside. Everyone else had crammed into the gym; Jason tossed me my sweater, to put it on. Mr. Boyle then went inside, there was clapping as he made his way to the stage. Mr. Smith was talking, saying how proud he was that we traveled a long road. And that road was long over due; it had been two years since they had been in the finals. He gave a speech about how we started off, and how we developed into this year's contender for the Centennial Cup.

The school was charged up, they gave a deafening roar. I was feeling nervy, as did the guy's, hearing the students and teacher's sent chills up my spine. Then Mr. Smith did his intro for Mr. Boyle. In only his first year as Coach, he made prospects of us all. How he made the team where it should it be, that he was to make us champions again. "Without further delay, I present Mr. Boyle." And they applauded as he made his way to the podium. He thanked everyone for gathering for us. And he had said without them supporting, the team was nothing. We were to face the Melville Millionaires, starting next week Tuesday. He talked for five more minutes or so, and then he introduced the team. "Let's hear it for our Mohawks." As the boys walked into the gymnasium, they played "Animal" from Def Leppard. The students and teachers cheered applauding.

One by one they entered; Waylon stopped me as I made my way in. He motioned for me to wait, too be last. I felt funny when it was time for me to walk in, I was afraid. My heart pounded almost out of my chest, my hands were shaky and my legs now were wobbly. I barely opened the door I was so weak. Walking into the gym, I stood there frozen like. I then took a few steps, and then I had seen students and teachers rise, as they began to cheer louder. I stopped in my tracks feeling emotional it was loud.

My vision began to blur, my throat burned. I tried to smile, tears streamed down my face. I raised my arm into the air to wave for thanks they gave a thunderous roar. I slowly walked across the gymnasium I wasn't expecting this welcome. I'm not sure how long my ovation was but it had me in tears. As I seen some of my teammates wiping their eyes to hide their emotion.

Mr. Boyle was moved as well, and I thought he was made of iron. Who knows maybe I returning touched most, when it seemed inevitable I wouldn't be back. I thought I wouldn't be back, Waylon had come and gave me a hug, and he stood by my side. Then the whole team came and shook my hand, greeting me back and stood with us. This would send the gym into applauding frenzy. Then they started chanting "ROBBY, ROBBY!" It was a rally all right, a welcome back thing and a boost to keep us striving for the championship. It was our dream, our glory to win the Centennial Cup. To have that banner once more, and then we all raised our hands to victory. The gymnasium was electrified, and it was booming.

Then Mr. Smith announced that we were to have sock hop after the festivities. The students cheered, and the music man played on. It was pretty cool of him; he became the good guy in our books. School was put on hold because of us, and we enjoyed it as much as we could. Lana would join me along with Waylon and Darryl. We just stood around not dancing; it wasn't that the music wasn't good. It was what we normally did at dances. And I felt peace within me, after all that had happened. I knew I was home, I was with Lana and it was all I wanted.

The next day I would spend most of it in the guidance room. I had a lot of work, more than I can handle. I had to catch up and it may take a month. I stared at that pile and wondered if this guy was serious. I had asked if there was a better way of catching up, he suggested summer school. Summer was for break, away from school. I thought about it, and if it was the only way to pass. I said I would think about it, until then I took homework home. And it was a lot. It wasn't so bad though, not as much I thought it would be. Lana helped me in some subjects, like Native Studies and Geo. The other two were not mandatory, so I shrugged them off. But it was two more credits, easy ones at that Phys Ed and shops. I would have to put aside my activities with the guy's. But I would go to practice, meeting with Melville once again. This time for the cup, they were good but so were we.

McCormick would feel my wrath; this time the giant would have to fight for what he thought was his in the first place. He had it easy in my absence, but now I'm back. I was healthy as a horse, agile as a panther, and I had the strength of a bear. In between practice and homework, I would be at the gym working out; Building my power, my confidence. I needed to be ready for anything that might hurt. I worked on my shoulders and upper body. My legs I worked very little, I had enough work out on them skating. I would spend hours in the gym; Lana would have had to come see me there. I pushed myself to the limits; it's been five or six weeks that I have been gone. I just wanted to be prepared for Melville.

That whole week I spent in the gym, skated three times. So I worked on my legs more. Tuesday was days away; I would also go to the hanger to prepare my sticks. I had seen some aluminium shafts; this was the first time I held one in my hands. They were lighter than my sticks, so I figure I would try one. I went to see Mr. Boyle to ask if he can open the barn for a light skate. Try out my new stick and practice a little. He gave me a smile and agreed. He called one of the teacher's Mr. Sheldon to come, bring his equipment.

When we were on the ice, he gave me one to one drills. He coached me privately, giving me instructions. I was doing drills shooting on the goalie, going in and out of pylons. He was making me skate the lines, like in hockey school. We were doing the stuff I learned in hockey school, but they were hard. Mr. Boyle pushed me, and skated along side of me telling me not to give up. Going down towards the goalie we passed it back and forth. Then he would make me skate around pylons in the slot, shooting from every angle. He would pass it to me, and I was to one time the shot. "All this to try out a stick." I grumbled to myself. But I needed to skate as well, and I continued on. Sweat pouring; I was only in my skates, my equipment at the hanger. I skated until I literally fell over in exhaustion. I crawled to the bench; I stood and heaved over the boards. My stomach hurt, dry heaving I wished for water. Mr. Boyle chuckled along with Mr. Sheldon.

"That was a good skate…Bruaack! Cough…cough." I said with my eyes watery.

"I'll say," Mr. Boyle smiled. "Are you a little out of shape McKay?"

"What gives you that idea?" I looked at him wiping my eyes.

"Here have a shot." Mr. Sheldon handed me his water bottle.

21

After skating for an hour and a half, I went to the gym. I went to see Waylon, he and Darryl were playing floor hockey. I lay on the bleacher's watching, catching myself dozing off. The guy's were bugging me to play, but I had already had a work out. I then went to Mr. Boyle's, as I was tired; it was where I stayed for the remainder of the school year. When I had got there, I went straight to bed. When I had woken the next morning, I remembered I was to phone Bill after the game. It has been a week already, I forgot about him so I figured I better give him a call since I had promised. It was at the school where I had called him, before going to shops using the last of my change. It was eight-thirty in the morning. He answered all croaky, sort of losing his voice.

"Hey loser."

"Hey…what you doing up so early?" His voice was all crackly.

"We won the game the other day. I scored the game winner in over time."

"Cool, but you were supposed to call me then. Loser…You're a loser." He catches on.

"Yah!" I laugh. "We're in the finals! Man it was something when I came back."

I explained everything to him, how it was emotional for me. I never thought in a million years they would greet me like they had. I was glad to have gone back, I made the right choice. He was happy for me, and wished me luck in the finals. And to call him to let him know what was going on; so he could tell the guy's. I agreed and said if I didn't forget because of all the distractions of the excitement from the games. Then I said "Till next time." And then I hung up the phone. I then felt sort of lost; maybe it was just that of calling an old friend. Thinking of what I did, to come back. And the same time memories started to flood back, mom was in my thoughts, as I was now feeling lonely. It didn't matter if I stayed home; I would have felt this way as well. Wiping away my tears, with nowhere to hide. I slipped into the boy's room.

Resting my hands on the sink, my head down, I had fought with my emotions. That lump hurt the back of my throat. Sniffing I washed my face and stared at myself. Just then a student walked in, I made it look like I was washing my hands and face. I went to the paper towels; he congratulated us on our victory. Leaving the rest room I debated on whether I should go to my class, trying to shake my feelings. I then went to find Lana she was in Biology. I stood at the door trying to get her attention; waving one of her friends noticed me. I pointed out to her and she chucked a pen at her.

I laughed to myself, as she hit her on the head. Her friend put her hand on her mouth, smiling she pointed to the door. I just needed a little distraction from myself, and it was working. She came to the door, and asked what I wanted. She stood in the hall with me; I told her I was thinking of her. She smiled and said she had to get back, and then Mrs. Higgins came to the doorway. She told me to go to class, that Lana was very busy and then shut the door. It was Friday April 5th and so I went to class, although I didn't want too. The day seemed to drag, but my mind was on hockey. I drew some pictures to pass up the time, more like doodling. When lunch came I went to see Waylon and Darryl. Waylon was putting his books in his locker when I approached him.

"What's happening for tonight?" I asked.

"Same old thing, you know! Drink down at the docks." Waylon said.

"Jeez, can't you guy's find something else to do? Besides drinking!" I smirked.

"Hey," Waylon looked at me closing his locker. "It's me!"

"You guy's man…You're something else." I chuckled.

I acted like it wasn't what I wanted to do, but I missed those parties with them. I never really drank like them; I couldn't drink hard stuff straight up. I preferred coolers, beer tasted awful. Well the beer they bought anyway, who drinks OV? Not me, it was Bud for me. Besides it was there so I helped myself. I had a point to my drinks; I didn't want what had happened to me with Lori. No memory of things, so I just played it cool.

Just then Lana showed up, she came and hugged me. And asked what we were up too. Her arm around me, she told me her parents were going to Winnipeg for the weekend. I instantly thought we were alone, and my mind raced with stuff. Then she looked at the guys, and said Crystal was to have a little party. She'll invite some of her girl friends, but Waylon and Darryl would have to buy all the booze. Waylon popped me one in the arm, all geared up and excited.

"I guess you found something else." I looked at Waylon with a smile.

"Nah! Somewhere else." He grinned.

"Awesome, it would be just like out of a James Bond movie!" Darryl added.

"Huh," We looked at him.

"What do you mean?" Waylon asked.

"Pussy Galore…" Darryl gave a devilish grin.

We laughed; even Lana found that funny where he came up with the stuff I don't know. But being with them took loads off my mind. Although at times I was still had felt sad and lonely, but it was them that kept me smiling. When school was out, Waylon had come looking for me in the shops. He wanted to get going into the Pas, to get the booze. I really didn't feel like going, I told him I was going to hang back and wait. He then left with Jay and Crystal along with Darryl. I sort of ditched my little crew; I only wanted to be alone with Lana for a while.

As I was cleaning up my department in metal class, making sure I had put everything back. Lisa stopped by to see me. I was stunned, "What on earth would she want now?" I wondered. She waited in the hall as I finished up. I was more curious than anything, so I went to her. She had stood there for a moment giving me a glance here and there. She mostly had her eyes fixed on the floor. I looked at her waiting to hear what she might have to say. Then she looked at me with tears in her eyes, and fought with her words. She then said she was sorry for what I went through, and the things she had done to hurt me. I only listened; I had no intentions to hold her. If that was what she was expecting, leaning against the wall, with my hands in my pockets. I nodded to accept her sympathy towards me. She was going to give me a hug, but I put my hand out. I give her a small smile, and then I held her hand for a moment. Lost I just stared into her eyes; I wipe away a tear with my thumb. "It's okay." I tell her, I then let go of her and then smile.

The feeling I had at that moment was remorse; my feelings for her were maybe still there. I had felt her sadness, as I was still vulnerable. She slowly slipped her arms around me to sort of comfort me or comfort herself. But I fell for it, I found myself weeping in her arms. My grief was pouring into the wrong hands. I lifted my head from her shoulder, and I wiped my eye. I looked at her, and then I told her that I was with Lana and I wanted to remain true to her. That maybe we could be friends, because we shared a moment of despair. In my moment of loneliness and in that little time I relieved it with her. I gave her one last hug and departed. I thanked her and then left to find Lana. Again luck wasn't on my side; I couldn't get the breaks when I needed it the most. She wasn't at her locker, I strolled over her place but she wasn't home. Then I thought she went to town.

It was where she probably was. Hanging out with Crystal and the guy's to get to know them I suppose. After all, she was going to get her girl's to come over. I began to worry about Darryl, what on earth could he be saying. "Chic's" was his only vocabulary of a girl. I then headed to the cafeteria, to the lounge. Maybe play some table soccer to pass up the time as I waited for the group to get back. I was a worried wart, sick about those two; Waylon was down to earth at times, but Darryl…He was oblivious. He might ruin the chance to party, kill the mood. "Wait a minute," I thought. It was what I wanted in the first place, he kill the mood so I could be alone with Lana. So I didn't worry as much, but in a way Waylon could get laid. I had never seen him with a girl period. Maybe now it might loosen the fellow up a little, be on solid ground. Talk to me normal without being cheeky. Then again I might be wrong about the silly bastard; it could set off a total idiot. Who was I fooling, for all I know he might of gotten a girl while I was gone?

I was getting bored as I waited, and I started to feel like depression was setting in. My head was filling with my past and present, combining together. I felt like crying all of sudden, I was confused and starting thinking maybe I made a rash decision on returning. I felt sort of lost and I made my way back to Mr. Boyle's. I didn't feel like going out, I needed time to reflect. I stood for a moment in my room, realizing I stand-alone from now on.

I could only try to imagine what uncle would say to me, as I was feeling down. I lost part of me, my family. Sitting on the bed I felt tears roll down my cheek as I remembered mom. My dreams, I wanted to share my glory with her. Try to make something of myself, just so that she wouldn't have to work so hard. Feeling like I have fallen out of reach, I cried to myself, holding most of it in. I then had seen uncle's Dream Catcher lying on the dresser. I then stood from my bed, held it in my hand as I looked down on it. Then I remembered parts of his words from when I last spoke to him. Moving away from home has its ups and downs; he'll always be with me spiritually. I clasped it against my heart and cried, knowing they both are with me. I carry them in my heart.

I lay on my bed thinking of them, remembering. It was just like I time warped back in time, watching uncle play. The big game against Selkirk Steel men, it was the final game. The Tomahawks were down two goals going into the third period; we stood and cheered them on. There was mom, aunt Jean Lil Terry and I, clapping to try to motivate them. Uncle was a winger on the left. He never wore shoulder pads since that game with the Dune Buggies. But it looked like he had some on, his broad shoulders.

He was six foot, and bulky from his muscles. Probably didn't need shoulder pads any way, always powered his way to the net. I really wanted to be like him, he showed me some moves and some hits that would hurt. "Need to toughen you up." He always said after running over me, no mercy for his nephew I tell you that. I guess that's how I learned to be quick, thinking and always have your back against the boards.

The puck drops and they play hard, senior hockey was far more physical than you can imagine. Oh man there was this one guy, who was streaking in on the left. He danced around "Stingy," Kevin Bear's nickname. And right into the path of uncle's, he hit him so hard the boards wobbled. Auntie and mom screamed, hoping the other guy was okay. The play stopped, and uncle after he creamed the guy, had helped him up. They would nod at each other, and begin to play again, True sportsmanship. Later on in the game uncle would get set up in the slot. Jim Meeches passed it to him; he leaned into a slap shot and ripped one past their goaltender. Soon after as the game was winding down, uncle would go on a break away. He skated in hard and he winds up drilling a powerful shot that would push the goalie back knocking him over, giving up a rebound. He just skates in and flicks it in as the goalie was left scrambling to his feet. Tying the game up, with only minutes away from the end.

Uncle was coming out of his end; he gunned it down towards their end. Fending off checkers he came one on one with their defender. Uncle had made him look stupid, he dips and doodled him. Then he cuts to the net, seeing another defender he did a spinarama on him, then dishes the puck off to "Ducky" who deflected it past the goalie. The crowd cheered when the Tomahawks scored. "Ducky," Vince Delorme's nickname too, had scored the game winner. It was then when they took a photo of them winning the championship. Uncle had included Lil Terry and I in the photo beside him. Remembering that photo now, the one auntie gave me. It gave me warmth and soothing to my heart.

22

As I lay there, I now had a smile on my face. Feeling better I went to wash up, I slipped on a collar shirt and threw a sweater on over it. Fixed my hair a little, left it like a messy look and went over to Lana's. As I got there Jay and them would pull up saying they were looking for me driving around town. I jumped in and we drove over to Crystal's place. I looked over to Waylon who looked a little disappointed. I asked what was wrong.

"He's just mad we couldn't get the booze." Darryl had said.

"Ah, don't be bitter," Jay, added. "We have some liquor here."

We had went in to Crystal's and sat around for a while. Soon people began to arrive, Lana made a drink for me. We mingled around the place, and she tended to her friends. After a while the party was happening. I sipped as I chatted with others and even played that floor game twister. We had a ball, especially the guy's. They drooled as the girls would bend and arch around.

Then I noticed Melanie making conversation with Waylon. I watched as the big goof ball tried to talk; maybe he had a little too much to start with. He barely stood there, as he teetered back and forth. I laughed watching him, waiting for him to fall over again. Feeling I should intervene.

So I walked up to them, and asked if he was feeling okay. Melanie looked at me with a smile and assured me things were fine, that I get back to Lana. I glanced over to the guy and I was certain he was ready for bed. Then it hit me; I guess that was her plan.

I laughed to myself, never saw that coming the day Waylon get laid. But what girl in her right mind would even consider, Melanie? With Waylon even now I think I'm jealous. Yeah right. Moving around the place, I was starting to feel out of place. I just didn't feel like drinking, so I put down what I had left. I looked for Lana, to sort of split the scene. When I found her I smoothly put my arms around her from behind. "Hey you," I whispered in her ear. She turned to face me, putting her arms around my neck. Our foreheads touching, I gazed into her blue eyes.

"What do you say we split?"

"Why? What's wrong?" She asked now adjusting my collar.

"Nothing." I smiled. "I just thought maybe we could have some alone time."

"It's possible." She had said as she was finished adjusting me.

"Maybe we can see that movie I promised you."

"Now how can I resist that offer." She smiled.

"And you can make me those brownies," I twirled her hair. "I've been only dreaming of them every night." I smirked.

"You certainly have a way with words Robby," She looked me straight in the eye smiling. "Okay, lets go."

I chuckled, lost for words. As we left she asked me why I had wanted to leave, feeling something was wrong. I explained to her how I felt earlier, but I really did want to be alone with her. And I didn't feel like drinking at the moment. I guess I was just getting bored of the same old thing. We had walked over to her place, and I had told her I was thinking crazy that my mind was playing games on me. I wasn't sure if I came back to soon, and I was lonesome.

My eyes filled with tears, as I was feeling lost. I told her about my mother, what she had meant to me. She wasn't exactly like her mother, close and all. But in some ways it was, as she tried to be open. But I loved her; she was at some games in the city. I knew she was busy, but it was all for me, just so I can play hockey. She shared what little dreams I had, and now it…it doesn't seem right. I sat on the stairs of her porch; wiping my eyes I sniffed holding back my feelings. I was afraid to fall apart like I did at mom's funeral. How would Lana react if I did? As I sat there whimpering, she sat next to me and rested her head on my shoulder, rubbing my back up and down. She assured me, things were fine that it was normal for me to feel this way. I smiled at her and thanked her, and then she held on to my hand. Lana soothed me; she was everything to me, my foundation. She held me in place and I loved her. Lost time that I missed with her, I made it up to her as we spent the whole weekend alone, away from friends.

Game day, April 9th

That morning I went for a jog around the track, leaving Mr. Boyle's around seven. I ran with thoughts on how I am going to make an impact. I only wanted to win; the cup is only games away. "I hope we can win." I thought as I ran around the track. We had home ice advantage, but our games will have to be played in the Pas, since our arena was too small for their crowd and ours. Then we ship off to Melville Saskatchewan for games 2 and 3, Mr. Boyle had a meeting with the Commissioner. And the rest of the board members on the situation we faced last time we played there. He just didn't want us to go through the ordeal again, some rude fans may have spoiled it for every one else. He argued to change the location of their games to somewhere else other than Melville.

But it wouldn't work out to his disappointment; Melville was hockey capital in Saskatchewan. And it won't seem right for them to play in another arena. Ah it didn't matter to me, it was only words as Waylon had said. And it would put a hole in their wall if we were to win in Melville. "Oh it would make them crumble and I, would love to see that. It would be my place to make a stand, and show their world I am a gladiator and I am going to slay their giant." I thought this as I finished my run. I stopped and slouched over, with my hands resting on my knees. And then I stood up and took a deep breath; this series is going to be one to remember.

We fight the top team in the league. Melville had won three years in a row, can they make it four. I doubt that, we had a good team as well and we were hungry for that trophy the Centennial cup. With this thought I only remember uncle's words. One phrase that had kept me going, if it never burned in my thoughts; I sometimes think I probably would have quit. "Follow your dreams." Feeling a smile on my face, I ran around the track once more. As I was finishing the end of my run, I noticed Waylon coming towards the track. Thinking maybe he was going to run with me. I stopped at where he stood, and asked if he was going to run along side of me.

"Nah, I'm still too sick to run. And the headache…Ooh my head hurts."

"So," I smiled at him. "Did you luck out or did you get laid?" I chuckled.

"Oh man…I have no memory. Lucky I guess."

"Oh yah, what's his name?" I asked laughing.

"Nice, if I wasn't so sick I'd kick your ass." He grunted.

"Don't feel so bad. If its any consolation, that happen to me before I came to Cranberry."

"Yah, another story there Rob?" he asked mockingly.

"Hey, lighten up you big goof. So where's Melanie? Did you see at all this weekend after Friday night?" I smile at him.

"Not really, I just kept drinking when I awoke naked beside her."

"Man, what I give to see that. Her sweet ass I mean Mm, raunchy." I smirked.

"Rob, you need help." Waylon chuckled. "Probably enjoyed it too, to see my crotch again," he laughed.

"What! Get lost…Melanie has more bulge than you." I laugh, my tongue hanging out now.

"Rob I swear, you've become one of us." He snorted.

"Hey let's go to the hanger for a bit, you can tell me all about it. Besides I want to get my sticks ready for the big game."

"Yeah okay! And what's with you and this getting sticks ready?" he asked.

"Just a little ritual of mine, mental preparation."

"Mental is right, you do need help." He grinned.

"Yeah, yah! At least I can get some." I smirked.

"Ooh smooth, real smooth Rob."

"Like your privates?" I chuckled.

"Man, what's with the comments? Is this pick on Waylon day or what?"

"I'm sorry dude, I was just messing with you." I said.

"City slickers," He muttered. "Ah forget it, come on I'll race you to the hanger."

"Well you better tie your laces first." I said to him.

He looked at down at his shoes and I took off running laughing. And then he chased after me. I barely ran as I was laughing the same time, we ran across the field to the hanger. Well he bolted and I ran, he caught up to me and pushed me over, losing my balance I fell to the ground still laughing. I sat up wet from the ground, he laughed and helped me up. Telling me I never stood a chance anyway, reminding me that he was the 100-meter champ. And then he groaned about his headache, I just smiled and said. "Drink again." And then he punched me in the arm. When we were inside, I rubbed my arm, as it was still sore. I grabbed my new aluminium stick and re taped it. Waylon had only went through his gear, to make sure it was all there and packed them in his bag. I followed his actions and did the same.

We were talking about the party; well he was telling me that I didn't miss a thing. Nothing exciting happened this time, just a bunch of drunks out to get drunker. I asked if he remembered Melanie flirting with him, he looked at me and chuckled."Yeah," He smiled. "We're a couple you know, for about a month now. She's a real party animal, I'd say I'm dating myself." I laugh at him. Just then Mr. Boyle walked in, he looked at us and saluted. "Boy's." was all he said as he entered his office area. Mr. Boyle was about in between the height of Waylon and me, he wasn't very tall, but an athletic type. Slim and always wore gym outfits around campus, well he was also the gym instructor. I think the only time we see him in suits is at our games. We all had to dress to code, no jeans or t-shirts. It made us look important when we dress like this, but before we get there.

Mr. Boyle came back into the room; he smiled and asked if we were ready for the game against Melville. Waylon and I nodded, "Yes sir." Then he gave me a meek look. And asked why I was soaked. I look at Waylon with a smirk, and point with my thumb.

"He pushed me." I laugh, like I was tattling.

"It's going to be great," Mr. Boyle said jotting his hands. "Scouts will watching you boy's. Just keep one thing in mind; they will try to disrupt you anyway possible. Say things to knock you off your game, anything to win. Remember this, and only this. The important thing is to have fun, that's what hockey is all about."

"Scout's?" I look at Waylon. He looked more excited than I was and anxious.

"Just think Robby, we could be in the WHL next year." He now had a big smile as he looked up thinking it.

"Yah!" I watch as he is daydreaming. "That would be cool eh!"

"This is our time Rob. I dreamed it," He now looks at me. "Its ours you have to vision it."

And his eyes tell me so, that look that stare. It shuttled me to a place I forgot existed, a realm where my dreams, are waiting for me to extract them. Our dreams are way to point us into the direction we were meant to be. But sometimes other dreams get in the way from our right ones; Bad dreams try to take over. Which is why our people made Dream Catcher's, so all the bad dreams get caught in this sort of web like ring and let all our good dreams through so we can see and live what they show us.

23

My dreams were to be in the NHL, and if I was to be scouted for a team in WHL. This would be the next step to stardom. I too was daydreaming thinking of playing side by side with the great one. Imagining myself getting that hug from him when I score that goal he set me up on. We both stand there in our trance, and then Darryl walks in interrupting our visions. "What you girl's doing?" He asks jokingly. "First class is about to start. Thought you chic's might be in here."

"Whoa…is that time already?" Waylon asks.

"Chic's!" I nodded my head. "Haven't changed a bit." I smile.

"Blah, blah, blah. Quit judging me and lets get to class."

"You better run home there Rob, get changed up unless you want to look ragged." Waylon smiled.

"Yah! I guess I should. Wouldn't have to if you didn't push me down, you big jerk."

"Hey, easy on the language." Darryl chuckled.

I laughed with them as we finish up with our gear and headed out to class. I wave at Mr. Boyle as we pass his office. And chat amongst ourselves, laughing and teasing as we walk towards Mr. Boyle's so I can change. It would be just another normal day before game time, but I was anxious to suit up for battle. The day seemed to drag as I kept looking at the clock, thinking what kind of game will we face.

What will the out come be, and will McCormick be present. He has to be, I'm sure he just wants to punish us, destroy what thoughts we might have had. The more I thought of the giant, I became sort of intimidated. My mind was on the game as the day went by, not paying any attention to what instructions we were given on our subjects. I was beginning to get nervous, and jittery. Feeling my heart flutter I just wanted to play and dazzle the crowd once more. Finally, when school was out, I went home to get ready. Putting aside my friends for a moment, I sat on my bed thinking. Waiting for departure, I then caught sight of my Dream Catcher. I stood there lost in it, trans fixed on my vision. Memories were flooding back, what uncle had said. I stare into my deep thoughts, reflecting what this means to me. Then I kneel before my bed, and say the Lord's Prayer.

I ask for guidance and peace within my heart. To help me through my troubled time, and I thank God for giving me the strength to come back to finish school, and to play hockey once again. I ask for, forgiveness on my thoughts that I had when I blamed him for taking mom and uncle.

"Forgive me Lord, reconstruct my broken heart, mend it so I can play with all my heart. I play for honour, my pride, and I give you my glory lord. Keep me strong as I go into battle. For I know I would face words that hurt, keep me strong I praise and I thank you, amen."

Now feeling a warm glow within me I smile as I wipe away my tears. I washed up and headed to the hanger and then the cafeteria to have supper with the boy's. After supper we had went to the hanger, to load our gear. Before boarding the bus, I noticed Lana coming down the lane. I couldn't help but smile and so I quickly ran to her. She had small bag and then she planted me with a kiss and wished me good luck. She had made me brownies; I smile and touch the tip of her nose, "Later." Was all I can say before Mr. Boyle whistled for me to get on the bus. I turned and she slapped me in the ass pinching it; I look at her as I jogged to the bus and then she blew a kiss.

"McKay…I thought I told you. Lay off the girls." Mr. Boyle grinned.

Smiling I only gave a shrug, and before I can sit down Waylon swiped my brownies from me. Teasing me about that little spectacle, Darryl then leans over the seat and grabs a brownie adding into the conversation.

They continued with the teasing as they both devoured my snack. I look at them as Waylon handed me back an empty bag.

"Thanks for saving me some guy's"

"No problem," Darryl says sucking his fingers. "Mm best brownies I ever had."

"I agree." Waylon adds.

"You guys…" Was all I can think of saying.

I was left to only imagine what they tasted like. I just sit there staring at them in complete awe. Sort of upset but more amused. Waylon looks at me with a grin, and said he had some crumbs on his shirt if I wanted too and then he laughed. It wasn't long before we got to the city limits. The bus started to slow down; you can feel it as the driver shifted the gears down. We looked at each other, waiting for the bus to stop. And then we joked about Tim's bag, before darting off the bus. I sure didn't want to haul that big bag. He can haul it himself.

"Boy…and I thought you were kidding about the run." I said to Waylon as we waited.

"Still glad you came back?" He had said.

"Are you kidding? And miss all this excitement." I said as I threw a bag over my shoulders.

It wanted to rain, but that didn't bother me. The mist would cool me off as I ran the 2km. I ran adjusting the bag the same time. And then Waylon came up side of me, pushing me and telling me I was starting to slacken. It made me pick up the pace, as it now seemed like a race between he and I. "Let's go ladies." Mr. Boyle calls out on his blow horn. The bus drove with his flashers on, we were behind it. Cars honked at us passing by. When we finally reached the end of our run, we tossed the bags into the back and jumped on the bus to change. My clothes were damp and were sort of sticking to me as I pulled them off. I was thinking that what person would make us run before we get into town, especially when we have a game. Mr. Boyle must have been mad with us yet, but he never showed it. He just stood there smiling at his clipboard making the lines with Mr. Patterson.

"Look on the bright side," Waylon slaps me on the back. "We've could have been wearing our dress clothes running."

"I guess...probably look funny too," I chuckle. "Hard to run in dress shoes you know."

"You tried?" He laughs.

"No!" I act in response.

As we approached the arena, I had butterflies in my stomach. I was feeling scared for some reason. My nerves were acting up, as I was getting tense. I tried to shake them, but McCormick was rattling them without me knowing right away. I stared at the entrance as the bags were being unloaded. My thoughts were on the game, and I told myself. "Just another version of David and Goliath." Then Waylon tossed my bag at me, knocking me off balance and out of wind. I gave him a stare, and he just laughed.

"Wake up city slicker," he said

I can only smile, his way of distracting me away from my thoughts. Heading towards the rink entrance, I thought of Pops and my friends back home. I wished they were here to watch. As I thought of the things they did, the way they wanted me to continue my journey. Those second thoughts of my choice of coming back, they were erased. I would honour them by playing my best. I would imagine them in the crowd, rooting us on. Melville was already here, and again I found myself staring at their bus, thinking of the game. Trying to get myself pumped up again Waylon starts yapping to me to not think too much. He and Darryl keep me occupied.

Game 1. 1994 playoffs.

One hour before game time, some of us get our skates sharpened. Slowly getting ready, I would notice my Dream Catcher. I wondered how it got there, sitting comfortably between my gear unmarked. I pulled it out from my bag, thinking I must of have put it there. I then hang it in my stall, for all to see. Waylon stared my way for a bit as did others, watching as I tied it up.

"What' that?" Mr. Boyle asked.

I only get to open my mouth.

"It's a Dream Catcher." Waylon explains for me.

"You lost me." Mr. Boyle is uncertain.

"It lets the person who dreams of something, to catch what they dream of. Sometimes we have bad dreams, nightmares. And we have good dreams as well, but there are times when the bad tries to over run the good. To keep us from our dreams of what we are to become. Sometimes messages from loved ones, but it's hard to see them. So dream catchers are a way of getting that message. It's a symbol of our heritage."

"Really." Mr. Boyle is impressed.

I was motivated by his words. But in a way, he hit the mark with his explanation of my dream catcher. There are different meanings, but his was more interesting, and it revealed my uncle's words "Follow your dreams." Not out loud though. It just pushed it out there where I can see. Waylon came and stood in front of me. Waiting for me to finish and he asked about my dream catcher. I looked up at him, and said my uncle made it for me. Smiling I said I liked his description of it, and it fit the bill.

When I was ready he hit me in the shins with his stick. And I do the same to his, and follow him out. You can hear the music playing. My blood was over flowing, my heart pounding so hard it feels like it would rip right out of my chest. The guy's all followed behind; one by one we jump onto the ice. Racing around the rink, preparing for battle. The music man was blaring the tune, "Jump," from Van Halen. It was our supplement, a boost and it sent a surge up my spine as it played. And then Waylon instructed us to do the horseshoe on Tim, to get him warmed up.

Melville would make their way to the ice surface, popping out from the other side of the rink. One by one they walk onto the ice, slowly skating around. Every once in awhile they would glare at us as they circle past center. I watched as they skated by, then Jamie Houda hollered my number, and said for me to keep my head up. I smile and point at him and pretend to slice my throat, indicating he's a dead man. Skating by center we would meet and exchange words, filthy ones and he just said some racist remarks to me. Stopping along the boards he would skate by once more and again say things to me, only this time he would include my mother.

"Hey Houda, Why don't you come say it to my face. You chicken shit!" He riled me.

He stops and coasts my way yapping and smiling. My blood was boiling; I can feel it in my face. He gets so far before one of his teammates skates in front of him. Blake pushes Jamie towards their bench; I continue to call him on. Wade skates to us, and tells Jamie to shut it. He listens to him, and then Wade looks down on me.

"You have quit the mouth for a little guy." He stares at me with his steel grey eyes.

"You got a problem?" Waylon intervenes, Standing toe too toe with McCormick.

"Fuck off chief. I'm talking to the dwarf." Wade pushes him with both hands on his stick.

Waylon pushes him back, and they both exchange words shoving each other before it sends them into a fight. Their team and ours are pushing as some try to stop them. Then a brawl breaks out, they are throwing fists and wrestling each other. I try to stop Waylon, then Houda blind sides me and I go hairy. I rip off his cage and he did mine. I begin to throw my fists connecting a few times. The crowd is in an uproar, they scream in fear as the horn buzzing trying to stop us. Officials now come onto the ice along with our coach's stopping the brawl. Some of us are bloody, and they too. I wipe away my bloody mouth with the sleeve of my sweater.

My blood tastes of iron and is bitter. But now I thirst for blood, their blood, that Millionaires blood. I am now transformed into a predator seeking my prey, and that prey is Houda. In the dressing room, Mr. Boyle is enraged at us. He screams at the top of his lungs, not sure of who or what started it. But he is more irritated at the other team. He shouts at us that we are not baby's. He asked Waylon what happened since he was in the middle of the brawl. Others try to speak on our behalf, but he points at them to shut it and gives a stare. And then he proceeds to ask Waylon. He is quiet for a moment, and then he stutters his words.

"What was that? Can you speak more clearly Mr. Clarke?" Mr. Boyle barks.

"I was sticking up for Robby." He finally gets it out.

"What! Robert…You have to tell me what's going on, this has to stop." He scratches his head.

"It's bad blood, from what happened the last time we met." I said.

"Houda said shit about his mom, and I draw the line at that." Waylon blurted.

Then the guy's all interrupted, standing up for me. Leaving Mr. Boyle speechless for a second before he smiles. He is then called outside the dressing room by the ref's. He and Mr. Patterson leave for a few moments, and then come back into the room. Mr. Boyle then speaks, lecturing us.

24

"Okay boy's, the ref's are going to call everything and anything that looks disruptive from both teams. Its hockey out there boy's," He points towards the door. "Not cage fights. I am going to tell you this once and only once. This is hockey. We play with grit and honour, and what ever you face on the ice. What ever happens here tonight on that surface, it stays on that surface. I don't want any of this bullshit coming back to school. You got that…We are here to win a championship. We are here as a team as you showed me by sticking up for your fellow teammate, we've come a long way to get here. Melville players will do anything to get you riled up, get you kicked out perhaps. But this is play-offs, you get kicked out its just for one game. This doesn't mean I want you to go out there and fight, the only fighting you will have is for that puck. Show them grit; show them power. This is best of the best boys, and scouts will be watching. Its up too you if you want to go the distance, now…Lets get out there and play some hockey. No guts…No glory." And he puts his hand out.

We all put in our hands, and on three. "MOHAWKS." And then we head out of the dressing room. Jason is at the door bumping gloves, as we stroll down the hall you can hear the crowd and the music playing. Those tingles that run through your body pumping you up, the crowd gives you energy, the power to perform. We are now the stars of the game, all of us. The crowd fancies a show and we are going to give them one, a series to be talked about 10-maybe 20 years from now. The ref's are at the box, waiting for both teams. We are the first ones out, and are instructed to go to our bench. Mr. Boyle has his first line waiting on the ice; Tim takes a shot from the water bottle and then sprays his head before putting on his mask. My heart is racing and I am charged up. Standing in the bench, I feel the hatred within me. I am ready to pounce on Houda, Jamie took it to far when he called mom a whore. I can feel my blood boiling as the Millionaires made their way to the ice surface. They go to their bench; McCormick is half way to the bench. And he demonstrates his moves with an imaginary puck, and then points our way giving a fist pump. I nod with exception, "Yah, I have moves of my own." I think.

Its only game one, I can imagine what kind of series it would be. We are hungry for the cup; it's our chance, to become legends. The Pas arena now became a battle zone; we are at war with Melville. We suited up our Armour once more for combat. We fight for Cranberry, as it were our Queen. We are on a quest for the Holy Grail, and that is the Centennial Cup. We stand for the Queen, as the anthem plays, waiting to slip on our helmets. Waiting for battle. I drop my head for a little prayer, and then I kiss my hand and look up to the heavens. I imagine mom and uncle, as if they were here watching me. I hear nothing but my own heart beating, it begins to slow down from a rapid one. As I now become more relaxed after thinking of mom. I see their smiles and it eases me, without warning a slap on the back brings me out of my dream state.

The music is loud, playing before the puck drops. The place is packed, as some were standing behind the nets. The two centers square off; the ref shows the puck to both goalies. He stands in between them and then drops the puck. A quick draw and Melville wins it. They cycle the puck back into their own zone, and set up a break out. Mr. Boyle screams for our player's too pick up a man.

McCormick goes in behind and picks up the puck, he flies up toward our end. He throws a nice pass through center to Stevenson who bolts to the net; he goes wide as Brian tries to hit him. He blows by him and drills the first shot on net. Tim saves it giving a rebound; there is a scramble in front. Houda picks up the loose puck and dishes it back to his defence. They set up passing it back and forth, like they are on a power play. With one quick pass low to Blake Stevenson, with a one-touch pass to the slot. McCormick leans into it and hammers one. It hits Waylon as he dips in pain, and tries to stay in the play. Almost falling he tries to come to the bench, but collapses. They play is stopped as Mr. Patterson dashes to his aid.

Our players on the ice surround them; Melville's trainer is there as well. We watch in despair hoping he is all right. The crowd is silent, so quiet you can hear a pin drop. McCormick has the nerve to come over, he's bent down as if he is trying to help. Then I see movement from Waylon, he sits up nodding his head as they ask him questions. The crowd cheers, and their bench bang their sticks on he boards. And he is helped back to the bench; McCormick skates along side of them. He has Waylon's stick and hands it to Mr. Boyle. Waylon sits on the bench winded, as Mr. Patterson checks him through. The game continues and then Mr. Boyle is talking to him, I can't hear from the crowd and players yelling. But I see Waylon gesturing yes. And Mr. Boyle then pats his shoulder. As I look his way and when he saw me, he gave thumbs up. I then knew he was okay and I turned my attention to the game.

The Millionaires have control of the puck; they dump it in and then exchange lines. Our forwards race to try to take the advantage, and streak out of our zone. Darryl burns up ice with Dwayne trailing. Ryan skates into the play, he now acts as forward as Jason dropped back in his position. Dwayne and Darryl fight for the puck in the corner, and when Dwayne plucked it free. He throws it to the front where Ryan deflects it on net. The crowd woos, as Rapaport makes the save. We still have the puck, as our guys pass it around. Ryan hesitates as he coasts in; he winds up faking, passing it to an open winger. Darryl fires a one timer and hits the back of the net. The crowd roars, and the music is pumping. Our bench jumps as he scores, Mr. Boyle sends out a new line, and they high five the line that scored.

I sit and wait for my cue, I bump gloves with Darryl as we shuffle waiting for the next change. His name is being announced and the crowd cheers, I smile as the excitement from the crowd over whelmed me. I couldn't wait to get out there; I had a rush from that goal.

"Back door Swan." I smile at Darryl.

"That's priceless." He smiles back.

Both teams are waging war on every hit, and every shot. It is a true battle between giants, Lords of hockey. We are boys during school, but when we touch the ice, we become Kings. It is our time to dethrone the giants. It is our time to become legends, we've come this far, we can't lose grip of our dream. My dream is to hold the Cup and celebrate as if uncle were beside me.

Melville changes their lines, as the play now heads down in our zone. They keep the puck away from us. And they give hammering hits with brute force. It sends the crowd into a deafening roar. Our players never give up; we keep playing rolling with the punches. The game is half way through the first. I sit and wonder when I am going to play. I sometimes look at Mr. Boyle, hoping he give me the okay. But he doesn't look my way; he stands on the bench hollering out plays.

My heart begins to beat faster as I was getting anxious. The third line heads out for the change. Melville is trying to run us over, but the guys keep getting back up. Finally Mr. Boyle sends me out with the next line change. I stand with Charlie and Ronald. The defence keeps getting juggled. Mr. Patterson wants to keep up with Melville's top line. Then the whistle blows to stop the play as Tim covers it. Stepping on the ice, I felt those butterflies. I coast to Charlie's left wing, and square off.

"Make sure to back check McKay!" Blaine blurts out.

Before I can answer or even look at him, the puck drops. Charlie wins it; Blaine takes hold it and pivots back two strides. He passes it across to Ryan who carries it through center before shooting it in. We hustle after it; I chase it into the corner. And deliver a hit, the defence absorbs my hit and whacks it off the boards behind the net. Melville digs it out and head up ice. Their smooth as the carry it in, nice crisp passes. Almost like their gliding as they storm the net. A quick set up and a blistering shot on Tim. I am mesmerized by their skill; they became more puck handlers now than enforcers. Tim deflects it to the corner, as the defence fight off the checks being thrown. Melville now becomes enforcers, blowing over Ryan. Their crowd roars as does ours, Charlie is in there to help, I hang high waiting for a pass.

We scramble to get it out of our zone, I then skate back and then cut across to the other side. Looking back for that break away pass, Ryan passes I receive it. As I turn to look up ice, I see a blur then WHAMO! The place goes dim, and I see stars. I can feel myself sliding on my back. I then slowly get up. Dazed I hear muffle from the crowd, I see Blain yelling at me. I hear nothing, just my own breath inside my head. Finally I get to my feet, but I'm dizzy. I skate back to the bench on my own will. My ears now come to life as the crowd is roaring; Mr. Patterson opens the door for me. He checks me out; his light shines in my eyes. I'm not sure what he's doing, but I'm knocked stupid. I ask if he got the license plate. He looks at me biting his lip holding back his smile. "I see you still have your humour." And continues to look at my pupils. When I reached the point of getting my senses back, I look around to the guys. Darryl grins at me, and teases.

"Now that was definitely rock 'em sock 'em." He chuckles.

"Didn't hurt!" I wipe my cheek.

"Wow, now that rocked the place." Waylon adds.

"Wait till you get rocked. No mercy from me." They laugh at me.

The period ends with us still up 1-0. Strolling down the hall to the dressing room, Mr. Boyle is already talking as I enter the room. He discusses the drills we practiced, and the defensive ones. Battered I sit in my stall, feeling defeated I am drained. My body feels like it wants to stiffen up. The defence asks questions and Mr. Boyle answers. He goes over some plays, and adds a few suggestions. We want to win this game, Melville only plays to intimidate. It works on some, as I felt what was only the beginning.

When the ref blew his whistle to start the second. I felt discouraged, forgetting all the positive things I used to motivate myself. I was slow at getting up; having my brain rattled that period. It was just the start of things to come, the series. We walk out to the rink; the crowd's satisfaction was blood. My mind was elsewhere; it was fixed on Candice for some reason. I thought I was done with her. Why was I thinking of her? I had Lana in the crowd cheering for me; Candice just lingered in my head. What was wrong with me? I needed to get my head rattled again, maybe that will erase her. But that was merely a suggestion to myself.

I watched the game as she drifted in and out, but when McCormick took to the ice. He intrigued me, he moved like a shark. He smells the blood, but waits for the right moment to attack. Weaving in and out, he danced around our players. Making a mockery of us, the crowd loved him as he carried the puck. He walked in on Tim, and he stick handled gracefully and then scores. The house erupts into a thunderous roar; he looks our way and pumps his fist.

He was playing mind games with us. Melville was now in the game, McCormick added another point to his standings. The giant now took control of the game and the crowd. Whenever he stepped on the ice, they cheered him, praising him. Sitting there I forgot I was playing against him, it was though I watched from the stands. I caught myself loving him along with the crowd. How do I stop this guy? I wondered this as the game went on. After a while I was put in on the next shift. McCormick was on the ice. As I coasted to my wing, I stared at him. He stood there, looking down at me as I passed him. I can see his eyes, those steel colour eyes. And it sent shivers up my spine, I have to admit, I was intimidated. I can feel him looking at me long after I was past. I now became the prey. I squared off with Houda just outside our blue line, and I can only feel those Grey eyes on me.

The puck drops, McCormick over powers Charlie as he goes forward. He has it and dances in, then as he passed over the blue line. He gave a saucer pass over to Stevenson on the right. Blake turns on his jets and guns in on the net, he scurries toward it and then passes it back to the trailing giant. Without a pause he leans into it, and he lets go a zinger. It's a blur, but it rings off the post hard as it echoed through out the arena. The crowd Woos, Blaine now handles the puck out of our end. Handing the puck off to Charlie as he streaks down the left carrying it in. McCormick zones in on him as Charlie flips it in. Like a shark McCormick attacks and delivers a huge body check. Charlie is thrown into the bench of the opposition. The crowd roars with glee, and they're on there feet cheering the total destruction McCormick had made.

He sets the tone now as he is in charge. Late in the second as the time is winding down, I get out there and try to help our defence. The play is in our zone. I skate in behind the net to scrape up the loose puck, as I hustle about. Houda charges towards me. I see him coming and brace for the hit as I protect the puck. He comes at me full throttle and we collide, the puck slides in the open. I cross check him and the play is still going down. We exchange words behind the play; I haven't forgot what he said. I was waiting for the right moment, now wasn't the time.

The horn sounds to end the second, and the score is tied at one. The ref is there to stand between Houda and I. Now he's braver as the zebra's stand about. He says things to me and the zebra's do nothing, they push me towards our bench. I am riled and Mr. Boyle hollers at me. I focus on him and he points to the dressing room. "Forget it kid!" He pats my shoulder. "The time will come." And I stroll down the hall to the room. In the dressing room he goes over plays, I sit there with no thoughts on the game. Candice again pops into my head. I tried to shake those thoughts, thinking of her made my heart sore. I don't know why I had her in my head, but it wasn't long before she faded out. Maybe one last memory as I try to move on with my life. My heart ached, the way I felt with Candice, wasn't the way I did with mom. I missed her dearly, wishing she and Terry were here. I felt tears trying to over load my eyes, as I remembered them. Those pep talks with him, and the way mom had hugged me. I took a deep breath and covered my head with a towel. If I was to shed a tear, no one will notice. I breathed in once more, visualizing my performance.

25

Then I hear the whistle and my teammates as they shuffle to the door. My heart beats a little faster. I wait to be last and I don my helmet. I stand and look at my Dream Catcher; I'm not sure how long. Mr. Boyle calls my name, snapping me out of my daydream. I glance at him and start for the door. He stops me and asks if I'm okay. I nod and put out my glove; he bumps it and pats me on the back.

Walking toward the rink, once again the music playing sends chills down my spine. I stop for a second before I touch the ice. I look around the rink and the crowd cheering, I look for Lana but there are too many faces to spot her. The players are skating around as I make my way to the bench. Tim does some stretches in his net. Melville players skate around loosely, McCormick is leaning against the boards at his bench waiting for the period to start.

I try to ready myself, prepare for another battle. It is a long road ahead, and I feel defeated. My emotions steer me away from the game, I sit and wait for the period to begin. Mr. Boyle probably sensed it, as he calls my line to get ready for the next shift. He asked if I was up to it. Shaking my head I stand and watch the game. McCormick's line is out there, and whatever line was matched with them. They manoeuvred around us, like we were pylons. Melville wins the draw, and they storm into our zone. They dump and chase, Waylon foot races with Blake, they both go in hard and Waylon over powers Blake hammering him hard into the boards.

McCormick is behind them, and delivers a check of his own. Waylon falls after he bounces of the boards. The crowd roars with excitement, McCormick retrieves the puck. He stick handles around Jason, as he tried to play the puck instead of the body. McCormick has a quick look, and passes it to Houda as he tried for the one timer.

Tim sprawls to make the save. The play is now in our possession, Darryl carries it out. He pours on his speed down the right side. He cuts for the trolley tracks and with a quick move he jumps back to the right. He's around the defence and leans his way to the net. He snaps a shot and Rapaport has quick hands and gloves it. The play is whistled down and we exchange lines. McCormick's line stay out longer, we face off with them.

I stand with Houda, I look at him and he has a grin. He begins to yap at me, but I don't pay attention. We win the draw, as I skated to get into the play. Houda whacks me across the back of my legs. It stings and I look at the ref, but he does nothing. The crowd boo's I nod and I am ready to cream him. As the play goes down to our end, I give chase after Houda. And when he skates around the back of the net. I stride in lining him up, and I throw my body into him with all my weight. Colliding I spin through the air, as does he. The crowd erupts into a cheer. I now got even and I jumped up to get back into the play.

But now my shoulder hurts, I tweaked it with that hit. I quickly race off before I can injure it more. I tell Mr. Patterson, he examines my arm and moves it around. I am mad at myself; I ended my night with that hit. As much as I wanted to play, I knew I had to sit. Mr. Patterson said I was okay to play, but I nodded "No." I benched myself in order to stay in the play-offs. As the game went on, I move my arm around hoping it will pass. The time on the clock now showed nine twenty-five. I still was a bit sore; I debated with myself if it was worth it. To go out and try to cream Houda one more time. My heart thumps like a drum, the score still tied and my teammates look beat. Tim stays strong in net; He's brave enough to face McCormick's 100 mph slap shot, I'm not sure if its that fast. Waylon did say it hurt like hell.

I stand and decide I'm ready for one more shift. I call to Mr. Boyle to put me out on the next line. He gives me the okay, and I stand with Darryl and Jay once more. We are matched with McCormick's line. I feel energized now knowing I'm up against Houda. On the next whistle we shift the lines. I coast out to my wing, and glare at Houda. He comes to the circle, and gives another rap. I nod my head in disdain. He calls me a squaw.

I wait till the puck drops to start the game. When it does, I push his skates out from under him with my stick. Melville wins the draw, it comes my way. I quickly retrieve it and dump it in. We give chase; I look to see who is coming. I skate hard in after it. Their defence only gets to shoot it away, as he turned with his shot. I jump up and fly into him with all my weight, dead square in the chest. Knocking over the big defensemen sent the crowd into thunderous roar. I'm pumped up and give my all, the play then goes down to our end and McCormick leads the rush. He gets past center and blisters a powerful shot on net. It catches Tim who is caught off guard. The crowd cheers and Tim nearly let that one in.

I skate back to help, and Houda runs interference with me. I look at him and pursue after him. He turns to me and we exchange words. "Lets go." I said to him. He spears me in the gut; I grab his stick waiting for the ref to call it. Nothing happens, I slash at him back, and then I drop my gloves and take my helmet off calling him on. He hesitates, and the crowd booing and hissing makes him do it. My heart is racing as I wait for him to ready himself. The crowd is on there feet chanting us on. Wait...wait...and then we fight. All my anger came out from what was said. And we threw fists connecting, my head rings at every hit. I pound at him like I was fighting for my life. Then he crumbles after I hit him once more; I fall on him as he pulled me. The zebra's now separate us and I am escorted to the box. I am bloody but the crowd cheers for me, I roll my fist like I am hitting a speed bag.

Waylon comes and give my equipment to me, and says I smacked him good. He grins from ear to ear. I'm lit up as he skates away. The door remains open; the refs are at the timekeeper's box. Then head official turns and indicates to me I'm ejected. The crowd boo's I receive a fighting major, roughing major, game misconduct and instigator penalty. A 21-minute penalty, and I feel great. Great that I clocked Jamie Houda, but now we were short handed. I regretted the decision on fighting, but I had too. This means I would sit from now on till when I didn't know. All I knew was, I was in trouble. As I skated off, the crowd cheered for me. Strolling down the hall to the dressing room, some workers patted me on the shoulder. "Way to knock 'em around." They said as I past.

While I am getting undressed, you can hear the crowd's moans and cheers plainly. I'm scared for the out come; I left my team short handed. I sit there and listen, chills go up my spine as I hear them scream and then woe's. And then moments later, there is a loud mixture of cheer's and woes. Some one scored, but whom. I am left to wonder as I sit there loathing. I feel sick as I wait for the team to enter the room. The buzzer goes to end the game and the arena is filled will cheers. My heart sinks as I push my hair back with my hands. I am only in my shorts as they enter the room. Some are angry and toss there sticks to the corner. No one speaks to me, I now know, we lost. They grumble to themselves, I sit there and watch as they fill the room. Mr. Boyle enters, and I feel scared. He waits till every one is on the room. He looks around at everyone, and then he puts his clipboard under his arm. Suddenly he claps, and gives us praise for our efforts. "Was it worth it?" He looks at me as he puts his pen in his mouth. I'm not sure what the answer is; I just sit there for a long pause before I nod my head. He then smiles and tells us he enjoyed the game, that we've given our best and to shower up. Darryl comes and tells me McCormick scored the winning goal. That he went one on one with the defence and faked a slap shot, then waltzed right in on Tim and did some fancy stick and foot work. And then he backhanded it top shelf.

"Man that guy is good." He added.

Some of the guy's agree, almost like worshipping him. But Wade controlled the game, and the crowd was entertained. They loved him and he even stole our fans as they screamed on his goal. He demonstrated his puck handling skills along with his power. He showed us he was a monster when he could hit. But he was the master of playing keep away. For a guy his size, they're usually clumsy. Not him, he was a magician. After leaving the dressing room, I was feeling down about our loss. As I strolled out, Lana was there waiting for me. Her smile erased those feelings and I was drawn to her like a moth to the light. She had different colour hair; she now had red strawberry hair. She looked so radiant, much more beautiful.

The way I felt at that moment was like I had never seen her in a long time. She made my heart skip a beat, and I was mesmerized.

"What's wrong?" she asked

"Uh, Nothing," I grinned. "It's uh…"

"What?" She giggled. "Don't like the hair?"

"Wow…you're beautiful."

"Mm yah!" She wrapped her arms around me and looked up at me. "Am I?"

I felt compelled to smother her with my kisses. She adored me when I loved her up. She just giggled and kisses me back. And when the guys came out, they whistled and cheered us. I just looked her in the eye and gave a wry smile. I felt a little embarrassed, and I can feel my face go red. Lana just smiled and kissed me again.

"I'll see you…later." She rubbed my face as she bit her bottom lip.

I stood there and watched her walk away again, how does she do that? Leave me wanting more. She had her way with me, and I loved it. Waylon whacked me in the back and teased me. Telling me I should ask for a job at the rink, I cleaned the ice pretty good. I smirked and chuckled at him, I had no come back. We just boarded the bus back to Cranberry. I would sit out for next three games, I had a one game suspension, and Mr. Patterson felt I should rest my shoulder for two more. I was a healthy scratch, as some might say. I still had to travel with the team regardless. But it was hard for me to see and watch my team play without me; it really hurt me.

As for the series, well it was rough. We would play the next two games to a packed house in Melville and lose game 2, but fought hard to win game 3. Melville was a place to be when it came to hockey. They loved hockey, and they loved Wade McCormick. That arena was something else. We played game 4 at home and lost. Facing elimination, it would spark a fury within us. Down 3-1 in the series, we stormed back winning game 5 at their house and game 6 at home. Game 7 would be played at Melville, hockey town and seventh heaven. This was it, a win away from the cup. McCormick led the scoring race in the play-offs. He had wrapped it up. He mopped the floor, dazzling the crowd. Scouts would be proud, probably buying him out already.

With 23 goals and 23 assists and total 46 points. Wade averaged 3 or 4 points per game. He was magnificent to watch. Going into Melville we were ready, and we battled through our injuries in the series. They punished us, hurt us, and nearly devoured us. We stood our ground, weakened a little. But now our energy was restored as we had a three-day resting period before we headed to hockey town. It was Wednesday April 24th when I then decided to give Bill a call, there was no answer but I then called Mark at the drop-in. I was glad when someone was there to answer. Kim answered, and when I said hello. She was excited to hear from me. She asked how things were and I told her where we stood in the play-offs. I told her that we played in Melville, Saskatchewan. If she wanted to know where that was. I told her about the games and she gasped on how it was. Later I told her we were to leave Friday, for Saturday's final game. But also tell Mark I said hi and then we both said good-bye.

Saturday, April 27th. Game 7.

My stomach had butterflies again on the ride to the rink. I felt nervous but more terrified. I unknowingly kept rubbing my medallion Lana gave for good luck. This was it, the last game. It was a quiet ride as some of the guys were napping. I looked over the seats to Waylon and Darryl, to see if they were up, and so I can go rap with them for a while. But both were dozing, so I just tried to occupy myself. Thinking of the game and Wade. I just hoped I could survive another tongue-lashing from Houda. I hated those words. I am just a person like any one else, why can't he see that. The last time we were here, we played against the ref's. This game would be no different. But at least it was the end of a long road. Half of our school seemed to follow us into Melville, which made us stronger at heart.

As we were pulling in the parking lot, my heart started to beat a little faster. I didn't know if I was anxious. Mr. Boyle hollered to others to let them know we had arrived. When we were gathering our gear, I just looked up to heaven. I thought about mom and Terry. With that it brought a smile to my face as now walked toward the arena. Then the other bus pulled in, you can hear them as the bus rolled to a stop. Our booster bus, and it brought smiles to every ones face. I looked back as I was walking to see if Lana had made the trip. They were loud and cheered for us as we entered the building. People were still unloading the bus, but I couldn't see if Lana was there. We had to go to the dressing room.

26

My heart thumped, as I got ready, thinking of that tune that was played in Rocky part 2. "It's the eye of tiger, it's the thrill of the fight." This lyric repeated in my head. Getting ready, as I was sliding my elbow pads on and slipping into my shoulder pads. Before I don my jersey, I turn to my Dream Catcher and say a little prayer. We wore our red sweaters; we had usually worn them at home. Red was a symbol of power; we wore our sweaters with pride. Red was dominating. When I was ready I sat there for a moment, I rubbed my medallion one more time and kissed it.

"Lets go boy's, get out there and stretch those legs." Mr. Boyle said loudly.

Going out for warm up, the crowd was noisy already. The arena was packed, and we had our fans there and they wore red as well. To keep us striving for glory, our colours stood out from the crowd and they shouted as we entered ice level. The music was playing, the ref's stood along the timekeeper's box. I grinned, making them do their jobs. They were afraid of another brawl, as they guided us to our end. This was a play-off; it's what hockey is all about. Fighting was just part of the game, it was our way of being sheriff. "You mess with our guy, we straighten you out." The atmosphere was different in some way, like it wasn't real. It felt strange; I stood there and looked around one more time before participating in our drill.

We did the horseshoe on Tim and then the two on one drill. Then Tim wanted to practice going side to side. He was pumped as he slid side to side gracefully. He was sharp on his glove; I looked around the rink hoping to spot Lana. Then the buzzer sounds to end our warm up. Again the ref's guided us to the door. It was definitely going to be war out here. In the dressing room Mr. Boyle went over some plays, and put me out on the first line then the signal came. We all put our hands in the middle. "One, two, three, *MOHAWKS*." We shouted.

Tim was the first one out leading us to the ice. Leading us like he did the whole way here. Jason was at the door bumping our gloves as we strolled out. Walking down the hall, my heart pounded, was I anxious or was I scared. Then I heard an old song playing as we were stepping on the ice. "Rock you like a Hurricane." It made me feel powerful and I exploded onto the ice. Skating around in our zone, I gave quick bursts of speed here and there. I was now charged and ready to go and it made me feel good inside. Then the music faded out and played "Thunder Struck." The crowd roared as the Millionaires made there way to the ice. They chanted "Thunder..." as it played; they skated around in their end. The crowd singing to there delight, because it sent a message that they will be like thunder, and they were ready to rumble.

Then the announcer welcomed everyone to the rink. Home of the Millionaires, and announced little draws to be made. And then he asked for everyone to stand for the Queen and our national anthem. I stood at center ice, holding my helmet. I stared at the flag as it waved while the anthem was played. My heart pounded while I waited for it to be over, I was now restless.

And when it was over, the crowd cheered loudly as we raced around the rink once more. The music man plays the song "I like to move it, move it..." It sends a vibe through me. McCormick coasts to center waiting; the ref blows his whistle to start the game. I square off with Blake Stevenson now. The centers square off, the ref signals the goalies and they slouch their positions. Like a loud slap the puck hits the ice. Melville wins it, and McCormick holds up Jay. Darryl goes after it forcing the play. I skate along with Blake. The defence skates through center, throws a nice pass rink wide to Houda as he flies in.

He goes in on Waylon his feet are quick. He cuts to the middle, and with a move I haven't seen before. He spins around on the spot; Waylon is caught going the direction he thought Houda was going. The crowd goes wild, Houda's in alone; he snaps a shot on net. Tim gobbles it up as the Millionaires storm the net. Then "You can't touch this…" Plays getting the crowd hyped up. We face off on Tim's right side. Jason tips it past McCormick, he lounges forward getting the puck. He backhands it out of our zone. The Millionaires go back and set up a break out.

McCormick swings into the right wing, exchanging positions. He receives the puck and skates in. He goes wide on Blaine stick handling around him. Blaine tries to grab him; Jason skates in to check him. McCormick dance's around him, the crowd is on there feet cheering. Darryl skates in to play the puck, and McCormick plows into him sending him to the ice. The crowd yells in excitement, McCormick draws all the attention to him, and then he gives a beautiful saucer pass to the slot. Blake cups it then lets a wrist shot go Tim saves it. Houda skates in whacking in the rebound, it sends the crowd into a roar. The town's favourite son's score, the place goes wild as their air horn sounds. They loved hockey, they loved the Millionaires, and they loved McCormick. With that, it felt like they sank their teeth in. It hurt; I was caught admiring them as we now changed the lines. Mr. Boyle patted our shoulders as we came of the ice. "It's only the first period Boy's," he said loudly, but the others didn't hear from the noise of the crowd booming. Then they chanted "Charge." To the theme that was now playing.

Through out the first half, they led by one. And they showed skills with the puck, they skated blissfully, dazzling the crowd. Dodging the hits we threw, they set up for shot after shot. Tim came into his own, making save after save. Melville charges our end, a perfect pass to the point. The defence passes it across to the other one. He looks, gives to the winger down low. He pivots backward. Then he gives a hard pass to the slot, a one timer. Tim blocks it, there's a scramble in front. They scuffle; the puck squirts free.

A Melville player jumps on the chance. It dings off both posts. The crowd is frantic; we are on our toes. Those chills I got, goes through me rippling from my head to my toes. Charlie now has it, as he desperately tries to carry it out. He is met with a hit that rocked the house. Charlie is one of our bigger players, and he gets sent to the ice. We over turn the puck. But they dump it and go off for a line change. Our line races out, Jason speeds in behind the net to pick up the puck. Darryl and I switch positions as we pass each other. Jason flies up ice. Taking a small advantage on Melville. Jason feeds Darryl as he now pours on his speed. He skates to the top of the hash marks; he looks to see if were coming. He fires a slap shot on Rapaport. He deflects it into the corner and I give chase, beating my man to it. Blake checks me and holds me up. His defence wraps it off the boards, behind the net.

We force them, not letting them set up. McCormick is weaving high waiting like a shark. We forget about him, and he gets the puck. The crowd cheers as he storms down to our end. Waylon is behind him two strides. We all race down to our end chasing the play. Tim comes out a bit, to challenge. Wade gives a fake, Tim goes down, and then he sprawls reaching out. McCormick lets a backhand go; it hits Tim's stick. The crowd goes mad; Tim stopped the giant from scoring. The whistle goes to stop the play; I give Tim a smile and whack his pads commenting his save. He lifts his mask and takes a shot from his water bottle. We change the lines, before the period ends. A few minutes were left on the clock, which was a close one. The atmosphere was pleasing; it was just like a dream. It was unbelievable. They cheered on the chances we had, but gave thunderous roars on theirs. It was enchanting; they were still leading by one when the period ended. And a good one at that, we head to our dressing room pumped up. The crowd was hungry for more, they applause as we exited the rink.

In the dressing room, we were quiet as Mr. Boyle went over some plays; he drew them on the chalkboard. Melville played the puck the first period, were they going to play like that through out the game. I wondered it was probably just a decoy. No one speaks, just silence in the room. All you could hear is Mr. Boyle's pen scribbling on his note pad. We sat waiting for the ref to signal us. Then the whistle, we get up and wait for Jason to go to the door, and we follow Tim out. Bumping our gloves again, we stroll to the ice surface. The crowd cheers as we take to the ice. The music plays loudly, we are charged up from this multitude of people watching and cheering. They get even louder as the Millionaires step out onto the ice.

The feeling I have at this moment is unspeakable. The way they cheered, they made it seem like we were in the NHL. It was like a dream, Melville rocked; I never experienced this feeling till now. The ref blows his whistle again. Charlie faces off with McCormick, the two giants exchange words as they both nod. Charlie wins it; he gets it back to Ryan on defence. Who in turn passed it to Brian; he skates back a little. Brian looks up ice, then circles back setting up a break out. Ronald skates back for it, and drives out of our zone. He flips it up ice, chasing after it. Dwayne skates to his wing, attempting to recover the puck. They get it and skate far as their blue line. Before loosing it to Melville. They come in hard, and play the puck with ease. They drive the net, and throw it back to the point. Their defence looks, he coasts in a bit. He holds for a second or two, and then fires into a screen. It rings the post; the crowd woe's Tim doesn't know where it went. He looks around franticly, but we dump it out.

As the second period went on, both teams exchanged shots on goal and a shared number of penalties. The crowd was pleased with the effort we put in. it was pure puck handling this period. But the king himself showed us up. Wade danced around us, he sheltered the puck; dodging our hits, he showed us he was a phenomenon. And before the period ended, he blistered a shot so hard it shattered the glass. Tim looked on in shock; we looked each other for a second. "My God." I thought.

This guy means business; I shook it off thinking it was old glass. As we headed to the dressing room, the score was still 1-0. The guy's talked about McCormick, discussing that shot. I sat back in my stall, tired and drained. I looked up at my Dream Catcher, feeling strange. I saw a different room through it. I blinked my eyes shaking my head. I looked again; nothing...my mind was playing tricks on me.

I rubbed my face, to wake myself from my daze. I went to showers, and splashed some water in my face. I thought of Pop's and my friends back home, wishing they were here. I wet my hair and pushed it back before I don my helmet. This was it, the last period. Mr. Boyle gave us some plays on the chalkboard. We watched as he instructed us through.

And then he stopped for a moment, and looked at us. He grinned and said he was proud to be our coach, that he never coached a better team. We have all the ingredients for a dynasty. Suddenly he was choked up, anyone nor I seen this side of him.

"We've traveled a long road boy's. And I can't say it wasn't worth the experience," He wiped his eyes. "I'm proud of you all, now what you say we go out and give it all. But remember one thing, and can you tell me what that is?" He looked around the room.

There is silence at first.

"Have fun…?" Someone had said.

"What's that? I can't hear you."

"HAVE FUN," We said aloud.

"Great…" He nodded. "Now on three, one, two, three."

"*MOHAWKS!"* We shouted.

Then the whistle sounds, we follow Tim for the last time. My heart pounds like a drum. Nearly drowning out the crowd as we enter the rink. I feel jittery as I skate around the rink. I go to the box as my legs feel wobbly, weak from the fear of losing. I rub my medallion, and I wonder where Lana is. Now feeling better, I just sit on the bench. I look around in hopes of spotting her. I can't make the faces in the crowd; I rub my eyes and look again. I can't see her, but I know she's here. The ref signals the start of the third. My heart is racing as I wait in the bench. The anticipation has me worked up. The crowd has me going, I want be noticed. I want them to remember me. The puck drops, it seems quiet as I watch it fall in slow motion. The centers slowly whacking away at it, then…it's back to normal. The crowd's roar snaps me out of it. Melville wins the draw, and dumps it in. They chase after it; Waylon turns to fire it out, he banks it off the boards. A Melville forward, skates in hard and hammers Waylon knocking him to the ice.

The crowd reacts with satisfaction. Charlie carries it through center. He flips it in for a quick line change. We leap over the boards on the fly, chasing the play in their zone. Hoping to catch them off guard as we charge in. I skate in with Darryl; we force the turn over. Darryl plucks it free and then dangles one and dances around the other. He cuts to the front of the net, and passes to Jason.

He one times it and Rapaport makes a blocker save. The crowd cheers, as we still control the zone. The puck goes back to the line. Brian barely keeps it in play as he dumps it in again. Jason fights for the puck in the corner, it goes behind the net. McCormick throws his body into Darryl as they both went for the loose puck. Jason again picks it up; he dishes it back to the point. Waylon drifts in and lets a wrist shot go. It hits a player in front. I skate for the loose puck, turning and spinning I fire a shot on net. It hits Rapaport, and he covers it. We go off on the whistle. The chances are there; it's just a matter of when.

We have them running around; we just need to stay focused. Again we try to crash the net, but their goalie stops us cold. Rapaport is playing solid, but we would catch a break later in the period. Houda would get a slashing penalty at 12:52. Mr. Boyle sends out Jason, Dwayne and Charlie. Brian and Waylon were on defence. But the Millionaires keep us from getting a good shot on goal. Melville would attempt to shoot it out; Waylon blocks it from coming out their zone. He quickly bats it down and leans into a bouncing puck; it's a knuckle ball. Like a pinball, it bounces off a few players before hitting an unexpected Rapport. Dwayne pounces on the rebound, he scores. The place goes wild; we jump up from the bench. We scream in excitement and high five the line as they come to the bench. They've done their job and they glorified in it.The score tied at one, as the game continued and with only five minutes remaining now. Both teams pour on that extra drive. Melville changes their game from finesse to enforcers; McCormick would throw a hit that brings the house jumping to there feet. It's crazy, and loud. Those last five minutes seemed to drag, like time was standing still. Time was on their side.

Our line is out there now, trying to play there game. Melville would force their way to the net; Blake crashes the net knocking Tim over. The play is still on and the puck is loose, there are bodies in the crease. The crowd is so loud you can't hear yourself. Bodies get pushed around as they scramble. We shoot it off the boards desperately trying to get it out. Tim is still fighting his way back to the net. They keep it in, I see him winding up. He leans in to it, I go down to block it closing my eyes and turning my head. It stings at first then pain shot through my body; I slid on the ice in pain. The crowd is mad, as this block would create a turn over. I force myself up through the pain. Just so the ref won't stop the play, I clench my teeth as I push myself up. I watch as Darryl and Jason fly up the ice, Darryl leading a two on one. He passes it quick to Jason, the Melville defence drops and slides. Jason uses him as a decoy, fakes a wrist shot, and passes to Darryl. He redirects it...everyone is watching. I'm biting my bottom lip as try to get to the bench nearly fainting from the pain...and then the house erupts into thunderous roar. Darryl scores, he leaps into the glass in excitement. All eyes are on him now, as my line mate's surround him.

I get to the bench; they bump me as I sit in pain. Mr. Boyle came and said something like way to take one for the team. A sacrifice that I hope was worth it, the arena is filled with cheering so loud, you hardly hear the whistle. Time gets closer to the end, so close...can we hold them.

"One minute remaining." We barely hear the announcer.

In a desperate attempt, Melville pulls Rapaport. McCormick leaps over the boards and yells for a pass. He carries it in. No flaws as he weaves the puck in and out. Dancing around Charlie skipping by Dwayne. Waylon skates in with him; he dips his shoulder and hammers the giant into the boards. They rattle and the place goes nuts, Waylon holds him there. Brian whacks the puck off the glass and out. Then the crowd starts counting down, three, two, one...and it's pandemonium. We clear the bench and pile on each other. It's like a dream come true. Then the crowd starts singing "We are the champions..." hugging one another some of us start singing too.

And when time came to present the trophy, when they announced us. The crowd cheered for us, it was unbelievable. Jason would grab the Cup and call us to join him carrying the trophy; the guys skated around showing it to the crowd. And when it was my turn, the feeling I had holding the trophy, as we skated around the rink. It was glorious, and I looked up to the heavens. I had tears in my eyes, "This is for you mom...For you uncle." Closing my eyes as tears streamed down my face.

These moments I wanted to share with mom, to hug uncle, too see their faces. I passed the cup to Waylon, and as we skated around the rink. I wished mom and uncle could see me. When Mr. Boyle came and hugged me, I broke down and wept. All he could do was pat my back. Tears streamed down my face, I was emotional. As I watched every one else, I close my eyes and smile. I open them and I was some place else.

I awoke with tears in my eyes holding uncle's Dream Catcher, and I wondered "Why am I here at Pop's? I just won the cup." My Dream Catcher now lay on the bed. I pinched myself to see if I was dreaming, it hurt. But it all felt so real, everything that happened. Those talks, those feeling's. Mark, Kim…what was the meaning of this? And those games, or Lana…those moments with her, it all seemed and felt real.

Then it occurred to me this was all a dream. I stared at my Dream Catcher for a moment. I smiled to myself wiping my eyes. My Dream Catcher showed me my moment of glory. Just what I needed, "Dreams of glory." I needed that to get by, during a tragic moment in my life. It seemed like a lucid dream of some sort. But in reality, I had a vision. It was the morning before I left, to join my teammates in Neepawa. I would go back, to fulfill my dream. My Dream Catcher was the key to my return. A dream that would change the course of my life, and I suggested we wear our red sweaters on the road as it held its promise and we did win the cup. My dreams of playing in the big league would also come true, the summer of 95, the same year I graduated. I would be drafted in the 3rd round to non other than Chicago. The following year I went and played in my first NHL game against Detroit.

A lifetime achievement and I owe it all to my uncle Terry who had envisioned this. I owe it all to my lovely mother, God bless her. She had worked two jobs so I can play hockey. And last but not least I thank Mr. Boyle for believing in me, and making me remember one important thing, to have fun. Wade McCormick was plucked right out of high school. Three teams would fight over him but it was Philadelphia that would claim him in the end, or what I think bought him out. As for Lana, in case you're wondering, she was my anchor, my foundation. My guide back to Cranberry Portage, she was one of my reason's to return. When we finished high school, when I left to play in the NHL. She had left everything behind and followed me to Chicago. We were married in 2000; we now have two lovely children, Terry and Sylvia. Named after mom and uncle, my mentors. Dreams, they have a way of communicating with us, a guide to our future. Sometimes we see it, feel it and pursue it.

Sometimes, we misunderstand them. And sometimes we miss that calling, our chance. In closing I would like share these words, what my uncle Terry once told me.

"Listen to your heart, follow your dreams. Never let go, and never…give up."